GIRL
IN A
RABBIT HOLE

(Book 1 of the five-book series)

By RJ Law

Chapter 1

"Have you noticed any insects behaving strangely?" the man asked, his pen tapping the table in consistent rhythmic beats. "Avoiding you, perhaps?"

"No," Claire answered.

"Good," the man said. "That's different from the other subjects."

He scribbled something onto his clipboard.

"What about sleep? Have you slept yet?"

"No."

"Interesting," he muttered. "That's 72 hours."

He scribbled again and set the clipboard aside. He removed his glasses and placed them flat on the table.

"And how do you feel?"

Claire glanced down at her hands. The leather straps had cut flawless red circles into her milky white wrists.

"I have a headache."

"Well, that's to be expected with the dehydration."

She looked at the two guards standing by the door, their bodies impossibly large and still, as if they'd been cut all at once from two granite hunks. The man rubbed his eyes and sighed.

"Let's hurry this along. I don't want to be here any longer than you do."

"I doubt that," Claire whispered to no one in particular.

"Fine then. Let's proceed." He put his glasses back on and collected his clipboard. "Any itching of the skin?"

"No."

"What about sudden blindness, visual impairments?"

"Nothing."

He pursed his lips and nodded approvingly.

"Are your fingernails growing?"

She looked at her hands.

"I have no idea."

"Fine," he said.

She cocked her head to the side and assessed the man before her. He was bald and his Adam's apple jutted forth like a misplaced elbow, its sharp point bobbing with every spoken word. She lowered her head and sucked the saliva in her mouth.

"Water."

The man looked up and frowned.

"I'm afraid it will be a few hours more at least."

"Why?"

He frowned.

"Let's continue."

The questions came quicker now.

"Any lesions? Is your stool strangely colored? Abnormal hair loss or growth? Have your feet begun to curl?"

"No."

He released the clipboard and took the pen by each end, his elbows propped up on the table, a look of embarrassment taking root within his pale gray eyes.

"Have you passed any fluids since the injection? Urine, sweat, anything?"

Claire shook her head from side to side.

"None?"

She shook her head again.

"Are you sure?"

"Yes."

He looked at one of the guards.

"98.6," the shadowed figure said. "We check hourly."

The man nodded and wrote furiously on his clipboard for several minutes, only stopping to brush away a fly that had somehow entered the facility.

"Well then," he said as he stood. "I'll return tomorrow."

He turned and took a couple of steps toward the door.

"Wait," Claire said. "I need water."

The man stopped without turning around. He looked at the guards and shook his head from side to side. Then he passed through the doorway, leaving her alone with the two hulking men, their stony faces unmoved and uncaring, scars throughout.

Both stood stoically until the door closed and then each one relaxed. The larger one removed a pack of cigarettes and worked two free. He handed one to his partner and set fire to them both. He looked at the other man and gave him an elbow, a smile unfurling beneath his broad mustache.

"I can get you water," he said, as big spindles of white smoke curled from his fingers: the thickest Claire had ever seen.

Claire stared at the floor, her long hair draped around her sulking head.

"I'm serious," he continued. "I can bring you a big cup of cold water. It would take me five seconds."

He glanced at his partner and they exchanged smiles.

"You be nice to me and I'll be nice to you."

He approached her from the front and looked down at the back of her neck. The fly circled his head as if it smelled something familiar. He swatted at it and cleared his throat.

"And, of course, you'll have to be nice to my friend here, too."

Claire raised her head and looked up at his face, her mahogany eyes boring forth, jaw undulating beneath the skin. The guard smiled boldly and drew from his cigarette. He started to say something else, but before he could, the door swung open and Demetri entered.

Both guards looked at their cigarettes and nearly swallowed the smoke in their mouths.

Demetri waved his hand against the stinking fog and coughed.

"Outside," he said without looking at either.

The two men rushed past him, heads pointed down, a telling fear within their watering eyes.

Demetri shut the door behind them and approached. He had a small plastic cup of water in his hand, and he held it so it could not be missed.

"I'm honestly surprised to find you here," he said, as he took a seat across the table. "I thought you would have left by now."

Claire pinched her eyebrows together and raised her wrists against the leather straps.

"Please," Demetri said, as if truly insulted, his black eyes like little holes behind the glasses he wore.

He leaned back in his chair and sighed, his expression casual, as if he sat across an old friend on the most ordinary of days.

"So, why are you still in this room?"

4

"Where would I go?" she asked. "How would I even know?"

Demetri frowned, his dark Latin features bold and handsome despite his age.

"Let me tell you a story," he said.

He brought his chair flat and placed the water on the table. He removed his glasses for a moment to massage his nose and then replaced them with care.

"I come from a place unlike your home," he said. "It is a choiceless place controlled by cruel men. There, children are made to work like adults. Sometimes with men standing behind them, pistols strapped to their waists."

He cleared his throat and put his hands together, his forearms resting on the table, a stern look in his cold, hard eyes.

"I was born into this place a fatherless child. My mother looked over me and my brothers and sisters as best she could, which was to say inadequately. I spent much of my time taking things that were not mine, a common thing in this place. Even at a very young age, children must learn to steal if they hope to survive for very long. Those who do, do. Those who don't."

He shrugged and turned his palms upward.

"One day, I took something from a soldier. A gold pocket watch that looked very important. Very valuable. Having a practiced hand, I easily lifted it from his jacket and casually made my way through the crowds. Simple as always. One of a thousand times."

He leaned forward in his chair.

"Except this time, another man had seen me. This man, a colonel of the army. As I cleared through all the humanity, there he was to snatch my wrist with his gloved hand. I looked up and saw his face, entirely marred by scars, a thick black beard snarling in all directions. Then I saw the butt of his rifle as it came into my face, and then darkness."

Claire looked down and shook her head slowly.

"I don't care about any of this, Demetri," she said.

He gave a patient smile and continued.

"When I awoke, I found myself shackled to a stone wall in some sort of dungeon cell. On this damp wall, a very colorful algae grew to make a stench that nearly choked the oxygen from the room. This I remember the most, even more than the beatings, which were substantial and severe. For five years, I lived in this place, without any way out. Without any sort of hope."

He frowned and looked thoughtful.

5

"And each day, I became more trained, and with time, my obedience became ordinary. A thing that was taken for granted. And with this apathy came opportunity. More than enough, in fact. And yet, despite these possibilities, I remained a prisoner, because of fear."

He pointed a finger at her.

"Men of power know this one true fact: that more than knives and guns and bombs and steel walls a hundred feet thick, fear is the one true controller. And so it was with me. Until one day, when I finally took my opportunity and freed myself."

He folded his hands and bit his lower lip.

"I had to kill three people to do it, one an old woman who happened across my path at the wrong time. I had never dreamed myself capable of such things. And yet, there I was with a blood-soaked shirt and gore and death in my wake. And do you know what caused me to risk my life and my soul on that one particular day and not the others leading up?"

He waited for a moment as if he thought she might answer, and then he removed his glasses once more and studied her with his naked eyes.

"Because one of the guards I trusted very much told me I would be subject to heinous things if I did not. You see, the bearded colonel who took me by the wrist so many years before had made regular visits throughout my stay. And, each time, he brought some new misery with him. Miseries which left me broken and scarred for weeks following. And this guard told me with earnest words that this bearded colonel meant to visit again in one day's time to make a toy of me in such a way that would have surely left me dead."

He shook his head once.

"And that was when I acted."

Claire looked up and his eyes sunk deep within hers.

"You see, for five years I remained paralyzed with fear. And had my hand not been forced, perhaps I would have died. Or, perhaps I would remain in that place, still alive, even today."

He smiled and put his glasses back on.

"Thankfully, we will never know."

He stood up and dusted his slacks.

"For one hour, you'll find yourself undisturbed," he said, his eyes serious and bold even behind his glasses. "Then the guards will return to do as they please. I will not stop them. The cameras will be off."

He collected the cup of water and looked it over. He took a small sip and set it on the table.

"Of course, that will all depend on whether or not you still occupy this room."

He turned and took two steps toward the door.

"Wait," Claire said. "Please don't do this."

Demetri smiled and put a finger to his lips.

"Sometimes, you cannot win," he said. "But you can still decide how you will lose."

With that, he exited, leaving the door open and unprotected, the hallway outside bright and white and smelling of disinfectant.

Claire bit her lip and wrestled against the straps, their edges biting down on her flesh, blood trickling from her veins and splattering brightly atop the tile floor. From the corner of her eye, she saw the fly land on the table and rush forward, an invisible trail of filth in its wake. It stopped immediately before her and pawed at itself before taking flight once more.

Down the hall, voices murmured, the guards chuckling to themselves, foul plans rooting within their twisted minds. She glanced at the clock, its pace the same for everything in any circumstance: the guilty, the innocent, animal, insect and man. She took several short breaths and reengaged the restraints. But even after 15 minutes of fury, they remained as they had been: firmly fashioned around her bloody wrists, the leather thick and without seams.

She dropped her head to sob, and when she did, the fly landed on the nape of her neck. Without thinking, she jerked her head back and whipped her hair around. The insect took flight and orbited her head a number of times, its buzzing made loud by the hollowness of the room. In a rage, she shrieked and jerked at the leather straps, the chair squealing against the bolts that held it to the floor.

All the noise brought laughter from down the hall, and now the guards whistled and made crude comments, one shouting the time every five minutes.

She settled in her chair and cried dryly, her body aching for water the way the drowning ache for air. But even as she cried, the clock kept ticking, its gentle racket like a train whistle inside her head.

She thought she might take her own life if given the power, but this was a wasted thought. And more came with it: her childhood, her father's face, a boy she once loved. And time held its pace through it all, unmoved by the problems of men, the clock on the wall tracking its progress with gentle, rhythmic clicks.

At last, she resigned to her fate, her body resting weakly, eyes fixed upon the cup of water. They'd enter the room shortly, she thought. And there was nothing within her to stop them. And no one would be coming to her aid.

She rested her head against her shoulder, and when she did, the fly set down on her cheek and scuttled over her nose.

As if poked by something electric, her weakened body jerked to life. She writhed about, but the insect stayed affixed to her skin, its vile extremities tickling their way across this new terrain of supple flesh. At last, something within her broke and she screamed until her lungs ran empty and her mind went black.

Seconds later, her clarity returned, the fly within her right hand, the leather confinements broken atop the floor. She looked at her free hand as if it had just grown from her wrist, the wounds gone, faint bruises where there had been open sores not minutes before.

She glanced at the clock, but the time was gone. In a panic, she gathered the other strap into her free hand and pulled. With little effort, the thing came apart like something made of paper. She held the fragments and studied them, her face pallid and awestruck.

Suddenly, footsteps gathered outside. She stumbled from the chair, her body wavering atop infant-like legs. But before she could take even one step, the two monstrous guards appeared in the entryway, their jaws made unhinged by her inexplicable freedom.

For what seemed like several minutes, she stared at them and they at her. And then all three looked at the cup of water.

In a panic, both men raced toward it, their hands reaching out, eyes wide as dinner plates. But before they could close the distance, Claire threw herself forward and bent over the table. She gathered up the cup and brought it to her lips, even as one of the guards took her right arm and twisted it backward.

By the time it reached her mouth, the cup had nearly emptied, but for a few drops which splashed onto her face and slipped between her open lips. Soon she was on the ground, the two men restraining her, one clubbing her face with what seemed like a two-ton fist.

But even as he whaled away, she felt a growing heat within her body. And soon, she was on her feet, one of the great, giant men cowering against a wall, the other clutching a useless arm that now bent in all the wrong places.

"Please," the other guard said, as he pressed his body flat against the wall. "I'm sorry. Just go, please."

She approached him and bent low, taking his bristly jaw in her small, delicate hand. And then his screams invaded the halls and traveled deep and far throughout the facility, where Demetri sat at his desk, sipping coffee and smiling.

Chapter 2

(9 months earlier)

Claire Foley slept under warm blankets in a cold room. Below her, floor vents whispered. Outside, the sky grew purple and soft. On her nightstand, an alarm clock threatened to sound in 30 minutes, but this didn't matter much. The birds would cut through everything soon, puncturing the serenity with their thin little cries.

When the first one came on, she turned over her body and worked the covers between her naked feet. She watched the clock keep time as her mind made the murky path toward full-on consciousness. She reached out into the coldness and flipped off the alarm just seconds before it brought more unwanted clatter. She withdrew back into the warmth and listened to the ballad of tweets and calls, the birds growing ever louder as if they believed it necessary to coax the sun from its wherever place. At last, she spilled out from the covers and rushed toward the bathroom, the cold tile floor stinging her little feet with every pattering step.

In the bathroom, she dressed, spread makeup onto her skin and studied in the mirror a young but serious face. She ate little before leaving for work, her car parked along the curb outside, abrasive morning radio voices filling the interior with a twist of the ignition key. She zipped onto the freeway and off the curled exit. She slowed to pay the homeless familiar and the ones that looked new. She cleared security without any eye contact. She slotted her vehicle in the parking space that said staff only without really meaning it. All this she did without thought, as if she'd practiced the sequence hundreds of times before.

And so it was, because she had.

For nearly half a decade, Claire had worked at Clairmont University, assisting a brilliant man, while he continued the research of another brilliant man who'd lived many years before. Like most brilliant men, Paul Devaney knew he was brilliant, but he didn't seem to notice that Claire was, too. Or if he did, he intentionally kept it to himself, out of pride or thoughtlessness, who could say?

Over the course of those five years, Claire worked alongside this disgusting man, while his big fleshy nose squealed like a teakettle with every breath. While she worked, he'd pace behind her, years of abrasion patterns marking the cut of his lazy, scuffling path.

"No, no," he'd say. "Do it again."

And she always did, while his tiny black eyes burned holes in the back of her head.

Nearly everyone at the university had contemplated murder fantasies for Paul Devaney; however, most seemed content enough when they learned he'd accepted a job at Viox Genomics, one of the most prominent genetic labs in the country. That was a big day. People passed cute little smiles as they crossed in the hallways: secrets between subjects, better times ahead.

In the summer, Claire had dreamed up a darker fantasy, but she must have wished too hard, because instead of showing to collect his things and claim his long-awaited glory, Paul Devaney just stopped coming to work all together and ultimately disappeared.

The people at Viox Genomics were concerned, the university heads, too. But no one dragged the world's reservoirs looking for Paul Devaney. Instead, they moved forward, the university slotting apt candidates into relevant vacancies, one to fill his void, one to fill the void made by the filling.

This brought opportunity for Claire, but not the opportunity she deserved. It turned out Paul Devaney had hoarded so much credit, she couldn't assemble a portfolio to prove her contributions. And so she took what came: a suitable offering that allowed her to continue the research which had become her life. And for the next several months, she spent each and every day ruining her eyes on microscopic particles and endless strings of numbers unintelligible to all but her.

She spent endless nights in that place, life getting away, neither dates, nor parties, nor invitations to decline. But then everything seemed to change, when a very important person from Viox Genomics called to offer her the job once promised to Paul Devaney. Without hesitation, she claimed the hand-me-down opportunity as her own, a broad smile cutting across her face, mahogany eyes beaming and wet. That night, she drank margaritas from a yawning, salt-rimmed glass, a rush of warmth flooding her core, newfound confidence at root somewhere within.

Over the following weeks, the past closed out with a wink. Free from Paul Devaney, the facility's social atmosphere bloomed. Attitudes improved and so did just about everything else. How-are-yous became commonplace. Smiles occurred out in the open. People transformed into themselves. Did the air smell better?

On this day, bright thoughts accompanied Claire into the building, an overwhelmingly tall man holding the door as she entered. She stepped inside and surveyed the footwork before her. People came and went across the linoleum floor on practiced feet made experienced by days prior. She sucked in a big breath and pushed her way within their ordinary every day.

For half a decade, she'd worked here, subordinate to geniuses, subordinate to fools. But those days were over, and she wore this truth on her bright, beaming face.

Stacey, the young receptionist with the nose ring, saw it at once.

"Hi you," she said through a broadening, slick little grin. "Getting excited?"

Claire nodded, Stacey up on her feet, face drawing soppy and wet.

"I'm going to miss you so fucking much. I just can't believe this is happening."

The young girl fled the desk and offered a hug. Claire forced a smile and bent so only their shoulders met.

"Oh, it's alright," she said. "It'll be alright."

"No," said Stacey, a stern look setting in. "It's fucking not going to be alright."

She looked over each shoulder as if she made a habit of qualifying her remarks by the presence of others.

"It's not alright." She began to cry. "I hate all these fucking people. Each and every goddamned one." She rubbed the back of her hand across her nose and it shined like polished brass. "I hate their faces."

Claire pulled free and patted the top of her head.

"O.k. Alright." She nudged the young girl backward. "We still have another week, don't we?"

Stacey's face went flat.

"Oh, right." She dusted her chest. "Another week. Sure."

She returned to her desk and started working her cellphone.

"That guy's got an appointment," she said, without looking up.

Claire looked over to the man sitting poised upon the lobby couch.

"Oh, hello," she said, taking a few steps to meet him. "I'm sorry. I didn't see you there."

12

"Hello, ma'am," the man said. He bowed a little and tipped forward his hat, a fedora that suited him well.

"I wasn't aware I had any appointments." She turned toward Stacey, but she was only there in body.

"That's perfectly my fault," the man said. "It was a last-second thing."

"Ok," she said. "Ok. Well, let me just have a chance to settle a few things, and I'll be right with you."

He put his hand up and regained his seat.

"You take your time, absolutely."

She nodded, her expression showing traces of confusion. Normally, she had few meetings if any, and as she entered her office and closed the door, a temptation to straighten overtook. She looked around for signs of loose organization, but there was already too much order, so she took some files from the cabinet and fanned them out on her desk. She opened one of the drawers, removed a handful of pens, set them on the files and looked around. Someone had given her a coffee mug that read, 'cancel my subscription; I'm tired of your issues,' and this she put in the wastebasket.

She checked the messages on her voicemail and then waited an appropriate amount of minutes to show that unexpected appointments must wait if for no other reason than to prove the value of her time. Then she buzzed Stacey, who let the man in.

He entered and gave a little bow, and Claire lifted from her seat slightly, because it seemed like the thing to do.

"Hello," she said as the man approached. He held a black folder in his right hand and a pen in the other.

"Hello to you. Do you mind?"

He pointed to a stiff little chair propped against the wall, and she lifted from her seat once more.

"Please," she said, as she looked over her appointment book. "Mr. Harris, is it?"

"Yes, ma'am," he said. He lifted the chair with one hand and spun it to face her desk. He sat down and organized himself as comfortably as the thing would allow.

"I'm sorry for the chair," she said. "Truth be told, I don't really get that many appointments."

He pushed away her apology with a flip of the hand.

"It's good for my posture."

Mr. Harris wore a bland gray sport coat that seemed too tight and slacks that seemed too short. Burgundy suspenders arched over his belly and

13

stretched thin against its forthcoming weight. He was handsome in the face, but his age and small stature stole greatly from it. Indeed, it took effort to notice his kind, square features over the plainness of the rest. But something about his manner suggested he might not care either way.

"How can I help you," she asked, her hands folded neatly on the empty wood desk.

"Do you mind?" he asked, hesitating to set the folder upon his side of the varnished barrier.

She turned her hand over, and he placed it flat.

"Now, Ms. Foley, I'm here today to offer you a proposal, and I hope you'll listen to me the whole way through even if at times, you don't feel like you need to, or want to, or whatever."

He had some sort of rural accent, but he didn't seem rural at all. She leaned back in her chair and it cried a little.

"I've got enough copy toner if that's what you have on your mind."

"No, no," he shook his head. "This is way better than toner, I assure you."

"Alright," she said. "Well, I think I should warn you that I won't be here much longer, so you might be better off taking your offers upstairs."

He shook his head and pursed his lips.

"No, ma'am. I'm here today to see you and you alone."

She put an index finger to her chin and lowered her eyebrows.

"Okay."

He smiled and wrinkles shot out from his eyes.

"Now, it may not look like it, but I represent some very powerful people. People who have the power to make dreams come true." He put both hands flat against the desk. "People who have the power to give people like you everything they need to reach their goals."

She frowned.

"Ok," she said. "That's an aggressive statement."

"Absolutely," he said.

She picked up one of the pens and set it back down.

"What makes you think I'd be interested?"

Mr. Harris leaned forward and scratched the back of his head.

"Well, because we know a lot about you."

She smirked without realizing.

"Really?" she asked. "What do you know about me?"

He tightened his lips and raised his eyebrows.

"We know plenty. You'd better believe it."

Claire chuckled and shook her head.

"Mr. Harris, is it?"

He nodded.

"Well, I'm not sure what you are selling, but you'll have to do better than this." She leaned forward and folded her hands. "If you really know plenty about me, you'll know I'm uncomfortable with ambiguous language. I deal in certainties, and I'd expect the same from anyone who hopes to do business with me."

He bowed his head and raised his left hand.

"I'm sorry. I'll be as forthcoming as I can."

"Why can't you be 100 percent forthcoming?"

"Because the people I represent don't feel it's in their best interest."

"Forgive me, but these people sound somewhat shady."

He placed his hand flat upon the folder in front of him.

"I assure you, they're as shady as your average corporate or political man, which is to say, somewhat."

He pushed the folder forward and sat back in his chair. He crossed one leg over the other with some obvious discomfort.

"Please have a look, and take your time."

She lifted the folder and flipped it open. A single loose page sat upon a stack of pictures, followed by more pages and still more pictures. She thumbed through the top three, eyes darting around, widening. She closed the folder and looked up.

"Who are you exactly?"

Mr. Harris put his hands together as if truly frustrated.

"Ma'am, it really isn't important who I am, I assure you. What's more important is who you are."

"Who do you think I am?"

He shook his head a little and pushed his hat back to reveal a balding scalp.

"Doesn't matter. It's what they think."

"Your employer?"

"That's correct."

She looked down at the folder.

"And who do they think I am?"

"I know few details."

She looked up.

"What do you know?"

15

He leaned forward and propped his forearms against his knees, face casual, eyes set.

"Just that you're headed for a position at Viox Genomics after working for five years under Paul Devaney, his death the main reason for it."

She set the folder flat.

"He's dead?"

Mr. Harris nodded without losing eye contact.

"From what I understand."

She bit her lip and closed the folder.

"How do you know?"

He shrugged.

"I don't know, but my employer does, and I have no reason to doubt it."

She put both hands on her desk, the sweat on her palms making suction for a moment.

"I think I'm going to pass on your offer, Mr. Harris. But thank you anyway."

He stood.

"This isn't unexpected." He pulled the fedora back in place. "Please give a look at the rest of the folder. You'll receive a call from me within the next couple months in case you change your mind."

He put his hand to the front of his hat and turned toward the door. She traced the folder's face with the edges of a finger.

"Wait," she said. "Why don't you give me your number?"

He turned and looked at her. She wore an uncertain expression as if her words still hung in the air waiting to be taken back.

"Because my employers don't feel it's in their best interest." He opened the door a crack and then shut it firm without leaving. "I will tell you this. The people I represent, they aren't the type to quit asking."

With that, he put his fingers to the front of his hat once more. Then he opened the door, acknowledged the receptionist and made his way to the elevator.

Claire eyed the folder and considered its contents. During her brief glance, she'd seen an oddly-worded cover letter, a few headshots and not much else. The remaining contents were a mystery and would stay that way for at least a little longer. The clock demanded action and she'd never been late in her life. She lifted the thing and looked it over once more. It was nearly an inch thick and heavy as a book. She opened a drawer and slipped it inside. She left her office and locked the door.

For the rest of the day, she went about the usual routine. But within her mind, Mr. Harris had found a place in which to live. She thought of his words while she ate. She thought of them during phone conversations. She thought of them while she worked in the lab. And she thought of them during her drive home, the file sitting alone in the passenger seat, a few subtle glances here and there.

When she finally arrived home, she gathered the hefty thing up and made her way inside. Without deterrence, she unlocked her front door and hurried to her bedroom, where she opened the folder and spread the contents across her bed. As she thumbed through it all, her heart picked up, its quickened beats audibly thumping within her ears.

No single piece was shocking in itself, but as a whole, the contents were terrifying. They had everything on her: credit scores, middle school grades, bank statements, orthodontic records. There were receipts and phone records. Letters she'd written long ago to people she no longer knew. Car leases, rental agreements, and somewhere in the middle, she found a picture she'd never seen before. It was her as a child, maybe six, maybe nine, brittle-edged and sepia, freckles on her cheeks.

What she didn't find was an offer, a job outline, a copy of her resume or letter of recommendation. The contents were deeply personal, not professional, and it became clear that what Harris had given her was no pitch at all, but a veiled, methodical warning that she should take their offer, whatever it was, whenever it came again. It was their power revealed and nothing more, and as she closed the folder, she felt the threat working within her as designed, and she did not sleep well or much, and by the time morning broke, she was greatly diminished.

The next day, Claire received a call from Gunther Billingsly, the man who'd begged her to accept the position at Viox Genomics in place of the prestigious Paul Devaney. Then his voice had been pleasant, soft and pleading. This time, it was terse, his words as if from a script.

"I'm sorry to say that Viox has withdrawn its offer and will be seeking other candidates," it said without any obvious inflections. And no questions

17

were answered, and no reasons given, and if she'd been a pleader, Claire might have argued on her behalf, but she'd have done so to a fallow receiver, the opposite party removed the moment his words crossed the wires.

In a daze, she left her office and stumbled outside. She looked about as waves of hurrying people split around her without regard. The air was cold against her skin, and as the pale sunlight disappeared behind a passing cloud, it grew even colder.

She walked along the street, alone and afraid, her mind so frayed and so long without sleep. She passed a cafe and stopped to enter, but the tables were all occupied, so she pulled her coat collar up and took a seat alone outside.

The waiter brought coffee to ease her predicament, and she sipped it gratefully, while the human rush moved before her eyes in a blinding mesh of wool coats and brightly-colored scarves. After a while, her disappointment gave way to terror, as she put the author to its effect.

This Mr. Harris worked for powerful people, indeed. Viox was a multi-billion dollar company with its own version of the CIA. There was no lie this behemoth corporation couldn't dismantle, and no person able to stand firm in the way of its goals. But somehow, this entity had gotten to them, made them do its will. And if Viox's defenses were but a day's worth of aggravation, what were hers?

The waiter appeared from inside, his demeanor strained against the weather's cruelty. He placed a bill on the table, the wind nearly seizing it before she could slap it down with her hand. She withdrew a credit card and handed it over. The tall young man took it and hurried to take refuge within the cafe's interior.

She sipped her coffee and thought, the caffeine rush lifting her spirits and sharpening her mind. She considered Mr. Harris and his people. What was her value to them? Where would they stop to get what they wanted?

Without Viox, she would have to withdraw her resignation from the university, but things could be worse. Whatever the case, she would not be won by coercion, and she nodded to herself to solidify the stance.

She looked up to see the waiter approaching, his soft, youthful face apologetic and somewhat sad.

"I'm sorry, ma'am, but this card has been declined."

She looked up, her cheeks growing red without permission.

"That's impossible," she said. "Are you sure?"

He squinted into the wind as it stung his face.

"Yes. I ran it twice."

She lifted her purse and withdrew another.

"I'm sorry. I don't know how that can be. Can you try this one?"

He took it and hurried away, only to return with the same results. After a third try, she paid with stray coins from the bottom of her purse, and when she took her place among the flowing mob upon the city sidewalk, she was truly afraid.

She walked to the bank, where she spoke to a bald man who resembled the Mr. Clean character from television.

"Let me look into this for you," he said, his voice dry as stale bread.

When he returned moments later, he explained that a hold had been placed on her account through legal means that were appropriate and neat. She would have to consult a lawyer for more information. He was obliged by bank policy. She asked for more information, for help of any kind, but bank policy was his god, so she gave up and left the building.

Outside, the winter wind licked her face, each cheek a healthy rose from the gathering daily same. She wept openly for all to see, few taking notice as they hurried on their way. She dawdled within the crowd for a while. Then she caught a cab and aimed it someplace safe.

Chapter 3

Claire wept as she hadn't in years, her mother trying to understand the muddled, furious words pouring from her mouth. The old woman stared at the dining room floor, sipping her tea, eyebrows pinched together, head nodding, judgments. When her daughter had finished, she stood and walked to the kitchen. Seconds later, she returned with two small plates of muffins that looked as if they'd been freshly made for the occasion.

"You need a lawyer," she said, as she centered a plate beneath Claire's chin.

Claire shook her head and leaned back.

"It won't do any good. These people, whoever they are, whatever they are, they seem too capable."

A garbage truck strained and gurgled out front, and they waited for the calamity of crunching glass and plastic to quiet.

Her mother frowned.

"This is why you should always put some cash aside."

Claire shook her head and looked down the hall.

"Where's dad?"

Her mother's mouth firmed, the corners descending.

"Just resting."

Claire turned and studied her mother's face, so weary and weathered by life.

"How is it?"

The old woman looked down the hall.

"Sometimes it's o.k.," she said, and that was all.

Claire tapped her fingernails against the table.

"Should I see him?"

For a moment, her mother's eyes grew pale as his, and Claire found her answer within them. Through the years, a cloud had grown over her father's mind, an unforgiving dementia at root within. At first, its subtleties inspired endearing little teases. He'd forget things, coin odd remarks, like who made ketchup so red? And how do you look at the stars long enough to count them? After a while, though, it became how is a shoe buttoned; why didn't the dog vote; and when will we eat anymore?

At first, her mother sought to best the doctors and all their certain words. But soon more and more memories went like bits of pepper in the wind, and her resolve ultimately fell away from the fight and settled on the caring instead.

"Maybe wait for a better day," she said, as she cleared the table.

Outside, on the stoop, her mother fiddled with her pocketbook under the shamed gaze of her genius daughter.

"This is all I have on me, but there'll be more. I just have to cash my social security check."

Claire took the money with a swift motion, abbreviating the moment.

"I won't need more." She held both her mother's hands, the skin like tissue paper. "I will return this with more upon more."

Her mother smiled.

"What will you do?"

Claire let go of her hands and straightened herself.

"Practical things."

The old woman put her palms on her daughter's shoulders.

"Long ago, I gave up telling you the ways of the world, my dear, but it wasn't because I didn't think they applied."

She leaned in and kissed the girl's forehead.

"Be careful. Life doesn't care about your abilities, will use them against you if it can."

Claire's eyes shot forth.

"Don't worry. The decision is made for me. I can see no way to resist."

They embraced as awkward friends, the bare treetops clattering above them in all the rushing wind. After a quick goodbye, she left in a taxi, the old woman outside, waving even after there was no one left to receive the gesture.

Claire sat back and watched the city flash outside the backseat glass. The driver tried to make conversation without success, so he pinned the radio to something foreign and off-putting. When they finally arrived at her apartment, she paid the man with money unearned, a miserly hand at the end of her wrist. He grunted and forced the gas pedal down, the tires spinning without much noise, despite his best efforts toward the otherwise.

She climbed the steps with a heavy heart and even heavier legs. She opened the door and let her keys splash against the kitchen Formica. She filled her lungs with the familiar scent of home, and for a moment, she was overcome by peace. But within seconds, the telephone broke the spell and brought the outside within.

She lifted the receiver and said hello.

"Ms. Foley?"

She breathed deeply, her stomach lurching at the sound of his voice.

"Hello, Mr. Harris," she said. "How are you?"

"Just fine, ma'am. Do you have a second?"

"Yes."

"Good."

She heard the rustling of papers.

"I'm going to read a statement to you given to me by my employer regarding the opportunity I spoke of the other day. Is that clear?"

"Of course," she said.

"Alright, begin quote:" He cleared his throat. "We'd like to offer you a lucrative position. We value your expertise and believe you can prosper with our organization."

She waited.

"End quote," he said.

"That's it?"

"I'm afraid so."

She dropped the phone to her waist and rubbed her left eye.

"Are you still there, Ms. Foley?"

She put the phone to her ear.

"Yes. I'm still here."

"I'm sorry I don't have more to offer, but that was the only thing given to me."

She said nothing.

"Are you interested, ma'am?"

Her mind worked over all opposing eventualities: risks, rewards and the forever lack thereof.

"I suppose so."

"Good," Mr. Harris said. "Very good."

That night, she laid in her bed with her eyes closed, mind frenetically turning stones at search for sleep. But it would not be found in its usual places.

22

And each time she drew close, it skipped away, her eyes rolling upwards and then snapping back, body flinching, palms bleeding sweat.

After a while, the light from the windows grew soft and purple; so she quit the enterprise entirely and moved to the kitchen, where she drank black coffee and drew sound, practical plans.

Chapter 4

Mr. Harris had said noon with an impactful tone, so she left at nine for anxiety's sake. The park wasn't within walking distance, but she didn't care. The journey provided room for thought and chances to reconsider. Cornered and sleep-deprived, she moved over the pavement, each step forced, yet terrifyingly productive. Something waited at the end, but its mystery was absolute. They wanted her; she did not want them, the former everything, the latter, a wrinkle under an iron.

She navigated the sidewalks, people rushing past, scarves whipping airborne, a mob of expressionless faces paled by the dim autumn light. Each made way toward his or her next thing, heads pointed straight with intent, as if its measure trumped all others, and as theirs, rightly so.

She bought a cup of coffee at the place with the smallest line, the cashier palming her mother's social security money like any other, no judgment opposite her shame. Outside, she drank as quickly as possible, wisps of steam curling up and wetting the tip of her nose. The caffeine ran its route, and she used it for its worth. But halfway to the park, the muscles in her legs caught fire, so she flagged a cab and rode too quickly the rest of the way.

At the park, on a bench, Mr. Harris sat against all reason, two hours too early, with the posture of someone anticipating an immediate arrival. She stood behind a big tree, watching him as if he mattered more than he did. But his decisions couldn't save her from this imposed destiny, and after a while, she stepped from her hiding and approached him from behind.

As she neared, he did not turn to face her, and for some reason, this brought relief. Despite his all-knowing, he could not predict the moment of her coming, and as she entered his field of vision from the side, he seemed to flinch.

He stood and outstretched his hand, and when she refused it, he did not seem offended. They sat quietly with good space between them, an obvious awkwardness at root. The weather so, few used the park for its designed purpose. But it made an ideal timesaver for the working lunch-goers, and mobs of white-collared people passed before them in regular flashes with middling breaks between.

Mr. Harris started to speak but shut his mouth at the break of her voice.

"Why the hell are you doing this?" she asked.

He pursed his lips and shook his head.

"I understand your frustration, but I am not doing anything."

She slapped her palms against her knees.

"Bullshit. You are ruining my life."

He shook his head again.

"I understand why it seems that way, but your life is not ruined, and I am not responsible for any of this either way."

A fat, whiskered man sold hotdogs from a wheeled stand nearby, the smell of flavored roasting meats traveling all the cold, surrounding air.

Claire pulled a tissue from her purse and wiped her nose.

"Do you have any idea how freaked out I am?"

Mr. Harris nodded.

"I can imagine."

She waited for something more, but he only sat, his face made no less handsome by its unsympathetic mold. She looked off somewhere and then back to his ardent stare.

"Well, what now?"

"Now, I give you the information you need, and you use it however you like."

She leaned back and rubbed her forehead.

"However I like?"

He nodded.

"Yes, ma'am."

"What I'd like is to have things as they were."

He frowned.

"The job you would've had?"

She opened her hands to the air.

"At least that, yes."

He squared his shoulders to face her.

"Ask yourself what you would have been there." He slid about an inch closer to her on the bench. "Just a background figure cooking up stuff for others to take credit for. That's all. And these places like Viox, they're corrupt.

They bribe politicians to get drugs rushed through trials. Next thing you know, you've got thousands sick or dead and you're responsible for it."

She shook her head and sighed.

"None of it matters, anyway," he said. "What choice have you got?"

She passed a glance at a blue-eyed girl wandering over the dead grass. The mother sat immediately across them on the opposite bench, her interest tied to some publication documenting the activities of the famous and those balanced along the fringe.

"At times, you seem like a nice man, Mr. Harris."

He nodded his head slightly.

"I thank you for the compliment."

She squared her shoulders to face him.

"Are you doing a nice thing now?"

He shook his head.

"I honestly have no way of knowing."

She rubbed her eyes and sat back on the bench.

"Tell me this," she said. "Why do you work for these people?"

He sighed.

"I would have thought you'd know that by now."

She looked off toward nothing in particular.

"Because you don't have any choice," she whispered.

He put his hand on her shoulder.

"If you want to continue what you've started in this life, want to be anything at all, you will have to do this." He took his hand away and moved it flat across the air in front of them. "You will have no consideration, elsewhere. They'll have you cut out until you're like a woodpecker in a petrified forest. No doors will open; nobody's going to want to touch you."

He frowned and scratched with his fingers the corners of his mouth.

"It is what it is."

From the opposing bench across the path, the mother attracted her child and gave her blueberries from a Ziploc bag. The girl winced from the sourness and then smiled with delight.

"Why did this have to happen?" Claire asked the wind.

Harris said nothing.

"Can't you tell me anything about these people?"

He shook his head.

"I'm sorry. All I can do is tell you where to be and when to be there."

He handed her a very small yellow envelope the size of a business card.

26

"Inside that, you'll find an address and a time." He firmed his position upon the bench. "Now, I need to give you some important information, and I want you to listen to me very closely. Are you listening?"

She nodded.

"Good. Now, I've warned you of the passive fallout that will occur if you refuse this offer, correct?"

She nodded.

"Okay, now I'm going to give you some important instructions, and you need to follow them, or desert this whole thing before you get started."

He waited a moment and then went on.

"If you decide to come to the specified location inside that envelope, you need to be on time, and you need to go alone. Don't bring someone else, or they will be in danger. Don't call the authorities, or you will be in danger. Do you understand?"

She took a breath and nodded.

"Do not disregard my warning, okay?"

"I understand."

He shook his head.

"No, I mean it. Violence to these people is like you or me having orange juice in the morning."

The two from across got up to leave, and Claire watched them go forward, the child at a stumble, mother at a considerate pace until they were smalled by the distance and lost in the flowing human mass.

"What's your first name, Mr. Harris?"

"I'm not allowed to say."

"Say it anyway."

He scratched hard the skin above his eyes.

"Henry."

She tipped her head back and closed her eyes.

"Henry Harris," she whispered.

The wind kicked up and desiccated leaves rushed between the benches, some whirling, some atomized under boots and heels.

She wiped her eyes, but they were dry.

"What's all this for?"

He slapped his hands against his knees.

"I don't even have a guess." He stood and smoothed the wrinkles on his shirt. "Something important."

She looked at him, his face suddenly grim and imposing.

"Just go along with it," he said, pulling firmly the bill of his fedora. "That is my advice to you, and it is sound."

With that, he stood and walked away, his figure square and smallish, and quickly lost in the hoard of passers.

She looked down at the tiny envelope in her gloved hand to make sure it was still there. She held it up to the light. She started to tear it open but stopped to make sure no one was watching. Someone was. It was a man on the other side of the path. Amid the grass, he stood alone, his hands in his pockets, dark sunglasses shielding his eyes. She lowered the envelope and watched him, her heart throbbing wildly within her chest. He kept watching, his face disappearing behind the people that passed and then reappearing exactly as before.

She pushed the envelope into her pocket and toyed with it nervously. She glanced to the left and the right, but there wasn't much to see. Her eyes drifted back toward the man, and she saw he was approaching. Her pulse raced as he closed the distance, her head growing faint, white flecks infesting her vision. Soon he reached the path and began sifting through the passing pedestrians, his face looking eager, mouth open and breathing.

After some difficulty, the man finally slipped through the human congestion and continued toward her. As he neared, Claire's body stiffened. She looked around. She started to call for help. But just as she opened her mouth, a young woman appeared from behind her and rushed into the man's arms. She buckled forward and breathed, her chest tight, hands trembling. She sat back and watched as the two entangled in what must have been a long-awaited embrace. At last, they separated and the man rubbed tears from beneath the girl's eyes. They smiled at one another and walked away, their hands interlaced as they disappeared from her sight and into their lives.

She sat a while longer until her heart settled and her hands stilled. Then she stood up, took the path a ways and caught a quiet cab ride home.

That night, she sat in her bed, the lights dim and considerate, her legs Indian-fashioned beneath the weight of her body and soul. The television ran live in one far corner of the room, but its offerings competed poorly for her attention.

She held the enveloped message in her hand, its secret at wait inside the cheap manila shell. Weightless and sharply rectangular, it was a part of something. Fractional to some greater purpose, but key to its actualization.

Inside this thing was the answer, and loath as she was, a terrible curiosity festered within. She was pursued by the influential and powerful. Forcible as it was, this entity considered her important, and a horrible,

28

unfamiliar satisfaction with that seemed rightly fixed to support the countering weight of her natural anxiety.

In time, it would all make sense; and she would cope and evolve and grow from whatever came with it. This was her destiny and bound by it, she seemed definitively so.

But when she opened the envelope, she found it empty, and no action could make things any other way. And she cried to her core for a long time. For more time than she ever thought she could. And she did not, could not sleep the night, her crisp, brilliant mind growing wild and frayed and spoiled with dark thoughts.

Chapter 5

The spring dusted the city in gold, the warmth eroding all the browning snowdrifts and opening lush pastures for children to play. Almost at once, the parks turned lavish with flowers and green-smelling things, the sunlight opening rich veins of pleasure for those who knew how to take it.

For others, the season came without notice, their lives ensnared by schedules, deadlines and obligations. Like oddly-uniformed soldiers, they marched toward their zombie enterprises, some fixated on rings of brass, others driven by the patter of wolven feet.

Claire's spring was spent at her parents' home, supporting her mother's efforts to care for her father as they safely guided him toward his end. Intent on mindlessness, she cleaned dishes and dust and physical waste, pacified his delusions, and thoughtfully exterminated her mother's notions of perceived improvement. Bonded together, they forced food into his mouth, and his body into bed, restrained his panicked aggression with smoothed voices, and when that didn't work, combined to forcefully hold his arms and legs together to keep him from stumbling outright into the open, uncaring world.

At night, they drank together, the two embracing over old notes, photographs and stories, their thoughts cast back to sepia times, two minds remembering for three.

The summer brought fresh worry and a whole new kind of ache as they became strangers to the man they loved. Now, he cowered at the sight of their faces, balling up in corners and sobbing, like a shattered child at the unsettling approach of foreign smiles.

After a while, his mind became less a child's and more a void, dull and vacuous and uncomprehending. Most of the time, he stayed in his room, his eyes tracing minuscule fragments of dust that danced on beams of window light. All day he'd watch them move about, like wisps of evanescent magic left by fairy wings. Free and aloft and always refracting, until they passed through the sunlight entirely and vanished into the realm of imperception. Invisible and unconsidered, but there just the same.

One day, she handed her father a cup of juice and he immediately turned it over onto the carpet. While he sat on the bed watching, she scrubbed the floor. The heels of her hands grinded against the carpet as soap suds foamed atop the sucking fibers. After a while she stopped and looked up at him, his face vacant, drool gathering at the bottom of his lower lip. She got to her feet and approached him. She took his whiskered chin in her hand and lifted his head.

"Remember me," she told his face, her fingers firming around his jaw. "Remember me, Goddammit."

But he only stared through her, the drool pulling downward in a wobbly string and then falling free. She fell to her knees, dropped her head into his lap and wept. But he only stared vacantly at the space she no longer occupied, his eyes neither focused nor unfocused, mind uninhabited.

They subsisted by sparse consumption, eating when and what they could. Claire unable to tap her bank account, they devoured her mother's monthly pittance with painful care, like the last morsels of a cruel harvest, picked clean by hollow-looking things with dark, sunken sockets and manifest ribs.

Claire's problems remained her own, and rightly so. Her mother was too tired and too lost to consider anything else for even a single moment. Over the months, Claire had met with lawyer after lawyer with no real success. The script the same in every instance: they'd listen, fingers tapping chins, stroking beards, foreheads firmed by thoughtful thinking. With confident steady voices, they'd make big promises, each outlining his or her approach in clear, definitive language that would have been easy for anyone to understand.

Undeterred by her warnings, they'd pursue the case, some with very real success, at least for a while. But then things would change. One after another, they'd end the relationship abruptly and without explanation, their eyes advertising worry. Their voices trembling, asking her to please go away. Doors shut in her face and locked shortly after. Phones unanswered, calls unreturned.

By this point, Claire had applied to many jobs that were beneath her, the interviewers confused by her interest and skeptical of her intent. Ultimately, most passed for fear that she'd turn over the position too quickly in favor of opportunities that were inevitable for someone like her. Still, others jumped at the chance to have her, those offers rescinded days later for reasons

31

that had become obvious to her, though mysterious and intangible, they remained.

One day in August, she made the last bowl of oats in a secondhand microwave she'd bought at a discount store. Her mother wouldn't touch the thing, older people having no use for those advances which serve to make their skills obsolete.

"It makes life easier," Claire had said to a sour face and shaking head. But this argument had died out among the sadness and fatigue, and now the thing sat upon the green kitchen countertop as if it had been there all along.

When the timer rang, she removed the bowl, added a spoon and toted the thing toward her father's room. Her mother met her in the hallway and snatched the bowl from her hands.

"Go out," she said.

"No. It's fine."

"No," her mother said. "Go out for a while."

She nodded and collected her purse, while the old woman carried the little bowl away.

Outside, it smelled of parched earth and dying grass, the sun's giving warmth now a nuisance to be wished away. She walked the neighborhood to the bus stop where all walks congregated for public transportation. After a while, the thing came, snorting and screeching, polluting the air with a foul, petroleum stench.

She ascended the steps and took one of the few empty seats. As the bus rumbled forward, her unblinking eyes pointed straight ahead, while the lewd gazes of strange-eyed, unwashed men itched against her skin.

After several blocks, the bus began emptying itself of all the wrong passengers, and soon she was left to ride with a pair of unwashed drifters who breathed through wet, open mouths. They watched her with covetous male eyes, their hands clasping the bus rails, gripping and relaxing, muculent prints of sweat left against the metallic chrome.

She noticed her stop approaching through the window and reached for the cord, only to take pause when she saw no other people outside. She glanced over her shoulder and reassessed the two men, her head conjuring images of torn clothing, screams and laughter, wide, gritting smiles. Without much thought, she released the cord and pushed back in her seat. Miles later, the bus entered a more cheerful area, and she finally tugged the cord and fled the vehicle to join a crowd of ordinary people dressed in sensible, coordinated attire.

She backtracked the way to her original stop, the sun intolerable, her blouse sticking against her sweating shoulders and back. After several miles, she crossed the street and entered a small café near a little grocery shop.

Inside, she found an immaterial line of customers that thinned quickly, and before she knew it, she held an iced coffee in one hand and a muffin in the other. Weak with hunger, she bit into the bread before the cashier could deliver the change. Errant crumbs fell against the coins in his outstretched hand, and she studied them with horror. The young man had a soft, handsome smile and he gave it freely, as she apologized through bulging cheeks.

"No worries," he said, as he poured the coins and crumbs into her hand.

She made a movement toward his plastic tip jar, but when his attention moved to another customer, she quickly placed the change inside her purse and turned to go.

Immediately, she saw Mr. Harris sitting in a far corner, his hat set upon the table, balding head tanned and glinting under the weak overhead light. He watched her like an impartial witness, his square face neither smiling nor frowning.

Without measure or hesitation, she crossed the room and bathed him in iced coffee, the foam settling on his face, the rest soaking the right portion of his sport coat.

Harris jumped to his feet, his stunned face studying the sleeve of his jacket as if a limb has been torn from underneath. An old woman gasped, a young couple gawked. The manager came out and asked her to leave.

"That's quite alright," Mr. Harris told him. "I had it coming."

The old black manager looked at one and then the other, his fists balled.

"Then I'm going to have to ask you both to leave, and immediately," he said, his jawbones at work beneath a layer of thin, coarse skin.

The two went outside, and Claire immediately turned and walked away down the sidewalk.

"Claire," Mr. Harris said. "Please don't go. I'm here to help you."

She kept walking.

"Claire," he said forcefully, his words cutting through the wind in a way that seemed beyond his capabilities.

She stopped and turned, eyes alive with fire, hate. She made the way back with fewer steps than before and struck him in the face. He staggered back and groaned, his palm against a swelling cheek.

"Who the hell are you? Once and for all, goddamit! Once and for all, who the hell are you?"

Mr. Harris steadied himself and removed his hand to reveal a gathering welt.

"I understand your frustration, but you have to believe that I didn't have a thing to do with that envelope." He spat blood. "I promise you, I did not know it was empty."

She moved toward him, and he flitted back like a much younger man.

"What the hell is going on?" she asked. "What do you have against me? Why the fuck are you destroying my life?"

He put his hands up.

"Not me," he said. "It's not me."

She balled her fists and screeched, passers flinching, birds fleeing trees.

"No more of that bullshit. I want to know what's going on."

He rubbed his face.

"I wouldn't even know how to lie," he said. "I promise you; I don't have the slightest clue."

She put both hands on top of her head, like a mother confounded by the ways of an errant child. Then she dropped them, staggered toward the exterior of the cafe and leaned against the brick.

"Why are you here?" she began to cry. "What now, for God's sake?"

He rubbed his face and spat again, his saliva looking pink against the pale sidewalk.

"I'm here to do what I've been told to do."

She shook her head.

"And what's that?"

He removed another tiny envelope from his pocket, and she moved toward him.

"Wait, wait, wait," he said, as he moved backward. "I checked this one."

She approached and snapped it up, tearing it open and lifting a white card from within. Her eyes burned forward as if to set it aflame.

"What is this?" she asked. "What is it?"

He put his hands inside his pockets.

"An address."

She looked at him.

"To what?"

He shrugged.

"I don't know."

She turned and tapped the card against the red brick.

"I'm sorry I struck you," she said. "That's not like me at all."

He took out his hands and dusted his shirt.

"I've been hit by people less angry than you."

She turned to face him and he flinched a little.

"Does the same hold true as before, Mr. Harris?"

He looked at her.

"I'm not sure what you mean."

"Before, you said I should come alone without telling anyone. Is the same true here?"

He nodded.

"Absolutely. Every bit of what you said is true and right."

She opened her purse and tucked the card inside.

"Then that's the end of this relationship. I don't want to see you anymore. Is that clear?"

He nodded.

"Perfectly, yes."

She turned and walked away without looking back. But once she achieved the edge of the building, she fled the walking path and retreated into a stairwell, where she wept for all that matters and all that doesn't, for her mother, for her father, but most of all, for herself.

How did you get so far in this life without any visible scars?

She pushed her back against a brick wall and sunk to the ground, crossed her legs and opened her purse. She removed the card and looked it over: it said 17 Copper Street and 2 A.M., and she took out a pair of old receipts and a pen and duplicated the address twice, placing one receipt in a pocket and one inside her shoe. Then she implanted the card back inside her purse, rose to her feet and shot back out into sun-drenched sidewalk that led the way home.

Chapter 6

17 Copper Street was on the east side of town, and she would have to leave early to make the deadline. Invested wholly in the overpowering history of her daughter's seamless reasoning, her mother threw up few complaints. Instead, she said goodbye in the way that mothers say goodbye to daughters when their children are all they have left in this world. And they cried like children, each and the same, the right words spoken in case of an untimely or failed return.

Her mother remained awake as long as she could before drifting away on the sofa, as television infomercials called softly in the dim pale light. Claire pulled a blanket over the old woman and placed a soft kiss on her wrinkled cheek. Then she shut the door noiselessly, leaving her mother alone to dream against unimaginable burdens and sorrow.

The taxi had come late, and Claire let the driver have it for much longer than he deserved. Soon they were both apologizing to each other, and then it was quiet except for the engine and the intermittent crackling from the CB radio.

At her request, the driver stopped a few blocks from her destination, and she entered the wind and night, where the street lights splashed weak hints of amber against the dark pavement. In that wind and night, indistinct shadows stretched outward, like ghoulish, spindly fingers across a vast and solitary urban terrain. But within that terrain, life moved all around her, and she knew it by the sound of clanking bottles and shuffling feet. As she walked, the downtrodden stirred in the shadows, pale-faced and curiously watching such a clean and foolish woman jog across their streets.

By the time she reached Copper Street, the fear and anxiety had taken its toll. She stopped and bent forward, her hands on her knees, lungs sucking hungrily the air. She wanted to go home, but it was too late. She stood up and rubbed the small of her back, her eyes darting about the shadows in search of dangerous men.

Then she saw them all scuffling about under a big pool of white light. She stumbled forward, her head turned slightly, the scene before her peculiar by context and setting:

At least a dozen men and women stood atop a dimly-lit basketball court that sat like a paved courtyard between three red-brick apartment buildings. Dressed professionally, they looked at their surroundings and one another through bewildered eyes, as if they'd suddenly appeared at this dusty, urban destination from thin air, or perhaps even another time. Claire crossed the street to join them, her heeled shoes applauding the pavement with thwacking noises audible to all. A good portion of the group unsettled, flooding toward her suddenly, like a shifting mass of migrating birds veering from the coordinated flock.

Claire stopped short of the curb, her feet tied to the dark, empty street.

"Are you one of us or one of them?" an approaching woman asked, her rotund figure laboring even at such an easy pace.

The small crowd filled in around the woman's shoulders, their faces eagerly awaiting a response.

"I'm definitely not one of them," Claire said, the words leaking through her knotted throat. "Whoever they are."

The backside of the crowd grumbled and turned away, leaving the woman alone to greet the newcomer.

"Oh," she said. "Well, come on then. We're all waiting over here."

Claire stayed fixed to the asphalt, a pair of small, brightening headlights bearing down on her position. The woman furrowed her brows.

"Are you coming, dear?" she asked. "You'd better get out of the street either way."

Claire turned toward the lights and jumped out of the road.

"I'm sorry," she said. "I'm just a bit flustered."

The woman gave her a tap on the back.

"Join the crowd," she said. "Figuratively and quite literally."

Claire followed the woman to the pack, many engaged in conversation and oblivious to her arrival, most of the men all together, one taking thoughtful drags from a polished wooden pipe. The fat woman joined two older, scholarly-looking women, and Claire trailed her and pushed into their group.

"What's your name, dear," the fat woman asked.

"Claire."

"And who are you with?" another woman asked, her jawline suggesting Scandinavian descent.

Claire's eyes washed over the group for a moment, their easy expressions offering no signs of fear or coercion.

"I worked under Paul Devaney at Clairmont University."

The asker's mouth firmed and her head nodded in approval.

"I'm Delores," said the fat woman, who then gave the other ladies' names and resumes in turn.

"Nice to meet you all," Claire said. "Do any of you know anything about this organization?"

The women traded looks.

"Not really," Delores said. "But we're all eager to learn more, everyone trading stories and such."

She raised an index finger and pushed her glasses back toward the bridge of her nose.

"Do you know what they're saying?" Claire asked.

The other women looked at Delores as if they themselves had asked the question.

"Oh, just a smattering," she said. "It's clear that no one knows anything substantial, but some have different attitudes than others. Some seem much more excited than others, than me."

Claire nodded.

"How did you come to be here?" she asked them all, but only Delores answered.

"They accepted an initial invitation. I resisted."

"So did I," said Claire.

Delores nodded and touched her elbow.

"I'm not sure everyone here understands them like we do," she said.

She opened her mouth to say more, but before she could, the faint sound of engines entered the quiet surround. At once, all the little social circles broke apart and each person lined up along the curb, some leaning forward and pinching their eyes to see deeper into the black yonder. The machine hum gathered in the distance until headlights finally broke over the horizon atop the paved hill. Through the bleary starbursts of shattered light emerged a train of five white airport shuttle vans, each spaced so evenly, they seemed tethered by samely-cut strands of invisible metallic cord.

As they approached, the vehicles slowed and turned their wheels, each pushing over the curb and onto the basketball court, shocks squealing, the drivers working carefully behind dark tinted glass that gave back the burnished street light, along with the faces of those who would attempt to look inside.

The watchers stepped back as the chain of vehicles looped around and steadied in an orderly line. Each man and woman stood waiting, their hair blowing in the wind, the engines idling softly, no signs of invitation or definitive reasons to run.

Finally, the door of the first shuttle opened, and a young well-dressed woman stepped out. She wore a broad, plastic smile across her beautiful, flawless face and she looked everyone over with high-voltage eyes.

"Hello!" She said as she stepped out to join them. "I'm so happy to see this great turnout."

She raised her hands and called them closer.

"Please, everyone, step forward, step forward."

They gathered around her.

"Now, if you'll just give me a few moments, I'd like to say some words."

Her impossible smile faltered for a brief moment, and then an even brighter one took its place.

"My name is Sherice, and I'd like to thank you for choosing this exciting opportunity to further your research and individual careers. Now, all of you are experts in your fields, and this has made you desirable to The Xactilias Project. What's The Xactilias Project, you may ask? Well, there will be time for broader explanations. In the meantime, I can say it is a mission dedicated to uncovering new discoveries aimed at advancing the human impact on the world."

She maintained her smile as she studied their faces.

"Now, I see a lot of different people from all walks of life, but one thing we all have in common is an insatiable desire to find answers to complex questions and, perhaps more importantly, the innate ability to construct the bridges that will take humanity from this plane to the next."

Her face suddenly grew somber, forming wrinkles and little bulges without affecting her beauty one bit.

"I understand you must all have numerous questions, but I'd like you to put a pin in those until we make our final destination."

A few of the attendees looked at each other. One man spat his gum onto the ground.

"Wait just a second," he said, all eyes turning toward him as he spoke. "What the hell is all this? You expect us to file into these vans and just go?"

He turned toward the rest of the party.

"I don't know about the rest of you, but I haven't been told very much about this organization, and I'd like to know more before I commit to anything."

The group turned its attention to Sherice, who appeared somewhat puzzled by the interjection, her eyes squinting toward the crowd, like a stage performer searching the darkness for drunken hecklers. After a moment, she turned and leaned back into the shuttle.

"Demetri?" she called. "Someone has a question."

The crowd waited for Demetri to appear, but he never did. Instead, the doors on the adjacent shuttle opened and three equally-built men exited, their thick, polygonal frames poorly concealed by dark suits, faces neither handsome nor ugly, expressionless.

As they approached, the free-willed man studied the increasing void between him and his colleagues.

"Please come with us, sir," one of the men said, the others bracketing him, sweeping him forward and into their vehicle, the whole thing swift and practiced, a thousand times refined.

"Now," said Sherice, her mouth regaining its familiar form, "while his individual concerns are addressed, let's talk about what happens next."

She stepped forward and the crowd gulfed. She turned her back to them and faced the shuttle train.

"All of you met with one of our representatives, and this is important because it will decide which shuttle you'll be taking."

She pointed to the left.

"If you met with Mr. Humphries, you'll be taking number five at the rear. If you met with Ms. Donovan, you will take number four. If you met with Mr. Grace, you'll take number three. And if you met Mr. Harris, you'll be riding with me in shuttle number one."

She turned to face the group.

"Obviously, no one will be riding in shuttle number two, except for existing passengers, of course."

She looked around as if she expected questions.

"Alright then. Let's all get into our shuttles and start this exciting adventure."

The groups within the group separated, some shaking hands, a few exchanging hugs, most content to keep their distance from anyone with features indistinct. They all lined up at their respective carriers and entered one by one, each vehicle equipped with white, leather seats and a steward to guide the incoming forth. At the front of the train, Claire fell in behind a line of tired,

40

beaten-looking people with haggard faces aimed nowhere but down. Each went up the steps and took a seat, Sherice grinning madly as they passed, like an insane flight attendant, happily at work upon a conveyor of doomed souls.

When the passengers had taken their seats, an automated voice bled through a pair of overhead speakers: toneless, preserved words thanking them for coming, asking them to please fasten their safety belts and remain seated through the duration of the ride. When all was set, the shuttle train moved forward, circling the paved court and carefully descending the curb one by one, the passengers jostling within darkened windows, their existence imperceptible to the few passing motorists occupying the city's sleepy streets.

Outside, the night saw the city evolve from a place of efficient business to one of sour noises and hard tastes. The deodorized flock gone to slumber, the streets now played host to a homeless breed, which subsisted off indirect charities and the plights of its anothers. One after the next, they passed by the windows of the racing shuttles, each one staggering loopily along the filthy gutters: Some heavenly gazing after a fix; others looking downward, their faces knotted, broken minds sorting deviant languages murmured from within.

The shuttles traveled a familiar stretch of roads, and many of the passengers already knew their destination long before the airport lights bubbled atop the westward horizon. But instead of taking the usual route, the shuttles veered down unknown paths that twisted and turned before finally spilling onto the runway itself, each trailing vehicle impossibly close in its pursuit.

The train wheeled past all comers, baggage handlers slowing their work, reflective clothing vivid under the passing halogen beams. Some of the guests rose toward the windows, fingers fiddling with their seatbelts enough to realize they were locked.

Finally, the shuttles wheeled to a stop near a military cargo plane, its impossible volume enough for squadrons of men with plenty of room left over.

A voice rang from the overhead speakers, startling the passengers as they leaned over one another trying to see out. It was Sherice, and she seemed no less enthusiastic than she'd been before the drive.

"Passengers, may I have your attention?"

Throughout each vehicle, a hanging cloud of mutters dispersed into a hush, as everyone calmed to listen.

"Good," she said, invisible to all but those in the lead carrier. "I'm so glad to welcome you to our intermediate destination. Next, you will all be boarding a flight that will take you to a tertiary destination, and I must ask that you hold all your questions until journey's end."

As she cleared her throat over the microphone, the shuttles filled with an agony of trebled clatter, and some of the passengers clutched their ears.

"I'm sorry," she said, regaining her pitch. "Now, as each one of you exit, your steward will present you with an envelope meant only for you. Once we exit, you'll have an opportunity to lightly disperse. At this time, please read your card and then place it inside a pocket or handbag. Now this information is meant only for you, and we must insist that you refrain from sharing any part of it with your associates. If I am able to impress one thing upon you during our brief encounter, it is that the leaders of The Xactilias Project value cooperation above virtually all else; so please heed all warnings that pertain to the sharing of information."

They felt her smile among them, as she said to rise and exit, the seatbelts separating at the break of her voice as if she by will controlled each one using the few mental powers jangling around her empty head. One by one, they stood and walked and claimed their little envelopes before stepping out onto the tarmac, the summer breeze warm and kind even at this crooked hour. When they'd all exited, the doors to the shuttles snapped shut, while the crowd dispersed as instructed.

Claire watched the train get going, Sherice's shrill voice still rattling around in her head, like screws in a coffee can.

"That woman's been holding in the same fart for more than a few years," she heard from behind. She turned to see a glad-looking man with handsome features that might have seemed threatening on someone from the blue-collar world. He smiled through a set of polished teeth, his deep brown eyes devouring everything they saw.

"My name's Nathan," he said, offering his hand like it was a reward.

Claire took it briefly before leaving it in mid-air.

"I really don't think we should be talking. They said we should disperse and read our messages."

He smiled.

"Sure." He stood same-placed as she turned to walk away. "We'll just put a pin in this. Nice to meet you."

Most everyone had already secured territory, and she hurried past them as if working against a stopwatch, a frowning man with his thumb hovering over the button, tenths of seconds wasted with every misstep. She finally breached the outer circle and found a private place of her own where no one would see over her shoulder. Across the way, she saw distant runway personnel stopping to watch the scene playing oddly before their seasoned eyes. She turned to see their perspective, the envelope moist inside her pocketed hands. Indeed, they all looked foolish spread out that way: high-shouldered and slouched forward, heads alternating from left to right. They looked very much like children involved in some sort of curious schoolyard game, each one hoarding clues for a contest that might bring licorice or tiny adhesive gold stars.

When she was sure no one else could see, the envelope came out, and she tore it open to withdraw another card.

"Welcome, Ms. Foley," it said. "We are very pleased you have chosen to participate and are confident you will find great success with our organization. That said, we must insist that you discuss neither the details of your recruitment nor that of other guests. Failure to comply will result in immediate termination. - Demetri M."

She put the card back into its container and studied the others, their blank faces giving up little. Some clutched their memorandums tightly, while others crumbled the cards and tossed them onto the tarmac. One man laughed aloud when he read his card. A woman put a trembling hand to her mouth.

"Hello!" A man said from above.

They looked up and saw him standing high atop stairs that cut into the belly of the plane, his figure looking rigid in a tailored military uniform.

"Welcome, each and every one of you."

He had a thin mustache that was shaved into a pencil line across his lip. They all watched as he sailed down the stairs with ease, the toes of his polished boots tapping each one for only an instant, as if they moved only to give the appearance of walking, while he floated upon a descending draft of air.

"Please, all of you," he said, as he hit the level ground. He lifted his hands high above his head and summoned them all together across whatever fictitious borders kept them apart.

"Now," he said, as they fell in before him. "My name is Bernard, and I will be shepherding you to your tertiary destination."

He scanned them slowly, each brown iris looking small upon his bulging white eyes. He kicked his heels together and crossed his hands behind his back, his body growing even more wooden before their eyes.

"Now," he said. "You will all line up in any order and board the plane using the stairs. Inside, you will enjoy free seating unless you require special assistance, in which case you will notify one of the attendants who will see to your individual needs."

43

He looked them over once more before smiling enough to show most every tooth.

"I'm pleased to be in your company and hope you will find your journey without discomfort," he said. "However, I must ask that you hold any questions until journey's end, when all of your individual needs will be addressed to your particular satisfaction."

He turned his body in an automated sort of way, his left foot sliding backward like some giant invisible finger had pushed against his right shoulder. He raised his arm and turned his palm upward as if to introduce to their eyes the plane for the very first time.

"Please," he said.

They all shuffled together to form Bernard's line, and he watched as they ascended the motorized passenger staircase, everyone avoiding his stare, eyes fixed to the back of the one before them.

Claire fell in with the laggers at the back of the line, finally taking a spot behind the person who did not want to be last and the one who did. When she finally reached the top of the stairs, a thin young Latin woman greeted her with a fierce smile before pointing the way to the seating compartment, which held three to a row on either side. She walked the aisle looking for a seat, moving past the rows of strangers toward the first vacancy she saw.

"Hello," Nathan said, his arm casually resting atop the backside of the open seat middled between him and an old man. "I'm willing to offer the window seat if that's something you're interested in."

She smiled politely.

"That's very gracious of you. Nathan, is it?"

He rose up and shrunk backward, the old man following suit; each allowing her to pass by and take his offer, her rear end brushing hard against each of their fronts, with all parties pretending otherwise.

"That's right," Nathan said. "And what was your name?"

"Claire," she said, as she claimed her seat. "It's Claire."

"Nice to meet you."

The old man leaned forward and outstretched his hand over Nathan's lap.

"My name is Alfred, madam," he said, a hint of an accent bending each word, its origination left unidentifiable by decades of proficient suppression.

"Claire," she said, as she took his hand, soft in hers and courteously gripped. "Nice to meet you."

"Thank you," he said, smiling somewhat bashfully. He wore round, thickly framed eyeglasses and a free-willed bush of a mustache that had grown Einsteinian, by coincidence or intent, one could only guess. "Mr. Nathan and I were just discussing the odd tenor of this evening. Although I must say, he seems to be most comfortable despite the countless oddities we seem to have witnessed."

Nathan placed both hands on his knees.

"Well, Alfred, I just happen to enjoy the anti-norm wherever I find it." He grinned, and Claire could see he was chewing gum. "What about you?" He turned toward her. "What's your story?"

"I don't have one."

"Ah," he said, dashing the thought with a flip of a hand. "I hardly believe that else you'd be sitting on another plane headed to a seminar in Nebraska or Iowa."

She shrugged her shoulders.

"Oh, I get it," he said. "You're one of these lab rats who's spent a life hovering over microscopic worlds pressed between slides."

"Hardly," she lied.

"Are you sure?" he asked. "I think I can see a microscope imprint around your eye."

Alfred touched his arm.

"This is how you acquaint yourself with a beautiful woman?" he asked. "In my day, young men approached women with poetry on their lips."

Claire smiled politely.

"I take pride in your error, Alfred," Nathan said. "However, I'm neither young nor am I trying to woo our seatmate. I'm merely making conversation." He turned back toward Claire. "So what is it? Do you have a story or not?"

She looked at Alfred and then back to Nathan.

"Well, of course, I do, but I believe we've been instructed to protect our information from one another."

"Ah," he said. "The babbling woman with the painted face. As I recall, her guidelines pertained only to our little personalized memorandums. Am I incorrect?"

He looked at each of them, palms turned upward. Alfred frowned, his mouth disappearing beneath a forest of twisted gray.

"I suspect the ominous nature of the warning itself was meant as a chilling effect toward all communication; however, I cannot disagree with your assessment." The old man looked over both his shoulders before hunching toward them. "Perhaps we should whisper, nonetheless."

They both looked at Claire, each of them eager-faced, as if the three sat beneath a fortress of sheets, trading slumber party gossip above a low-watt flashlight bulb.

"I'm sorry," she said. "I don't feel comfortable."

Alfred looked disappointed, but Nathan only smiled.

"I'll do it for you then."

He cleared his throat and framed his hands like a director setting a scene.

"You're an idiot savant fresh from your laboratory cage, where your hyper-systemizing resulted in countless breakthroughs, which brought you countless edible treats and, ultimately, freedom itself, and, no less significant, an opportunity with the mysterious Xactilias Project."

Alfred's wrinkled face grew somber as if the words had been pointed toward him.

"Such talk," he said without a follow-up. Claire smiled.

"It's alright, Alfred," she said. "I've heard worse from better."

Nathan's face grew worried.

"Forgive me. I meant to be funny."

"Please," Claire said. "It's perfectly alright."

A single tone poured from the overhead speakers, causing everyone to perk up in their seats.

"Welcome passengers," a voice said with a German accent. "This is the pilot speaking. I'm quite pleased to have each of you with me this evening. Our flight will take between seven to 12 hours to complete, depending on weather and other circumstances. Should you need to use the facilities, please flag the closest attendant, and she will escort you. Otherwise, we must insist that you remain seated for the duration of the trip unless you have a medical condition, in which case, you should notify your nearest attendant immediately following this message."

They waited for more, but nothing came. Instead, the engines roared to life and the plane crawled forward, no catastrophe procedures or safety demonstrations, the passengers furiously fastening their seatbelts on their own accord.

The tone rang out again, sending pulse rates ever higher.

"This is your captain again," a voice said. "I'm sorry to say we have no choice but to deviate from usual procedures and take off immediately. Please fasten your safety belts and prepare for lift-off."

As the plane gathered speed, more than a few faces grew pallid, some digging fingernails into armrests, others deep in meditative breathing exercises.

Claire shut her eyes, but this only made the engines louder, so she raised her lids and looked about the aircraft if only to read faces of the flight attendants for signs of calm or concern. Instead, she saw panic throughout the cabin: the passengers hunkered backward into the plush of their seats, the attendants themselves looking rattled, hands on their hats, bodies jolting side-to-side.

And then she saw Nathan calmly looking over the rest, his head shaking slightly, an amused smile on his face. He turned suddenly as if her stare had burned a painful impression on the back of his neck.

"Isn't this fun?"

Claire shook her head.

"Not for anyone but you."

The plane jolted and the cabin filled with little yelps and deep groans.

"Embrace it," he said. "You feel your heart beating? That's how you know you're alive."

She bit her thumbnail as the lights dimmed and reset.

"Preexisting knowledge," she said.

He smiled and touched her arm, his hand weighty and impossibly dry.

"There's no point in worrying. We're in no position to control this outcome."

She moved her arm.

"This type of worry is involuntary."

He looked at her and unfastened his safety belt just as the plane lifted a moment and clumsily bounced back to earth.

"Really?"

"Stop that," she said. "You're making me more nervous."

"Why should my personal decisions make you more nervous?" he asked. "Are you afraid my loose body might lift from the seat and render you unconscious?"

She turned her head to the window.

"Let's just not talk until this is over."

He nodded once.

"Agreed. If we survive."

"Stop it," she said, and he grinned.

"I can tell we are going to be friends," he said.

"Shut up, shut up," Alfred said. "I'm trying to keep from having a heart attack."

Seconds later, the aircraft finally gathered enough speed to ride the air upward, a terrible thunder reverberating from its giant smoldering engines. The plane climbed and climbed, its long wings dipping and rising, some of the passengers driven to nausea, the smell of vomit wafting between shoulders and heads.

Once airborne, the plane finally steadied, and the passengers began to settle. The attendants unbuckled their belts and straightened their little hats. One by one, they turned to face the passengers, their stiff faces replaced by preset masks, friendly and calm and pretty as the world could offer.

Alfred put up a finger and motioned one over.

"I think I'll have a drink, miss," he said, as he ran his hand through his dry, coarse hair.

"Certainly, sir," she said. "Each passenger is entitled to two alcoholic beverages. What would you like?"

"A vodka tonic, please."

"I think I'll have one, too," Nathan said. He nudged Claire. "How 'bout you?"

She looked at her wrinkled palms.

"Yes."

The attendant took out a note pad and made three checkmarks. "Three vodka tonics."

While they waited for their drinks, Alfred toyed with a coin.

"What is that, Alfred?" Claire asked.

"A very powerful good luck charm, my dear."

Nathan looked at him.

"You carry a good luck charm, Alfred?"

"Indeed."

Nathan shook his head, as the old man leaned forward and handed it to Claire.

"Please be careful with that," he said. "It is very valuable."

Claire took the coin and looked it over. Nathan watched from the corner of his eye.

"It's just a penny," he said.

Claire turned it over in her hand.

"Does it hold some sort of sentimental value?"

"Yes," said Alfred. "But that's not what makes it valuable. It's a 1969-S Lincoln cent with a doubled die obverse."

He looked at each of them as if expecting expressions of appreciation.

"So," Nathan said.

"So," said Alfred. "This coin is exceedingly rare. If you look closely, you will see a clear doubling of the entire obverse except for the mint marking, which would suggest a case of strike doubling. In this case, the doubling of the obverse without the doubled mint mark indicates a doubled die, which is what makes this coin so exceptional."

Nathan and Claire looked it over.

"The 'Liberty' looks blurry," Claire said.

"That's it," said Alfred.

"So you think this penny's lucky because it's blurry?" Nathan asked.

Alfred looked disappointed.

"No, it is only valuable because of this. Monetary value has no bearing on its ability to provide luck."

"How valuable is it?" Claire asked as she turned it by the edges between her thumb and index finger.

Alfred smiled, proudly.

"That coin is worth between 70 to 80 thousand dollars."

Claire stopped turning the coin and immediately cupped it with two hands.

"Jesus," Nathan said. "What the hell are you carrying it around for?"

Alfred shrugged.

"Because it is lucky for me."

Claire offered it back.

"Please take it. I'm afraid I'll lose it."

Alfred smiled and took it from her palm.

"I'd be rid of that thing as quickly as possible," Nathan said. "Take it to auction and be finished. I couldn't stomach the thought of losing something like that, lying in bed at night thinking about it passing from one take-a-penny/leave-a-penny jar to the next."

Alfred opened his jacket and pushed it into a pocket.

"I thought you weren't given to worry."

Claire smiled.

"Touché," Nathan said. "Still, I can't believe anyone on this plane believes in luck."

The old man looked at Claire and winked.

"It's bad luck not to believe in luck."

It was quiet for a moment, except for the tapping of Nathan's foot.

"The Secret Service confiscated the early specimens until the U.S. Mint finally admitted they were genuine," Alfred said. "Imagine that. All that expense to avoid the simple admission of a minor mistake."

Nathan dusted his lap.

"Well, that's the government for you. Where the hell is the alcohol?"

As if summoned by his words, the attendant arrived with their drinks. They slowly took liquor from the glasses, the warmth sweeping their bodies like a strong emotion, rushing through their veins and over their skin. Alfred wiped the wetness from his mustache.

"Tell us about yourself, Claire," he said. "If you will."

Claire rubbed her forehead and drank some more.

"I'm sorry, Alfred. I want to, but I can't."

Nathan flipped his hand.

"Don't worry, Alfred; I can tell you anything you need to know." He took a deep breath. "Our friend here is one of us without being one of us." He took the old man's arm. "You see, she is one of the precious few on this flight who is blessed with the genetic ability to succeed without barter. Look around you, if you will." He raised his hands over his head and made swirling motions with his index fingers. "All these passengers are busy giving their resumes to one another, their accomplishments, proof of their viability." He reached over and took Claire's hand. "Claire here has no need for such gainless strategies, because she automatically knows she is better than anyone here."

Claire ripped her hand away.

"I'm guessing most people don't like you very much," she said.

Nathan nodded.

"Perhaps. But you shouldn't trust anyone who is well-liked."

It was quiet for a moment.

"People at my lab dislike me because I don't use the e-mail," Alfred said finally.

"That seems like a very thin reason to dislike someone," Claire said.

"I leave notes for them," he said before downing the remainder of his drink. "On their desks mostly. I despise computers, though I'm forced to use them frequently to record data and such. But when it comes to communication, I wholeheartedly believe when someone puts a pen to paper, their words are truer than those placed in movable type, or electronic type as it were. To write by hand, it requires steady attention, at least if one is to craft legible script considerate of the reader's understanding. These days, few maintain the muscle coordination to print or scribe legibly, at least for long periods of time."

He leaned forward, his eyes growing wide and serious.

"Did you know they have moved away from teaching cursive in traditional public schools? Can you believe such a thing? You'd better because it is true."

He leaned back and looked to the ceiling for answers.

"It's archaic, they say. But there's so much more to it than simple facts and expressions writ to paper or digital storage devices. Ever so much more."

Nathan looked at Claire and smiled.

"Oh, simple thing, where have you gone?" he asked. "Quick," he addressed Claire. "Take this pen and scribe some coiling sentences to soothe our friend."

Alfred crossed his legs and raised a finger.

"Laugh all you want, but refinement for ease is not refinement at all."

He dusted his legs and looked from one to the other.

"You consider e-mail refinement for ease?" Claire asked.

"No, not at all," he said. "I'm a scientist, after all, not some old fool commit to useless relics that remind him of better days that never were."

He raised the finger again, as he seemed to do at the conclusion of every point.

"But when I want to send someone a message, I will have the consideration to raise a pen to the occasion."

Nathan tapped his elbow against Claire's arm.

"Wouldn't it be funny if his penmanship was indecipherable?"

Alfred shook his head.

"Oh, to be young and brilliant."

Nathan looked at him crossly.

"I'm 40, thank you very much."

The old man's face grew impressed.

"Oh, 40, my goodness."

Nathan raised his eyebrows.

"And what of smoke signals, Alfred? Will you be taking up their cause, as well?"

The old man leaned forward and took Claire's hand.

"Let me ask you this, my dear. Would you rather receive a love letter written by the very hand of your lover or one printed in New Times Roman?"

She smiled.

"I very much see your point."

His mouth grinned as he released her hand.

51

"And you," he turned to address Nathan. "Don't judge the old until you have gotten over the hill to see. And if your sweetheart ever writes you a letter by hand, you'd do well to regard the content with keen, attentive eyes."

Nathan put his hand atop the old man's shoulder.

"It's between the lines what counts, my old friend. True today as it was yesterday, machine text and handicraft alike."

The airplane bellied a thick pocket of air, loping suddenly and then falling just as fast. Some of the passengers groaned over the passing weightlessness, but Claire only felt Nathan's stare upon her while she gazed through the window glass.

"Tell me about yourself, Precious Few," he demanded.

"I have flat feet," she said without looking at him. "Is that the kind of thing you're asking?"

He bent over to take a closer look.

"At least they're only flat on the bottom."

She shook her head slightly, elbow on the armrest, chin nestled within her hand. Her eyes watched the moonlight pour over the tops of clouds, like an ethereal sun above a land of gossamer makings.

"I mean, what's your story?" he said.

She turned.

"It's not very interesting," she said. "Maybe you should just read that magazine."

He reached into the pocket on the backside of the chair before him and withdrew a Turkish publication called "Skylife."

"That's old news," he said. "It's been on the back of my toilet for weeks."

He rolled it up and began tapping it against his knee, as Alfred leaned back in his chair and shut his eyes.

"How'd you come about this little journey," he asked?

She looked at him crossly.

"Haven't you read your card?"

He reached into the interior pocket of his sport coat.

"What, this?"

He pushed the magazine back into the pouch and pulled his card from the little yellow envelope.

"What of it?" he said as he passed it over.

She pushed his hand away and looked around.

"I don't want that. For God's sake, put it back in your pocket."

A puzzled look spread over his face as he looked around.

"Jesus," he said. "It's just a little card."

She turned back toward the window.

"Let's not talk anymore. I don't think it's a good idea."

He took another look around the plane: most of the passengers trying to sleep, a few reading beneath pale little lights. He sat back down.

"Why?" he asked as he leaned toward her. "What does yours say?"

She did not respond.

"What does yours say?" he said loudly, another passenger clearing his throat at the disturbance.

"Shh," she whispered, placing her hand over his bare arm. "It says not to discuss myself with other passengers."

His jaw fell a little as her fingernails dug in.

"Alright, alright," he said rubbing the skin she'd just released.

His eyes grew suspicious of the woman before him, as if she'd just exposed herself as delusional. Just in case, he opened his envelope and withdrew his card to be sure he hadn't overlooked anything. When he was satisfied, he tossed it onto her lap, text up.

"Here," he said.

She flinched from it, her body turning wooden, as if he'd thrown a writhing serpent onto her legs.

"I don't want that," she said. "Please, stop this and take it back."

He shook his head and collected it in his fingers.

"Fine," he said, pointing it at her, his face stern. "You need to relax, Precious Few. This is going to be a long flight."

With that, he killed the overhead light and pushed his seat back, eyes closed, forearms wholly consuming both his armrest and hers.

She watched him for a moment, his mouth open and breathing. Dark morning stubble grew along his jaw and neck, but he was still a handsome man, with or without a shower, civility or refinement.

After a while, she turned her eyes back to the window, but her thoughts remained on his card, its message odd and troubling, the tone innocuous and soft.

"Welcome, Mr. Walker," it said. "We are very pleased you have chosen to participate and are confident you will find great success with our organization. Please let one of our agents know if you need anything during your trip, and thank you again for your commitment to The Xactilias Project. - Demetri M."

Chapter 7

The plane landed three times on its way to wherever it was going. Each time, its passengers remained seated without the slightest idea of where they were or how long they'd be there. As the hours passed, they muttered to one another and fidgeted in their seats. Outside the idle plane, they saw only paved tarmacs, the skylines empty of mountains or buildings, everything barren and lifeless and even as the blade of a knife. After countless hours in transit, the gravity of their choices had taken on size, whatever lives they had left behind growing both smaller and greater with every mile put between them and whatever was left behind.

Soon, little freedoms seemed to go away, attendants hard to flag, beverages and bathroom trips difficult to secure. Before long, a soft mutiny began its slow birth beneath the sustained quiet and order, but this was quelled by an unexpected announcement that they'd be landing soon and for the final time.

Within minutes, the plane began its descent, its passengers looking over one another out the windows, stiff-legged and aching and ready to get to their feet. Outside, they saw a forest land beneath them, tropical and lush, tiny toy motorboats zipping over the ocean along a flawless coast. They looked at each other with raised eyebrows and pleased expressions, some showing outright excitement, others the ease of relief.

The airplane rode the air downward and landed, the tires gripping seamlessly the runway as if caught up by an invisible corresponding track. The pilot brought the aircraft to a slow and wheeled it off the runway, settling on the tarmac and coming to a halt.

"I'm pleased to announce we've arrived at our tertiary destination," the pilot said through the intercom speakers. "Please unbuckle your safety belts and exit the plane in order, allowing those nearest the exits first opportunity. Once you've left the aircraft, Bernard will provide you with further instructions. I'm grateful to have had the opportunity to transport you and wish you much success with your new opportunities."

They exited the plane as instructed, the sun bright and centered above them, like a piercing white hole in the bold blue sky. There was an unfamiliar sweetness in the air, and it mingled with the scent of ocean salt, and as they descended the steps, a comforting wind cooled their sweating skin.

"Gather around me, please," said Bernard, his strict demeanor unaffected by the length of the flight. "You will all board shuttles, which will transport you to your temporary residences. In these, you will stay for three weeks."

He looked over them and smiled politely.

"It has been my privilege to oversee your journey; however, I must now leave you in the hands of Romero, who will be your guide over the next several weeks."

He put his hand out and a svelte-looking man stepped forward, his tanned arms and legs looking muscular and healthy against his white shorts and polo t-shirt.

"Welcome, guests," Romero said. "I'll be your host while you're here." He gave a crooked smile that made his perfectly symmetrical face seem more human. "I'm sure you are all very tired from your trip, so if you will all board a shuttle of your choosing, we'll be on our way."

Everyone looked at Bernard to see if Romero had erred in his orders, but the former had already begun walking the stairs back to the plane.

"Let's go," Romero said, and the passengers formed lines before various shuttles, many sticking with their seatmates from the plane. Claire took a place behind Alfred, and Nathan followed suit, his fingers furiously scratching the dark whiskers flourishing along his jawline.

"I need a shower and a shave," he said, as he ran his fingers through his hair.

"That sounds like heaven," Alfred said, as he took a seat inside the shuttle.

Claire selected the seat next to Alfred, while Nathan claimed the two in front of them, his leg draped across the other empty seat. Other passengers passed without seeming to notice and selected one of the many other seats available on the spacious shuttle bus.

When all the passengers had boarded, the doors clamped shut and the vehicles departed, the train's pacing far less precise than the one that had brought them all to the airport so many countless miles ago. The shuttles traveled along a sharp network of sculpted roads that ultimately devolved into dirt paths which could barely be called roads at all. The passengers held tightly, as the vehicles plunged over large water-filled holes, driving up great curtains of brown sludge that spread high and outward before spattering apart against oddly barked exotic trees.

Soon, the wildwood closed in around them, blotting away the sky before finally swallowing it whole. The headlights on the vehicles came to life; while unfamiliar bestial noises popped and shrieked in the not-so-far-away distance. As they burrowed deeper into the forest's heart, branches lashed out at the vehicles, breaking off at the windshield and stealing away some of the body paint. The passengers flinched at the sound of each metallic bong, the vehicles skidding left to right against the muddy earth.

"Where in the hell are we going?" Nathan whispered.

"Into a tropical forest of some sort, it appears," said Alfred, his hands clutching the cushion of his chair.

A crack of thunder shot across the unseen sky and rumbled into the distance. Droplets of rain followed almost immediately, slapping against huge leaves and pattering the roof overhead. Nathan showed gritting teeth as the vehicle jerked violently against a sudden void in the road.

"Any idea where we are?"

"Somewhere south of the equator," Claire said.

"How do you know?" Nathan asked.

"I noted the sun's position in the sky when we landed."

Suddenly the vehicle before them stopped in the middle of the road, its taillights burning red through droplets of dark mud. Alfred looked out the window.

"Something's going on."

"What is it?" Claire asked, but no one answered. "What is it?" she whispered.

"It's men," Alfred said. "Men with guns."

Nathan put his head out the window and quickly jerked it back inside.

"He's right. There are at least six on this side, all with machine guns."

Outside, the men fanned out around the vehicles, some barking orders to others in an unfamiliar tongue.

"What are they speaking?" Alfred asked.

"Portuguese," said Claire.

She passed a glance at one of the men through the window, his face heavily whiskered and bleeding sweat. Another man approached and stood next to him, each dressed in matching green fatigues, automatic machine guns in their hands. The two exchanged words as they peered into the forest, their eyes wide and seemingly concerned.

"What are they looking at?" Alfred asked, but none of the other passengers had an answer.

The driver of the shuttle turned and stood.

"Please, you must go now," he said in broken English.

Everyone looked at each other but no one stood. The driver pulled the lever and the door swung open.

"Please," he said. "Go now."

No one moved despite his request, most every seatbelt still securely fastened. The driver looked at them all through uncertain eyes, as Nathan stood and raised his finger.

"Shut that door," he said.

The driver looked at the door and then back to the American.

"Shut it."

The man shook his head and turned the lever, the door pressing shut, the other passengers closing their windows until the noise from outside reduced to a mutter.

"What do we do?" Claire asked, but she already knew the answer.

"I don't know that we have much choice but to sit still and hope our Mr. Romero can talk these people away," Alfred said.

They all waited in silence, the beat of the rain steady, like countless fingertips softly drumming atop the roof. While they sat, their heated breath fogged the windows until the outside world disappeared, its affairs seemingly distant and unreal.

Outside, the gunmen traded words, their conversations deliberate and slow. The passengers huddled silently, hearts throbbing violently within their chests. After a few moments, Nathan lifted from his seat.

"What are you doing?" another passenger asked, but Nathan didn't answer. Instead, he moved toward a window and used his finger to trace an eyelet in the condensation.

"What do you see?" Alfred asked. Nathan held up a finger and pushed his eye to the window. Outside, the gunmen busily emptied the other shuttles and lined the passengers alongside their vehicles, the rain picking up, mud hungrily sucking the soles of their dress shoes.

"They're taking the others from the shuttles, lining them up outside," he said.

A woman gasped and the other passengers quickly subdued her. Almost immediately, there came a hard banging against the shuttle door.

Without looking at the passengers, the driver turned the lever and the door swung open. The passengers stiffened as Romero stepped inside.

"I'm sorry for the surprise, my friends, but you must all exit the vehicle and join your colleagues outside." He took a step down before turning back. "Come on, now. Everything is perfectly alright. You have no reason to fear."

After hesitating for a moment longer, they detached their safety belts and shuffled toward the door. Outside, the raindrops seemed to fall in slow motion, before fracturing at last into countless water beads which melted against soil and clothing alike. Romero handed out green vinyl ponchos to each person as he or she exited the vehicle.

"Please, join the others," he said, as they slipped the rain gear on and pulled the hoods over their heads. When they'd all fallen in together, Romero stood before them and cleared his throat.

"Everyone, please, may I have your attention," he said. "I'm truly sorry for the inconvenience, but we must abandon these vehicles and travel afoot a short distance."

He pointed toward the gunmen, who were busy peering into the woods, rifle barrels pointing through gaps between trees.

"These men will be our protection as we make our journey," he said. "Without arising unnecessary fear, I can say they are an important defense against the potential dangers associated with the geography we currently occupy." He looked at their shoes. "I understand most of you are ill-equipped for this type of journey; however, we don't have the time to remedy this problem, so you will have to make do with what you have."

He turned and motioned one of the gunmen over. They spoke for a moment and then the man began walking up the road.

"Please follow me," Romero said. "You will all be well-served to trace the footsteps of the person before you. And please be kind enough to offer a helping hand to those who have difficulty staying up with the rest."

With that, he turned to go, adjusting his stride so his feet placed neatly in the lead gunman's water-filled tracks. Without speaking, the others followed suit, the rain popping against their ponchos and making a racket in their ears.

Overhead, the tall trees seemed to grow together to form a tunnel that choked out the light while disrupting the rainfall not at all. Beneath their waving branches, the men and women walked in a line with their heads down, eyes focused only on the path, minds calculating each and every step. As they plunged their feet into the existing steps, the foot holes grew deeper and deeper, until the mud tore the women's footwear from their feet, its suction greedily clutching the soles as they stopped to wrestle them free. Soon, most walked on bare feet, the road peppered with pricey pumps and loafers that jutted from the soppy ground like little hollow relics, as if the wearers had vanished without explanation, leaving only their shoes to declare they'd existed at all.

An elderly man buckled, his knees coming down hard against the ground. He struggled to his feet and moved on, only to go down again a few steps later. Nathan rushed forward and helped him to his feet.

"I'm afraid I can't manage this," the old man said, his fear concealed behind a thick pair of fogged eyeglass lenses. Nathan looked back at Claire and Alfred.

"Go ahead," he said. "I'll catch up."

They approached, their faces painted with concern.

"How can we help?" Alfred asked.

Nathan reached into his coat and removed a small pocketknife.

"Just keep up with the rest," he said. "I'll catch up." He looked at the old man. "Wait here a moment."

He slogged through the mud and stumbled onto the thicket's grassy edge. Claire and Alfred gave the old man a nod before moving forward, all the others growing distant in the murky curtain of drizzle before them.

They trod through the sucking muck, their figures swallowed up by the fog that lifted from the road. Through the rain, they heard nothing, not the birds, the strange noises from before, not the gunmen or even the sound of their own panting. The mud grew loose and deep, and they forced their quivering legs along, each one leaning against the other's body, pulling and pushing as necessary, not a sign of anyone before them, nor anyone behind.

Finally, Alfred stopped.

"I'm sorry, my dear; you will have to go on ahead."

"I won't hear of it, Alfred. Now, let's go."

He sat in the mud.

"I can't. These old bones just won't let me."

Claire sat on the ground beside him.

"I'm not going to leave you."

They waited.

"Will they be coming back?" Alfred asked.

She put her arm over his shoulder, and they leaned in together.

"Surely," she said.

Claire looked through the rain at all the lavish growth flowing in the wind, the tremendous leaves innumerable, tiny rivers flowing brown in the alleys alongside the road. As the water puddled around them, thunder rolled overhead, as if God impatiently thrummed the heavens at wait for their next move.

At last, they sat in the road, feet aching, skin made fragile by soggy shoes, peeling away in spots, stinging. Someone approached from behind and Claire turned to see the old man, his arm around Nathan's waist, a crude walking stick in the other.

"No time for a break," Nathan said.

Claire stood while Alfred regarded the old man's cane.

"Cut me one of those, and I'll see what I can do," he said.

An hour later, they crossed out of the fog to see Romero crouched over the ground, a small stick in his hand, linear patterns carved into the soil. To his right sat a pair of large armored military buses, their engines idling,

"I'm relieved to see you," he said, unconvincingly. He nodded toward the woods, and a pair of gunmen exited the thicket. "These men have kept a watchful eye on you; however, they are only being paid to protect and not to aid. Forgive me for your plight, but as I told the other passengers, we are taking special measures to ensure that we do not fall victim to opportunistic parties."

He walked over to one of the bus's giant tires and used the edge to cleave mud from his boot.

"Please," he said. "Join your colleagues. You will find towels and water inside."

As they entered the bus, each received a towel and a large bottle of water, which they nearly emptied on sight. As they moved through the aisle, they passed numerous weary faces, gaunt and timid and streaked with crusted mud that had given away its earthy tones and settled to an ashy gray. They found plenty of open seats near the middle of the bus and settled together, Claire and Alfred on one side of the aisle, Nathan and the old man the other. Nathan turned backward and addressed a pair of stupefied women.

"What did we miss?"

One of the women looked up and scratched a flake of mud from below her ear.

"He didn't really say anything. Just told us to get on the bus, take a towel."

Nathan nodded and turned around.

"May I ask your name, good sir?

The old man smiled.

"My name is Arnold."

He lifted his water and drank, his hand trembling. Nathan waited while the old man lowered the bottle and used his sleeve to dry his mouth.

"Thank you so much for your kindness," Arnold said. "I was once a formidable athlete, I'm ashamed to say. But in life, you lose things."

Alfred leaned over.

"I can relate, my friend," he said. "I once ran track and field, but I can hardly imagine moving that quickly anymore."

Arnold nodded. "Time has a quick hand, so it seems."

The bus began moving, its giant tires churning the soil and spitting up mud.

"I'm sorry. I haven't learned your names," Arnold said.

They introduced themselves and traded handshakes.

"Are you feeling alright," Claire asked. "Would you like some of my water?"

Arnold smiled and held up his hand.

"No, dear, thank you. I'll be fine. I just need to rest. Perhaps we can pick up our conversation when we arrive at wherever it is, we are going."

She nodded, and they left him to rest against the wall of the bus, his towel wadded into a makeshift pillow.

Nathan leaned toward the aisle.

"This whole thing is getting out of hand," he whispered.

Alfred nodded.

"Agreed. But I don't know what means we have to alter our course."

Claire scratched the mud from her calves.

"I agree with Alfred. It's only practical to wait and see what happens."

Nathan lifted his head and rubbed the stubble beneath his chin.

"I'll feel better when I can cut this down, have a shower."

They rode in silence the rest of the way, the old man asleep, whistling through his nose. Alfred slept, as well, while Claire and Nathan watched the scenery blow past through pink, wired eyes.

Two hours later, the buses breached the forest's perimeter and spilled out onto a long road that divided rambling fields of sugar cane. Almost immediately the rain ceased, the sun boring forth as if to welcome them from their journey through a dark and ancient land. The light evoked a stirring amongst the passengers, who climbed to their feet and gazed out the windows. Outside, they saw rows of plants flowing under the sunlight, the leafy blades bright green and whipping all around in the wind.

They continued through the fields, the ground turning hard and choppy, the chugging tires jolting the passengers for several miles. Finally, the buses climbed out of the fields and onto a stretch of flat, combed land. Soon, structures began to appear: silos, water towers and large storage buildings surrounded by tall electrified fences. Several miles later, they saw the coast appear in the distance, the water glinting brightly under the sun as it roiled against long away sands.

An hour later, they reached their destination, the buses slowing and then stopping before a gate, which gave access through a chain-linked fence that spanned the outer edges of what appeared to be a massive concrete dome. Security personnel guarded the entry, automatic weapons firm in their hands. Romero exited his bus and gave one of the guards a glossy little card. The man looked it over, his face broad, square and expressionless. He raised his hand and swung it forward and the gates drew open so the buses could pass through.

The dome sat at least 500 yards inside the gate, and as they approached, its mass seemed to both rise and expand, the passengers pressing their faces against their windows to get a better look at its size.

"This just keeps getting stranger," Alfred said.

"I agree," said Claire.

As they approached the dome, more armed men appeared, and the buses settled to a stop. Once again, Romero exited and showed his card, the guards nodding and then returning to their posts. Romero signaled the drivers, who opened the bus doors.

"Please exit carefully," Romero shouted.

The passengers flowed from the buses and gathered outside.

"We'll now be entering the enclosure," Romero said. "Please form a line."

One of the soldiers approached a keypad mounted on the sidewall next to a metal door. He typed something and the door popped open to reveal a steel grid walkway that led inside through a narrow hall toward a large elevator door. One by one, everyone entered and walked toward the elevator, their shoes and bare feet slapping hollowly against the cold metal below.

"Excuse me," Romero said, as he squeezed between them and approached another keypad positioned just to the right of the elevator. He typed something and the doors separated to reveal a large platform. "Please enter."

When all had done so, Romero typed against yet another keypad and the doors closed. The elevator dropped rapidly and without sound, a tickling in their stomachs upon its descent. Seconds later, they came to a stop and the doors opened to reveal an elaborately decorated lobby stocked with plush-looking couches, which were buttressed by end tables supporting stacks of varying genres of magazines. Directly in front of them, about 80 feet away, a very tall, beautiful woman sat behind a large curved receptionist desk, her attention fixed downward, hand furiously writing.

"Please exit," Romero said, and when they all had, the woman raised her head and smiled.

"Welcome," she said, as she pushed a stack of documents aside and moved to join them.

Romero held his hand out.

"This is Gretchen, and she will attend to all your needs during your stay at the spa."

The guests exchanged looks, as the lofty woman approached.

"For the next two weeks, you will reside here at our spa," Romero said. "During this time, you will be allowed access to a variety of relaxation services and recreational activities. The purpose of this time is to acquaint you with your new responsibilities, while providing you the opportunity to acclimate to your new surroundings and familiarize with your co-workers."

He turned to Gretchen and nodded.

"I'm very pleased to have you all here," she said, eyes gleaming and impossibly blue. "Here at our spa, we provide the best of everything. Should you need anything of any sort, you are to visit me or one of our other recreational therapists, understood?"

She turned to Romero and smiled.

"I know you all have plenty of questions," Romero said. "However, these are best kept for another time. For now, I'll be leaving you with Gretchen. In two weeks, I will return to move you to your permanent quarters in the lower levels of the facility and introduce you to the work area, where you will conduct your individual research based on The Xactilias Project's specific needs at that time."

Romero turned to Gretchen and nodded. Then he checked his watch and reentered the elevator. The guests turned to watch him disappear behind the doors. Gretchen returned to her post, her broad upper body towering above the desk.

"Please form a line and I'll get you each checked in one-by-one."

As they registered, she offered each a keycard labeled with a large number.

"This is the key to your quarters," she said. "Please do not lose it, or you'll be forced to move to a new room, as we do not issue new keys."

When they'd all registered, she instructed them to visit their quarters and clean themselves.

"You'll find suitable articles of clothing inside your closets," she said. "Each will be tailored to your individual needs if necessary. Just let us know."

The guests looked around but saw no staff lurking about.

"You'll find a button mounted to the wall of your quarters, adjacent to the door," she said. "Should you need assistance, press this button and a recreational therapist will arrive shortly."

She left the desk again and stood before them.

"Tomorrow, we will meet at 9 a.m. for orientation, when you'll be introduced to the spa area, cafeteria and recreational facilities, which include a weight room and racquetball court."

She folded her arms and smiled, her lips pressed firmly, eyebrows raised, as if she expected applause or some other form of giddy feedback. The others traded looks and then dispersed to search for their rooms, muddy feet staggering wearily down a bright, expansive hallway.

Claire and Nathan followed Alfred to his room and waited. He opened the door and tipped the light switch up.

"Not 5-star, but it will do," he said.

Inside, there was a bed, a nightstand, a dresser and not much else.

"All I care about right now is a shower," Nathan said.

They entered and Alfred walked to the bathroom.

"Standing shower," he said.

"Don't tell me you're a bath guy, Alfred," Nathan said.

Alfred shook his head and sat on the bed.

"I may just go to sleep without bathing."

Claire took Nathan's arm.

"Let us leave you, Alfred," she said. "Sleep well. We'll see you tomorrow."

Outside, the hallway sat empty, the red carpet fouled by wild trails of dried mud, as if it had been unevenly dusted with bucket-throws of cinnamon. Nathan followed Claire to her room and waited while she slipped her key card into the slot.

"I look a lot better once I've cleaned up," he said, as he gouged a hunk of mud from his boot.

"Too bad you can't wash your personality."

As she opened the door, he smiled and put his hand out.

"Thanks for the laughs."

She looked at his dirty fingers and gave them a brief shake.

"I'll see you tomorrow, Nathan."

He gave a trademark smile and walked away, sport coat thrown over one shoulder, lips whistling bright notes, as if he walked through his own home on the most ordinary of days.

She watched him the whole way, head poking further out into the hallway with each step, before he finally stopped and turned back to see only her hair flitting by, and then the shut of the door.

Chapter 8

Glenn Foley cannot read, but that is alright. For what he wants, it truly is. A truck driver and proud of it, he scrapes what leavings the world allows him into a life that makes him feel rich, valuable and whole. Others agree with his appraisal. Those others, not peers, but members of his family. For them, he gives everything. For them, he paves paths he never knew.

Before that, he is of the sorry and blaming, of the can't and never will. Born into the world strapped with bad genes, clueless parents and no mind of his own, Glenn middles along intentionless for a long while with no real reason to keep going, save the automatics working within his brain.

Out of school at 14, he spends the first part of his adult life working ditches, mowing lawns and laboring over endless conveyor belts for long hours and laughable pay. With no goals or angles, he is an odds-on favorite for nothing special, until he meets Dawn McWilliams, a local grocery cashier with a similar background and a future that seems parallel.

But Dawn McWilliams can read, and read more than the printed gossip in the magazines that seduce customers within her aisle. She can read people. And when she meets Glenn Foley, she reads his face and his soul and her future in the depths of his sad brown eyes.

Twice a week, he chooses her aisle over all others, giving no credence to the length of the line or his wavering will. See their flirtation, but don't judge its tranquility. Within it, there is stirring and bold desire, and the world is shut out by it, and the clocks keep ticking, though there is no time at all.

Their marriage brings a child and a reason, and Glenn works with Dawn on a lie that paints his abilities in false lights. He becomes a truck driver and stable provider, and his little family prospers, the world oblivious to their makings and throwing up few complaints.

In the beginning, he speaks of serendipity, of the nation and all its sites. He talks of the mountains, with their coiling roads, the bold ascensions and the terrifying drops, his boot against the brake, the pads against the rig's weight, the smells of burning rubber, of sore arms and foreign hotel beds.

He is gone almost all the time; but at home, on certain days and nights, the child sits at the feet of this hero stranger, while he speaks of faith and persistence, love and duty, the world's largest ball of twine and the St. Louis Gateway Arch.

Over a span of decades, he dips in and out of his family's life, not for want but necessity. If he could, he would be there always; but he can't, and they know it and understand. He goes on this way for as long as he must; his back constricting to a permanent arch; his soul grayed by all the missing, body ruined by years of bad food. By the end, he is broken down and used thin. But his victory extends outward; for his daughter is educated and pulled forth by the gravity of her promise, with abilities that are confusing to him, but wondrous just the same.

Claire hears this story enough until its weight falls against her every choice. A torch pushed into her diminutive hand at an early age, she carries a slim flicker of reason for her parents' woe and quickly becomes the embodiment of their hope. They know neither the inner workings of the world's secrets nor the strings that others use to make it spin. But they know enough to recognize that she wields the power to someday see each and both at the same time, and they recognize this gift while she is at a very young age.

At 13 months, she is talking in complete sentences. At 18 months, she has memorized the alphabet and knows the colors in English and Spanish: red and yellow, aureolin and fawn. At two, she can count to 20 in three different languages and do simple arithmetic using only her fingers. At four, her parents enroll her in a Montessori school, and she learns Spanish in just over a month.

Every day, she rises early with a constant, compulsive drive to learn, her mind receiving an almost sensual ecstasy from it, her brain like a heart in love. To her, learning is not of mastering; it is of experiencing. Vivid and absorbing, it penetrates and arouses, its absence causing pain, its presence, relief.

To her parents, it is a troubling addiction, and no amount of ordinary play will coax her from it. When knowledge is withheld, her mood turns gray and she becomes anxious and withdrawn. She must know everything about everything: lizards, grasses and planets, organic sediments, minerals and rock.

Sometimes she wants traditional cartoon stories at night. Mostly, she wants books on natural history. These, her parents use to train her in toilet habits, a sizable stack fixed strategically to keep her in place.

The schools are no good for Claire, a feeble curriculum, the lessons but pointless tasks. They ask her to solve 6+8; she makes 36-piece origami forms on her dining room table. They give her Frog and Toad Are Friends; she reads Les Miserable at home. How long can you anesthetize a child before you finally put them to sleep? This is the question her parents ask themselves every day.

The playground expounds on the classroom's folly, the other children distrusting of this odd figure before them, venomous in their response. She tries hard to be like everyone else, failing miserably in almost every way. At home, she becomes sleepless and depressed until her abilities turn from gifts into something to wish away.

At last, she is moved ahead several grades against the resistance of the school heads, their brows pressed with worry, mouths uttering warnings regarding social inadequacies. But in the end, her parents agree: what could be worse than this? For it is just as difficult to kneel or stoop as it is to stand upon toes.

At first, the move offers improvement, but soon, she is stretching the teachers past their abilities. The older students will spend a year on their textbooks; she sucks them dry within the first several days. Ultimately, they craft personalized curriculums and teach her on the side. But the more they feed this mind, the greater its cravings, until their cupboards are empty, and the deprivation returns.

They visit a private school for the gifted, and her test scores astound. There, they craft improvised parallel curriculums that soar above the heads of the gifted others. She ranges far beyond her classmates, mostly fixated on a newfound world of subatomic particles. At the conclusion of the program's fourth grade, the school heads agree she can go no further in such an institution.

Through personal connections, the headmaster secures a meeting with an influential representative from a prominent research university devoted to engineering and applied science. He is a doubtful man with big gray unkempt brows that have begun to hang over his eyes.

He meets with her parents and the headmaster for only a short time, and then she is placed alone in a cold sterile room before a tall varnished table that comes to her chin. There, the stern figure slaps a stack of papers under her nose, its questions requiring answers that will measure her IQ.

As he paces the width of the table, she populates each field, her hands appearing infant-like as she scribbles against the paper. When she stops writing, he snatches the test away, his eyes darting about the pages, his tired face made bright and pale by unbelieving. The exam's IQ distribution chart ends at 145; somewhere beyond, lies Claire.

Chapter 9

For nearly a week, the guests wandered the facilities without responsibilities, dipping in and out of hot tubs, taking massages, and drinking at the bar. In the mornings, the room lights would ignite automatically, a gentle combination of pinks and yellows that flared gently and considerately, until the senses enlivened, and the rooms took on a warm, comforting glow. For meals, they met together in a large but comfortable cafeteria, the food like something from a dream, with flavorful meats, brightly colored fruits and rich, flaky pastries that were always fresh, delicious and warm.

In the early afternoons, most gathered in the little round courtyard, where they sat among the sweet scent of flowers, chatting over coffee beneath willowy trees that shaded courteously the soft, green grass. Most kept tightly within the circles established during their journey; Claire, Nathan and Alfred no different, the three of them together the majority of the time, trading stories and theories, growing closer and happier for it.

At night, Alfred would usually retire early leaving Claire and Nathan at the bar, where they pried at each other's layers with subtle tactics both cunning and kind.

"Tell me about your research," he said one night, as he sipped a small glass of bourbon under an amber light.

"It mostly revolves around experimental research on human aging," she said. "Strategies to replenish DNA telomeres to make cells immortal and thereby prevent aging."

He pursed his lips and nodded.

"Have you made any strides?"

She sipped from a glass of red wine and nodded.

"Major strides; however, any sort of telomere-based anti-aging treatment is apt to increase cancerous growths and therefore increase mortality."

He nodded and lowered his head, his finger tracing the wet circle on the bar top where his glass had been.

"What's the nature of your research?"

He looked up at her and smiled.

"Experimental methods for cancer prevention."

They sat quietly after that, their minds pondering the meaning of these things and others. The mystery of The Xactilias Project. The mystery of each other.

The next morning, everyone congregated as usual in the cafeteria, where they filled their trays with thickly cut bacon, sausages, fresh berries, warm strudels, croissants and tarts. Like every other day, Alfred blended into the line and filled his tray with a wealth of rations, his face bashful and apologetic, as if he had taken each morsel from the plate of a starving child.

Once he'd acquired his share, he surveyed the tables and found Claire and Nathan sitting across each other, their trays samely glutted with far too much food. He hurried across the room and took a seat next to Claire.

"Every day I come into this room, my mind recalls the story of Hansel and Gretel," he said, as he raised a fork.

Nathan nodded.

"I've gained at least five pounds," he said, his words distorted by a mouthful of half-chewed food.

Claire watched him and scowled.

"Close your mouth. That's disgusting."

He smiled broadly, his cheeks pregnant with food.

Alfred took a sample from his tray and gently placed it inside his mouth. He lifted from his chair and took a long look around the cafeteria.

"Why do you suppose all the rooms in this place are round?"

Nathan glanced about and shrugged.

"Tell us about your research, Alfred," Claire said, as if she hadn't heard his comment.

The old man swallowed a mouthful of food and brushed a few stray crumbs from his mustache.

"I'm afraid it's not as fascinating as yours," he said. "It's mostly centered on practical solutions for utilizing water to produce hydrogen fuel." He stabbed his fork into a chunk of ham and held it for a moment. "Long before that, I was quite fascinated with neurological research. However, it didn't suit my abilities."

He raised the ham to his lips and then pulled it away.

71

"Sometimes, you have to choose to either pursue a passion in a limited capacity or apply your abilities to more practical endeavors that will allow you to acquire the lifestyle you desire."

Claire started to say something, but he cut her off.

"I did always enjoy neurological research, though. It was all I could think about as a boy."

Nathan passed a look to Claire, who gave a small apologetic smile for getting the old man started.

"When I was 12, I entered a school science fair with a project in which I manipulated rats into doing quite remarkable things."

Claire winked at Nathan, who grimaced a little.

"What sort of things?" she asked.

"Well, let's see," he said. "I taught one to stack blocks, and another learned to use a small key to open a door within a maze."

Nathan stopped eating.

"How?"

"Oh, it was really very simple. I got them addicted to amphetamines. They'd do anything for it. Plus, the drug itself made them quite adept at picking up new skills."

They all ate quietly for several minutes, others finishing up their meals and filing out the room.

"Well, did you win?" Nathan finally asked.

Alfred looked up, his face contorted a bit as if he'd forgotten the nature of the conversation.

"Oh, no," he said. "Another student invented a sock with a pocket on it." He shook his head and smiled. "The judges were captivated."

A man approached the table.

"Mind if I join you?"

Nathan turned to look at him.

"Howard! Good to see you. Of course, take a load off."

He sat next to Nathan and placed his tray on the table.

"Claire," Nathan said. "This is Howard."

Howard shook her hand. Alfred looked over Howard's plate, which held two hardboiled egg whites and some boiled asparagus.

"A meager appetite amidst such gluttony. Are you dieting?"

Howard looked at his plate.

"Oh, I'm afraid my stomach wouldn't tolerate much more than this. It's been a problem of mine for years."

They all frowned for Howard.

72

"It's not such a tragedy," he said. "I've grown used to it."

Nathan nodded, as he shoved a forkful of food into his mouth.

"Yeah, he's fine," he mumbled. "Don't worry about Howard."

They all returned to eating, a slightly uncomfortable silence between them.

"I know," said Howard. "Let's play useless facts."

"Fire it up," said Nathan, as he scooped another heap of food into his mouth.

Claire looked at Alfred.

"What's this?"

Alfred shook his head.

"Apparently, one attempts to impress the other with factual oddities which have no discernible use."

Nathan pointed his fork at Alfred and spoke through a full mouth.

"It has to be interesting, though. Otherwise, you lose."

Howard nodded.

"I'll start." He cleared his throat. "Flamingos get their color from the carotenoid pigments in the algae and crustaceans they eat."

Claire jabbed her fork into a pile of green beans.

"I can think of discernible uses for that information."

Nathan swallowed his food.

"Ignore her, Howard. She doesn't get it."

He thought for a moment.

"People have been chewing gum for more than 5,000 years."

"A blue whale's tongue is as heavy as a full-grown elephant," Howard said.

"A cheetah can run from zero to 60 in three seconds," said Nathan.

"Seahorse reproduction requires the male to birth the young."

"Anteaters eat 35,000 ants a day."

"An ostrich can move 16 feet in one stride."

"An ostrich can kill a lion with a single kick."

"Elephants can smell water from miles away."

Claire looked at Alfred.

"Why so National Geographic?"

Nathan glanced at her.

"It's more interesting," he said.

He thought for a moment. "Alright. This one's for Claire." He cleared his throat. "NASA's vehicle assembly building is so large, actual rain clouds form below the ceiling."

73

He looked at Claire and smiled.

"It has its own weather."

She shook her head and ate.

"Each person has two to nine pounds of bacteria in his body," said Howard.

He looked at Claire, who'd stopped chewing.

"Sorry."

Nathan grinned.

"When a male bee climaxes, his testicles explode, and he dies."

He laughed.

"You're ridiculous," she said.

"You go ahead, then," he said. "Illuminate us."

She set her fork down and used a napkin to wipe her mouth.

"There are more atoms in one cup of water than there are cups of water in all the oceans of the world."

They sat in silence for a moment.

"Boring," Nathan said.

She thought for a moment.

"Half of all humans who have ever lived on Earth died of malaria."

Nathan shook his head.

"Now, that's just depressing."

"Charlie Chaplin once entered a Charlie Chaplin look-alike contest and came in third," Alfred said.

"There you go," said Nathan. "Is that true, by the way?"

Alfred nodded.

"Owning a cat can reduce your risk of stroke by 33 percent," said Claire.

Nathan and Howard looked at each other.

"It's not uninteresting, but try something a little less scientific," Howard said. "Perhaps a shocking oddity of some sort."

She thought for a moment and pushed her tray aside. She leaned forward and all else followed suit until they were huddled in a circle across the table, like accomplices conspiring over some plot.

She cleared her throat.

"The Mexican General Santa Anna had an elaborate state funeral for his amputated leg," she said.

They traded looks.

"With speeches, poems, a 21-gun salute, a flag over the coffin," she continued.

74

Nathan shook his head.

"For a leg," she said.

They traded smiles and looked at Claire, but her eyes were fixed on what was coming up behind them.

"Ms. Foley," Gretchen said, as her towering body swallowed the space behind both men. "Mr. Romero requests your presence in the conference room."

Nathan and Alfred looked back at her and then to their friend, who pushed her tray away and stood.

"Of course," she said. "Would you be kind enough to empty my tray?"

Both men nodded as she followed Gretchen out of the cafeteria.

They made their way down the hallway, which curved sharply around a bare cement wall. When they reached the conference room, Gretchen opened the door and then walked away without speaking. Claire watched the mountainous woman retreat the way she'd come, then she entered the room to find Romero seated alone at the opposite side of a long conference table.

"Please, take a seat," he said, his hand pointing to the chair across from him.

She sat.

"Ms. Foley, I've called you here to prep you for your meeting with the head of our organization. Do you understand?"

"Yes."

"Good." He scribbled something on a clipboard and set it aside. "Most of your associates will take their instruction from the heads of the departments that govern their particular fields of study. A select few have attained special status for one reason or another. You are one of these select few."

He straightened in his chair and folded his hands neatly.

"Tomorrow morning, I'll greet you in the lobby at six. From there, we'll take the elevator into the mid-level division of the building, where you'll meet the leader of our project."

He waited for a response, but she gave none.

"Do you have any questions?"

She rubbed the back of her neck.

"No."

"Alright, then. Let's proceed."

He reached for his clipboard and read.

"You are to dress professionally with no jewelry of any sort. This means no bracelets, necklaces, earrings, pendants, hair clips. Do you understand?"

She gave a nod, but he never looked up to see it.

"Leave your purse behind. Carry no metallic objects whatsoever. Not even coins."

He looked at her.

"In fact, don't bring any money. That's very important."

She swallowed.

"May I ask why?"

He shrugged.

"You can, but I won't be able to answer."

She frowned.

"Alright."

He read from his clipboard.

"Don't bring anything edible, and this includes chewing gum. Wear flat-soled shoes and double-check to make sure they don't have any metallic clips or attachments."

He turned to the next page.

"You may wear lipstick, foundation and concealer, but no eyeliner or eye shadow. Do not wear perfume. Do not use hairspray. Pantyhose are fine, but they must be flesh tone. You can bring photographs if you have them, but you must not take photographs under any circumstances."

He stopped talking and passed the clipboard over, along with a pen.

"Now, please sign at the bottom if you agree to everything I've just told you."

She took the pen and signed her name.

"Do you have any questions?"

She shook her head.

"Good." He smiled politely. "I'll meet you in the lobby tomorrow morning at six. Please be on time."

They both stood and exchanged cordial nods. Then she left the room to look for Nathan and Alfred.

After checking the usual places, she finally found them drinking coffee in the courtyard, and when Nathan saw her coming, he stood.

"Everything alright?" he asked.

She approached with her head down, eyes darting softly at the handful of others that sat on benches or in the easy, delicate grass.

"I have no idea," she said as she joined them. "Things are no less strange, that's for sure."

"How do you mean?" Alfred asked.

She told them everything and they lingered quietly for a moment, Alfred smoking his pipe, the rich smell driving some of the others inside. Nathan looked up at the retractable concrete ceiling and then down to the neatly cut grass.

"This place is bat-shit crazy."

"When are you supposed to meet this person?" Alfred asked.

"Early tomorrow morning."

"I'd assume this is our Mr. Demetri."

Alfred pinched his bushy brows together.

"Demetri?"

Claire and Nathan exchanged looks.

"From the card," Nathan said.

Alfred reached inside his pocket and withdrew his welcome card. He turned it over.

"Mine's signed Dominic Betancur."

Claire took the card from his hand as if the old man could lie.

"I guess we don't know who's in charge after all," Nathan said.

They stood a while longer in that bright little place, talking about each other, about their past, about the lives they'd put on hold. But no one was really present. And no one seemed to notice when the conversation waned.

That night, Claire retired early, leaving Alfred and Nathan alone at the bar, long handshakes and good lucks, some reassuring smiles.

"It will be fine," Alfred said, as she walked away.

"I know," she said, with a nod. "Don't worry about me."

But later, alone in her room, she was different, an unforgiving anxiety in her stomach, like some breakaway sickness that could not be stalled. And it persisted while she showered, while she lay in bed, and into the late hours when a gentle knock brought her back from a close brush with sleep.

She sat up in bed and gathered the covers against her chest, her eyes on the door, ears straining for any hint of noise. Three more soft taps at the door. Then nothing. Then a whisper, "Claire." She escaped the covers and put on a robe. She approached the door and put her hand against it, as if she might learn the visitor's identity by a hint of warmth or lack thereof.

"Yes?" She said with a graveled voice not her own.

"It's Nathan."

She relaxed and took a breath.

"Just a second."

She moved to the mirror and tried to coerce her hair without accomplishing much of anything.

"What are you doing here?" she asked through the door.

"I wanted to see you," he said. "Can you just let me in?"

She quit the fight and moved to the door. She opened it and he came inside.

"It's late, Nathan," she began, but before she could finish, he kissed her.

She turned her head and pulled back.

"I'm sorry," he said, but his arm was still around her waist.

She looked down for a moment, and then her eyes drifted upward, and whatever he saw in them strengthened his resolve. He gathered her up in his arms and brought the tips of their noses together. This time, she lifted her chin to oblige, her body awash with chills and warmth all at once. Their mouths came together flush, his soft lips skilled and practiced, his touch so overwhelming, her head felt light.

For several minutes they went on this way, and then they were on the bed and she was atop him, her legs spread over his lap, nightgown pushed back over her knees. He took her lower lip between his and sucked it, while she clawed her fingers through his thick, black hair.

While she worked his mouth, his hands explored her body, his fingertips traveling slowly from her bare shoulders down to the small of her back. As he kissed her, the smell of his unfamiliar cologne made its way into her mind, like some invisible narcotic that would not be turned down.

She looked up into his dark eyes, an animal looking out from the other side. Then it was all seamless, their bodies together in an easy, relentless harmony, as if they weren't new friends at all, but familiar lovers after a long separation. When it was over, they laid together without speaking, their breathing heavy, bodies exhausted, and each one gathering up energy for a long night ahead.

Chapter 10

The next morning, she found Romero waiting patiently in the lobby, his usual attire replaced with a military uniform complete with polished black boots and a hat which he held at his side. When he saw her, his eyes traveled the length of her body.

"Very nice," he said, with a smile that seemed unfitting to her eyes.

She glanced down at her skirt and cleared her throat.

"Are you ready?" he asked, as he placed his hat on his head and pulled the bill low over his dark eyes.

"Yes."

He turned and tapped codes into the keypad and the elevator doors yawned open. They both entered in turn and he repeated the process in reverse.

"It will be a bit of a walk," he said, as they made the brief descent to the lower floor.

When the doors opened again, everything looked different. Before her eyes, a network of narrow metallic platforms seemed to sprawl in all directions. The floors weren't really floors at all, but stainless-steel grids lined to make a walkway over what? Who could say? The darkness below stretched down hundreds of feet or more.

"This way," he said.

He hurried forward without looking back, Claire following closely, like a child on the heels of her father in some dark, uncertain place. Every several feet, the platforms shot off to the left or to the right toward destinations that might be surprising to all but the knowing. To eyes like hers, the layout seemed ill-conceived to be anything else but intentionally confusing.

With every step, she held firmly the safety rails on both sides. As her hands slid atop them, a curious chalky dust bloomed up into the air and then quickly dissipated under the bold halogen lights, which effectively illuminated the steel walking platforms and not much else. Romero achieved impressive gains with each step, and she hurried along to keep up, her flat-soled shoes shooting off little metallic pings that echoed in all directions.

They walked for some time, taking lefts and rights through a seemingly endless maze of platform walkways that featured no markers, signs or numbers, nothing to tell you where you were going or how to get back. Finally, they arrived at yet another elevator and Romero accessed it by tapping more numbers into a keypad.

"Please," he said, holding his hand toward the open elevator.

She entered, but he did not follow.

"You'll take this elevator down to the third level of the facility, where you will meet with the head of our organization. Do you understand?"

She nodded, and with that, he typed against the keypad and the elevator doors pressed shut.

She barely felt the elevator move before the doors opened again, this time revealing a very dark, very long room. At the end of the room, an old woman sat at a small desk, and when Claire exited the elevator, the woman looked up and smiled.

"Come forward, dear," she said. "It's alright."

Claire approached the woman, her aged features poorly lit by a small work lamp, the only lighting in the vast room.

"I'm sorry for the darkness," she said. "Mr. Betancur is very particular about a great many things."

Claire stood before her desk. She looked for a chair, but there were none. The old woman finished writing something and then stood. She moved to the other side of the desk and made a complete circle around Claire, an old crooked finger to her lips, tongue making ticking noises against the roof of her mouth.

"Your makeup and attire look right," she said. "Did you wear any jewelry?"

"No."

"Good. Very good." She circled her again, this time stooping low to get a look at her legs. "Flesh-toned pantyhose, good."

She straightened with some obvious discomfort, a hand on her lower back, another on her knee.

"Did you bring any money or photographs?"

"No money," Claire said. "I have a photograph of my mother."

"Let me see it," the old woman said.

Claire withdrew the picture and handed it to her. The old woman held it by the edges and returned to her desk. She sat down with great care, as if her whole body were made of glass, then she held the photograph to the light and examined it.

"This looks alright."

She reached inside a drawer and removed a rubber stamp. She turned the photograph upside down and made a wet red impression of an inverted triangle.

"Ok," she said, as she fanned the picture in the air and passed it back to Claire. "You can go inside now."

She pointed to three equally sized steel doors.

"His is the one in the middle."

Claire approached the door and stopped. She looked over her shoulder at the old woman.

"Go ahead, dear," the woman said with a tender smile.

Claire nodded and turned. She grasped the handle and gave it a twist.

Inside, everything was dark, except for a very large desk that appeared to glow beneath the light of a small work lamp. Behind it sat a man, his hands folded neatly, a firm expression upon his face, like that of someone lost in meditation or a ticklish set of thoughts.

She crossed the threshold and closed the door behind her. She tried to speak, but he silenced her with a finger. He sat there a moment longer, his eyes fixed on nothing in particular. Then he picked up a very expensive-looking pen and wrote something on a small yellow notepad. When he finished, he opened a drawer, slipped the pad inside, and closed it without making any sound. He looked at her and smiled.

"Hello," he said, as he pushed his chair back and stood. "My name is Dominic Betancur."

He approached and stood before her, his height imposing, a Spanish accent dripping from his tongue.

"I am very pleased to finally meet you," he said.

He offered a handshake and she accepted it, her fingers disappearing inside his large, enveloping hand.

"Please," he said, "sit down."

He pointed to a chair that sat immediately across his desk and watched as she seated herself. Then he returned to his side of the desk and folded his hands.

"I'm sure you have various questions knocking around your head. I invite you to ask them now."

Claire squirmed in her seat.

"Anything?"

A smile leaked from the corner of his mouth.

"Well, let's move slowly and see how things go."

She looked him over in the low light, his dark features very rugged, eyes bold and brown.

"What is this place?"

He leaned back in his chair.

"A research facility, of course."

She crossed her legs.

"What sort of research?"

"All kinds, really. Certain varieties receive more funding than others. More attention."

"What sorts?"

He smiled.

"Nothing that could be weaponized."

She uncrossed her legs.

"Then what?"

"Well, we're interested in the same things you are. We want to cure diseases, extend lives, things like that."

She began to say something, but he interrupted.

"I'm sorry. It's very early and I didn't offer you any coffee. Let's have some coffee."

He tapped a button on his telephone.

"Carol, can you please bring coffee."

"Of course, Mr. Betancur."

They sat in silence while Carol brought coffee.

"Do you take cream or sugar?"

"Just a little cream," Claire said.

She poured them each a cup and then retreated from the room without saying another word.

"I'm sorry," said Dominic Betancur. "You were saying?"

"Why all the secrecy? Why the compound? The armed security?"

He sipped his coffee and thought for a moment.

"We have our reasons and they are sound, I can assure you."

She sampled the coffee, its flavor quite ordinary in relation to everything else at the facility.

"What is it you want from me?"

He sat up in his chair and placed his forearms on the desk.

"I want you to do what you do. I want you to continue your research. Or, I guess I should say I want you to pick things up where others have left off."

"You mean continue existing research?"

"That's correct," he said. "We've already made significant strides in your particular field of research. You're in store for some surprises when you get down to the third level of this facility. Suffice it to say, we've far exceeded what you've accomplished so far at your university. I say this with respect of course."

She drank her coffee.

"Whose work am I taking over?"

"I'm afraid we don't divulge this information. Just as we won't divulge your identity to your successor."

"I don't understand," she said.

"Well, I'm afraid our operation won't bestow you with any fame or glory. We work in a piecemeal fashion, with numerous researchers all contributing anonymously to one project for a certain amount of time and then surrendering their work to a successor. You will not receive any credit for your contributions. Not a page in the newspaper. Not even a letter of recommendation. You'll be required to sign a confidentiality agreement, and we will enforce it through any means necessary."

He sipped his coffee and waited for a response, but she gave none.

"What you will get," he continued, "is substantial monetary compensation, depending on how far you extend the research, of course."

She looked into her coffee cup for a moment.

"What do you mean by substantial?"

"Between one and ten million dollars based on how far you push the research ahead."

She looked up suddenly, and he gave a slight smile.

"We only want the best you have to offer. If you don't add a single thing, if you aren't able to advance the research one iota, you'll still receive a minimum of one million U.S. dollars. This will come at the end of a maximum 12-month commitment. That said, we may choose to relieve you from your responsibilities after only a few months or even a few weeks. But never more than twelve months. That will be the maximum duration of your involvement with our enterprise."

He shrugged.

"That doesn't sound so bad, does it?"

She sipped her coffee and thought for a moment.

83

"I can't say that it does."

"Good," he said. "Now I hate to cut things short, but I have others to see."

He stood and put a hand out.

"It was a pleasure to meet you, finally."

She stood and placed her coffee on the desk.

"Likewise," she said, as she offered her hand.

They shook and he followed her to the door.

"Carol will escort you to the elevator. You'll be moving to the third level of the facility in the coming days. You'll receive plenty of guidance when the time comes. Anything you need, you'll receive."

He opened the door to reveal the old woman, who stood straight and attentive, a kind smile decorating her weathered face.

"Come, dear," she said, as Dominic Betancur closed the door behind her.

They walked the length of the waiting room, and Carol opened the elevator doors with a few taps of the bright green keypad on the wall.

Claire entered and turned, her body finally relaxing, mind nearly exhausted from the stress of the engagement.

"Best of luck to you," the old woman said, as the elevator doors slid shut.

When they did, Claire leaned her back against the elevator wall and exhaled. She held her hands out before her eyes and watched the shaking cease. She breathed deeply and waited for the doors to open once more to reveal Romero, who would lead her through the maze of metallic grid scaffolding that led back to the facility's top level.

But when the doors opened, she did not see Romero. Instead, another man stood before her, his face like a hammer, eyes black as sucking holes.

She tried to look into them, but it was like looking into the sun.

"Hello," he said. "My name is Demetri Mendoza."

Chapter 11

They sat across each other in an empty room, a bare steel table between them, a long two-way mirror spanning the length of one painted brick wall. The smell of his musk cologne flowed over the table and stabbed her eyes.

"What is it you do here?" she asked.

"I'm head of security."

She placed her palms flat on the table.

"I thought Romero was the head of security."

He shook his head slowly, eyes small behind his glasses, but oppressive just the same.

"His role is limited to the surface. He has no influence in the subterranean levels of this facility."

She lifted her hands from the table, two wet prints reflecting brightly under the white fluorescent light.

He looked down and watched as they evaporated into the air. He did not smile.

"What exactly do you want?" she asked, her voice breaking in all the wrong places.

"I have questions. You will answer them. When I am satisfied, you will return to the top level. Understood?"

She looked down and nodded slowly, like a child before a figure of authority.

"Did you tell anyone about your interactions with Mr. Harris?"

"I met with some attorneys."

"What are their names?"

She swallowed.

"Will you hurt them?"

"No."

She gave the names, while he listened intently without writing a single one down.

He watched as she turned to face her reflection in the mirrored glass.

"Who's back there?"

He didn't answer.

"What about your mother? What does she know of your involvement with us?"

She looked at him.

"Nothing. Why?"

He adjusted his glasses.

"We must know."

"Listen to me," she said, as she placed her hands on the table exactly where they'd been before. "If anything happens to my mother, I won't help you. I won't do anything you ask."

He smiled briefly as if to intentionally soften his expression, but this only made his face gargoyalian for a terrifying second.

"Your mother is exactly as you left her."

He folded his hands.

"And that is the way things should stay."

She did not speak.

"Now, I want to speak frankly so you will understand what's expected of you here. There is much you will never know about the work we do, and that is for your benefit as much as ours. I can tell you that we perform a critical function for those who would defend its secrecy forcefully and at any cost."

He pushed his chair back and stood.

"Now," he said, as he removed his sport coat and folded it over the empty chair. "Mr. Betancur has his way of doing things and I have mine."

He unbuttoned his shirt sleeves without unlocking his eyes from hers.

"I know everything there is to know about every single person in this facility and that includes you."

He carefully rolled his sleeves up to his elbows.

"This knowledge makes me an especially good forecaster of behavior, and your personality profile tells me you will be a problem here."

She raised her palms as if to shunt his words.

"Absolutely not. That's ridiculous. I can assure you I've never caused a problem anywhere in my life."

He removed his glasses and folded them shut. He set them down and walked around the table, his footsteps light only to the ear.

"Now, when faced with an undesirable proposition, I take steps to prevent its occurrence."

She slid her chair back and moved away from his approach.

"Listen, you have nothing to worry about," she said, the words tripping over one another as if each one competed to flee her quivering mouth.

He seized her arm and gave it a cruel twist. She shrieked as he leveraged her face down against the cold, steel table until she came cheek to cheek with her reflection.

"Stop," she cried, her shoulder threatening to pop under the torque of his technique. She cried as his lips approached her ear.

"You will do your job and you will do it quietly," he whispered. "Do you understand?"

"Yes."

He gave another twist and she repeated the answer.

"Don't talk to any of the others about this or anything else. Do you understand?"

"Yes."

"Nothing to anyone. Only work."

"Yes."

He released her and straightened his tie. He returned to his side of the table while she cradled her arm like a dying child.

"Now," he said, as he slipped his sport coat back on," I expect our future meetings to be uneventful, but that is entirely up to you."

He slid his glasses back onto his pointy face without diminishing its gravity one bit.

"If you'll step outside, one of our security professionals will escort you back to the top level."

With that, he crossed the floor and exited, the scent of his cologne inhabiting the room for some time after, like some unseen phantom with life enough to stifle even the slightest thoughts against him.

When she arrived at the top level, she escaped the elevator with haste, rushing past several others who regarded her with curious eyes. She took the hall toward her room without looking at anyone, but a voice ensnared her before she could escape.

"Claire," Alfred called.

She turned to see him hurrying toward her.

"What's wrong? What happened?" he asked, as he settled before her, lungs sucking air over even such a slow and gimpy rush.

"Nothing," she said. "It was fine."

His eyes studied the way she held her arm.

"Please," he said. "You can tell me."

She removed her keycard and tried to use it, but it missed its mark under the trembling of her hand.

"No, Alfred. I can't."

The old man placed his hand over hers.

"Please, dear. Let's go inside."

She looked at him, eyes perspiring, hair in disarray. She appeared wild to his eyes, like some creature escaped from a box, eyelids flittering against the unfamiliar light.

"No, Alfred. Please. Just leave me alone."

He removed his hand and backed away as she fled within her chambers and shut the door.

When she had gone, he turned and made his way down the hall and into the lobby, where a sober-looking Gretchen stood in his way.

"Can I help you with anything, Alfred?" she asked, her mouth artfully composed to a dutiful smile.

He looked up at her big, broad face, the anger of youth bubbling up from places that were supposed to be gone.

"No," he said dryly. "Nothing."

She nodded once and turned sideways, her long muscular arm extending to award passage.

"Well then," she said. "Be well."

He moved past her swiftly and made his way to the courtyard, where he found Nathan under a crazed-looking willow tree, two women with him, their faces aglow over whatever bullshit he fed them.

"We need to talk," Alfred said without looking at either of the women.

Nathan looked at him over his shoulder.

"Can it wait?"

The old man turned and walked away. He sat at a bench and waited, while Nathan withdrew from his audience.

"What is it?" he asked, as he took a seat next to Alfred.

"Something's happened with Claire. She won't talk about it, but she's clearly upset."

Nathan scratched his neck.

"You saw her?"

The old man nodded.

"I waited by the elevator all morning. I caught her on the way to her room. She was visibly upset, and she held her arm as if it were broken."

Nathan looked around the courtyard.

"What did she say?"

Alfred shrugged.

"Nothing. That's the problem. I couldn't get a word from her. She told me to leave her alone, and so I did."

They sat quietly for a moment, while a bizarre-looking bird circled the sky above the retractable opening.

"I think we should respect her wishes."

Alfred looked at him.

"Aren't you hearing me?"

Nathan leaned forward and propped his forearms against his thighs.

"What can we do, Alfred? She's been mysterious from the moment we met her. If she wants to talk, she will. I don't think we're going to get very far pressuring her."

The old man removed his pipe and fed it with fresh tobacco. He lit it afire and drew from it hungrily.

"This place," he said, as he exhaled a big, white fog of smoke. "I came here because I had no other options. It was my only chance to have a worthwhile impact after all these years. Now, I'm not sure what I've done."

He smoked and looked off thoughtfully. Nathan put a hand on his shoulder and squeezed it.

"Don't worry," Nathan said. "I'll talk to her."

He took his hand away.

"But honestly, Alfred, if we're in a place of danger, there's probably not much we can do but keep our heads low and do our work. I mean, look around you. We don't have a lot of cards to play."

The old man smoked while Nathan watched Romero cross the courtyard, the man's dark eyes studying the two of them, his expression cold, as if he were privy not just to their words, but the very thoughts inside their heads.

"I'll talk to her," Nathan repeated. "Let me talk to her."

And in the days that followed, he tried several times. But she would not confide, and soon a distance took root between all three, until they were finally separated entirely and moved into the sub-levels of the facility.

Chapter 12

In the third level of the Xactilias's domed monstrosity, nothing went to waste. Lighting was kept to a minimum, food and words the same. People worked. People ate and slept. And in between, they moved about in orderly lines with same-paced footsteps and somber, bowing heads.

Within nearly every room, guards roamed, their faces dark and purposeful, automatic weapons in hand. All illusions of freedom went quickly, the bathroom breaks timed, the meals without menus, the conversations killed in their infancies, and all without even the slightest rustle of complaint.

In that place, recreation came infrequently or not at all, the people moving from their quarters to their labs to the cafeteria and back to their quarters, all without muttering much of anything to anyone unless the words related to the work at hand.

At first, there were whispers among the unprepared, but these were corrected in private little meetings that brought pale faces and trembling hands.

At last, it was all complete: a colony of geniuses, dutifully focused on their tasks, like a hive of worker bees, without will or way to corrupt the plan.

For Claire, the transition came with surprising ease, especially now that she had duties to occupy her mind. Despite its repressiveness, the third level offered a wealth of mental nourishment, the labs fully stocked with equipment and technology, the work a respite from the state of her being.

To move from one generation of researchers to the next, The Xactilias Project used transitional assistants, which worked with one lead researcher and then the next for only a short time. Claire's transitional assistant was named Karen, and she had previously worked under a man named Krystoph, who had advanced the organization's human aging research so far, he'd actually stopped the process entirely.

Claire had reviewed the man's work during her first two weeks in the third level, and the findings were so stunning, they brought her envy and shame.

"When I first began working under Mr. Krystoph, the project had met a bit of a roadblock," Karen said one day, as she worked alongside Claire in the lab. "But he eventually solved it quite ingeniously. Such a remarkable man."

"What was the roadblock?" Claire asked.

Karen looked over her shoulder at the guard who stood outside the containment glass.

"I can't really talk about it," she said. She turned and looked at Claire, her old eyes bright and blue behind her safety goggles. "You have to understand, I don't even know Krystoph's last name."

Whatever roadblock this Krystoph had conquered only brought on a new set of problems that now toyed with Claire's mind at all hours of the night. While halting the aging process, Krystoph had thrown the body into a constant state of disease, with cancerous growths and immune deficiencies plaguing those who had volunteered for treatments.

"Who were the volunteers?" Claire asked.

"Testing occurs in Level Four," Karen said. "We only get the results."

During the first month, Claire familiarized herself with Krystoph's research, her mind like a great sucking vacuum, consuming the information and putting it to use shortly after. The man's progress had been extraordinary, his instincts leading to clever discoveries she might never have entertained. But once she'd analyzed the data and digested his ways, she quickly found wrong turns and oversights that led to bigger, bolder advancements.

"I don't understand how this is possible," Karen muttered, as Claire seemed to equal and then surpass Krystoph's accomplishments overnight.

"My mind has always played quite well with existing research," Claire said. "Independent, original theories are a different story."

Except they weren't, or at least not that Karen could tell. Soon, Claire had taken the research forward enough to draw attention from The Xactilias Project's masters, and this brought an invitation from Dominic Betancur, himself.

Romero issued the summons during their lunch break.

"You'll both be forgoing the remainder of your daily schedule," he said.

Claire and Karen stopped chewing and exchanged looks.

"I can't do that," Claire said. "Today is important."

Romero's eyes narrowed.

"It is but for other reasons. Mr. Betancur would like to meet with you both to discuss the state of your research."

The two exchanged looks once more.

"Both of us?" Karen asked.

"That is correct."

Romero glanced at a pair of men seated at another table, and they immediately turned their heads to their plates.

"Following lunch, you'll each return to your respective rooms and change your clothing. I'll arrive to collect you in one hour."

With that, he turned and walked away.

Claire looked at Karen, whose pale skin had lost whatever blood was in it.

"What's the matter?"

Karen forced a smile and shook her head.

"Nothing. We should finish eating."

But they ate no more, and soon both found themselves alone in their rooms, thumbing through their closets in search of the right thing to wear for such an uncertain occasion.

Once she'd showered and dressed, Claire sat on her bed with a cup of water in her hand. She stared into it, her mind playing out all the potential scenarios to come. But in this place, there were no hints and no tells, everything obscured by humdrum routines, be they harmless ploys or calculated deceptions, confounding just the same.

A knock at the door.

"Ms. Foley."

She stood.

Another knock.

"Ms. Foley, it's time."

She answered the door to reveal an armed soldier.

"This way, please."

She shut the door and followed him down the tiled hallway, bright white motion-sensing lights flicking on ahead of them and dying quietly behind. They worked their way through a befuddling course of hallways and random doors until her feet began to ache. They entered empty rooms with doors that led to other rooms. They walked down hallways that led to other hallways and more hallways that led to still more rooms.

At last, they turned a corner and arrived at one last hallway, the walls white and sterile and indistinguishable from all the others in their wake. The soldier stopped and looked about uneasily. The walls were filled with plain white doors, spaced four feet apart, and he seemed not to know which one to open.

He looked at Claire, who immediately pointed her face away. Sweat leaked from the gills of his neck, and his throat bobbed as he attempted to swallow the void in his mouth. Finally, he pushed his hand into his pocket and retrieved a slip of paper. He looked at it for a quick instant and then pushed the crumpled thing back where it had come from.

He swallowed again.

"Here," he said, and he pointed to a door. "This one, here."

She reached for the knob and gave it a fruitless twist. She turned and looked at the soldier, who retrieved the paper from his pocket and gave it a second look.

"No, this one. This one here."

She stepped forward and reached for the knob, but before she could grasp it, the door flung open and Demetri stepped outside.

He glanced at Claire and then approached the soldier. He held out his hand, his face stony, jaw undulating beneath his dark skin. The soldier swallowed hard and then retrieved the paper from his pocket. He placed it in Demetri's hand.

"You can go inside now, Ms. Foley," he said without taking his eyes from the soldier's face.

Without speaking, she entered the room alone, the door nearly slamming against her as Demetri forced it closed.

"Hello," said Dominic Betancur. "Please, join us."

He sat on the far side of a wide glass table, Karen seated opposite him, a believable smile on her face. Claire approached and sat next to her.

"I'm very grateful you were able to meet with us today. I understand you're quite busy with your work, and I'm very sorry to have interrupted you."

Claire nodded.

"It's not a problem."

"Very good."

He opened a file and removed several papers. He thumbed through them and pulled one out.

"I'm extremely pleased with your progress," he said, as he looked the page over. "The two of you have performed well beyond expectations."

"All of the credit should go to Claire," Karen said. "She's remarkable."

Dominic set the paper down.

"Yes," he said with a smile. "She certainly is. We were very fortunate to obtain her services."

The door opened and Demetri entered. He straightened his tie and approached the table. He took a seat next to Dominic, and as he did, Claire noticed a touch of blood on the knuckles of his right hand.

Dominic traced her eyes to the hand. He leaned over to whisper something to Demetri, who immediately withdrew a handkerchief and wiped his hands clean.

"Where are we?" Demetri asked as he wiped.

"I was just complimenting these two on their fine work."

Demetri nodded.

"Yes, the two of you have been exceptionally productive."

"Indeed," Dominic said. "I'm quite eager to see where you'll be taking things." He frowned. "Unfortunately, although the work is promising, we're having some unpleasant feedback from subject testing in the lower level."

Claire furrowed her brows.

"What specifically?"

"Well, side effects, mainly, but we'll provide a thorough report with all the information you need, once you've returned."

Claire and Karen exchanged looks.

"Returned from where?"

Dominic smiled.

"Well, I'd like you to accompany me for an off-site project. I don't want to get into the specifics, but it's very important, and I need someone of your caliber alongside me."

Claire frowned.

"I'm honored, but we really do need to get back to our work, especially if there have been issues with testing."

"That can wait," Demetri said. "Tomorrow, you'll accompany Mr. Betancur's team for this off-site project. Karen will review the report, so she can brief you on the specifics when you return."

Dominic placed his hand on Demetri's arm.

"I do appreciate your commitment to your work, Claire," he said. "But this is pressing and I feel we just can't afford to approach it without you."

Claire glanced at Karen, but she only stared blankly at the table.

"Alright." She smiled. "I appreciate the kind words."

"Good," Dominic said with a broad smile. "Very good."

He stacked the papers and put them back in the folder.

"I am very sorry to burden you with unexpected responsibilities. I'm also sorry you had to navigate such an intricate maze to get here today. But that's part of Demetri's security gambit." He gave the man a soft elbow and smiled. "You must both feel a little lost, but you're actually quite close to your workstation, I can assure you."

Claire glanced at Demetri.

"I have an eidetic memory," she said. "I know exactly where we are."

Dominic placed his hand over Demetri's arm and smiled.

"Of course," he said. "How silly of me to forget."

He gave Demetri a hard pat on the back.

"Well, you two certainly deserve to celebrate your achievements." He stood, and the others followed suit. "I've actually arranged a little surprise. It's not much, but if you'll step outside, an escort will lead the way."

He smiled and shook each woman's hand in turn. Then he and Demetri left the room, the latter glancing over his shoulder as he disappeared from sight.

The two women exchanged looks, but before either could speak, another soldier entered the room.

"Hello," he said, with a dead, robotic voice. "I'm here to escort you to the diversions room."

They each offered polite smiles and then followed the man through yet another meandering route of same-looking doors and rooms and hallways, until they finally arrived at yet another same-looking door.

"Please," the soldier said, with his bloodless voice.

Karen twisted the knob and opened the door to reveal a warm, alluring room with dim lighting and comfortable-looking furniture. They exchanged looks and then turned to the soldier.

"You're invited to celebrate your evening here," he said. "I'll wait outside the door for the duration."

With that, he moved away and took a position against the wall, his rifle secure in his hands, eyes boring forward into nothing at all.

They went inside and shut the door. They looked around and took the room's inventory: a shelf jammed full of classic novels, three bottles of red wine on an antique wooden table, a dark brown leather couch, oak hardwood floors, a big, broad recliner and a deep, dark, supple green rug that spanned nearly half the room. In one far corner, a fireplace crackled and snapped, while a radio spilled a calm stream of classical music into the air. Karen approached the table. A wrapped gift basket sat upon it, and inside, she saw aged cheeses, cured meats, dried fruits and an assortment of nuts. And there were cigarettes, her brand of cigarettes, and everything looked new and fresh and completely unspoiled.

Karen immediately tore the butterscotch-colored plastic wrapping from the basket and collected the pack. She ripped it open and withdrew a cigarette. She placed it between her lips and snatched up a booklet of matches. She plucked loose a match and prepared to stroke it, stopping to glance up at Claire.

"Is this ok?" she asked, the cigarette dangling from her lips and bobbing with each syllable.

"Yes, go ahead," Claire said, as she took up a bottle of wine. She twisted a corkscrew into the top and pulled it open, while Karen set fire to her cigarette and smoked from it hungrily.

"Oh, my," she sighed, as she fell backward into one of the chairs. "I'm ashamed at how good this tastes."

Claire filled two glasses and handed one over. They each took several swallows, the alcohol spreading warm and evenly over their bodies, calming their nerves. Claire stood up and crossed the room. She approached the fire and sat before it, her legs Indian fashioned, eyes looking deep within the flames. She drank and studied the long fiery tongues as they lashed upward, the life within them so hypnotic after all the computers and sterile tile.

"I want to go home."

Karen sat smoking, her eyes watching the fire.

"Let's just be here for a while," she said. "Let's just be."

And so, they did just that, both of them drinking, eating, smoking and talking, as if they had somehow returned to the familiar existence they once knew. And for a while, the outside world fell away, the music filling its void and the growing voids within their lonely hearts. And for a few hours, they were happy. And then their minds and spirits drifted back to practical thinking and the inevitable promise of the coming day.

Chapter 13

"What do you know about Demetri Mendoza?" Karen asked. "Has he talked to you?"

Claire sipped her drink.

"That's the one thing I'm sure I don't want to talk about."

Karen gave a smirk.

"Yes, he's a character, isn't he?"

"He's a cruel bastard," Claire sniped.

Karen looked over the thick frames of her glasses.

"That and so much more."

She placed her drink on the table and stood. She put a finger to her mouth and turned up the radio's volume. Then she pulled her chair around the table and sat next to Claire.

"You don't have to talk, but you can listen. You can do that for me, even if you don't want to, right?"

Claire held her glass with two hands.

"If you wouldn't write it down on paper and sign it with your name, I wouldn't say it."

"Fair enough, but this knowledge I'd give you for your own well-being."

Claire looked away.

"You'd tell me things that would get me killed."

Karen took hold of her chin and pulled her face around.

"I'd tell you things that would save your life."

She removed her hand and reached over the table to collect her drink. She took a mighty swallow, while Claire considered the weight of her next choice.

"Whatever you tell me, they'll know," she said. "Then they'll take us both into dark rooms, and who knows what else?"

Karen set her drink down.

"Oh, they'll do worse. They'll torture us, maybe rape us, and then they'll cut us apart and feed our bodies to the starving people in the level below us. And if we're lucky, they'll do it in that order."

Claire started to cry.

"I just want to do my job and go home."

Karen shook her head.

"Pay attention," she said. "I want to tell you something that will make you understand what's happening to you and what you must do if you want to make it out of here."

Claire nodded and Karen took her hand, the radio pouring forth a racket of trumpet clatter as if to intentionally cheat the moment of its gravity. Karen waited for the violins to smother out the commotion, and then she began.

"When I first came here, I worked exclusively with Krystoph. At the time he'd been working in this facility for six years and he showed it, believe me."

"Six years?" Claire interrupted.

Karen nodded.

"Yes," she said. "I don't know what his original agreement said, but I'm certain it was adjusted based on his lack of progress. They kept delaying his release, if you will. Anyway, he knew he had to make a breakthrough to secure his freedom, and so that became his fixation. It was an obsession really, and it made him odd, but that's not really where I'm going with this."

She refilled her drink and took a sip.

"After about nine months as his assistant, I received an invitation to join a group that would accompany Demetri on some sort of project outside the complex. At the time, I felt Krystoph and I were nearing a breakthrough, and so I declined, partly for that reason and partly because of Demetri. I'd had plenty of run-ins with him over that first year, and I understood who he was better than most. Or at least I thought I did at the time.

"Anyway, when he heard I'd declined the assignment, Demetri summoned me to his office and asked about my reservations. I told him I had none and was only thinking of the research. I told him it was a bad time for me to leave the project, and I didn't think Krystoph could spare me at the moment. He listened politely and accepted my decision. Then he shook my hand and I returned to the lab.

"I finished out the day, had dinner in the cafeteria, returned to my room, took a shower and went to bed. But in the middle of the night, I woke up. I turned over and reached for the lamp, but a voice told me to be still. I sat up and pressed my back against the headboard. I peered through the darkness, and there he was, sitting in a chair in the corner of the room. I couldn't see his face, but I recognized the gravel in the voice when he spoke.

"He leaned forward and told me, quite simply, that he was disappointed I'd foregone the opportunity to join in his project. He then stood and left the room. That was it. He opened the door and walked out."

She took one last drag of her cigarette and crushed it into the ashtray over and over until all the little embers went dead.

"The next day, I asked a guard to escort me to Demetri's office, where I told him I'd reconsidered my decision. He accepted my answer without looking up, and I walked away. The guard took me back to my room, where I packed a bag of clothing and bathroom supplies. Then he escorted me to the elevator and up to the top level.

"We stayed in the top level for a week, and let me tell you, that courtyard was like heaven after a year down here. I remember the first of the sun on my skin and the way it made my heart pick up." She smiled to herself. "It's funny how much you appreciate the consolation of little moments while in the midst of hardships."

She collected her pack of cigarettes and thumbed it open.

"I still remember that first meal in the cafeteria, the texture of the bacon, the tart little pinch in the orange juice." She murmured the words almost to herself, her eyes darting off for a moment and then snapping back into place. "Thank God for life's little interruptions."

She withdrew another cigarette and held it for a moment.

"Anyway, after a week, they marched us out onto the grounds and put us in big military trucks alongside armed soldiers. We cleared the security gates and drove all day through all sorts of jungle land, and I saw animals I'd never seen before, and some of them looked unreal to me, though I'm sure they seem quite ordinary to anyone familiar with such things.

"That first night, they set up tents for us and other tents for the soldiers, and everyone gathered near a large bonfire that seemed the only defense against the forest even with the guns and the knives and the big strong men who would wield them. One of the men had a guitar and he played it freely and he sang songs in a language I did not know, and his voice was beautiful, though he looked like the type of man that might rape you if given the chance.

"The men had alcohol and soon became intoxicated and there was a great commotion and loud voices and fighting and those of us in the research group would have taken our chance to flee if not for the jungle which no sane person would enter especially in the thick of night.

"A group of men had been arguing about the very nature of the jungle itself and of phantoms and other metaphysicalities that might exist within it. Soon things were getting out of hand and that's when Demetri stood up before them. Immediately, every eye fell upon him and I saw eyebrow after eyebrow raise. He lifted his hand and silence washed over the company, the firelight making him appear iconic at least in the eyes of those strange men. They listened while he mused about their arguments and then he sat with his back to the towering flames and he told them a story that I'll repeat to you as best I can remember."

She cleared her throat.

"Long ago, a Spanish colonial army arrived on the shorelines of South America with the sole intent of seizing gold from the native settlements. Having raided the nearest villages, they grew frustrated by their petty scores and sought to push inward into the Amazonian jungle.

"Through their conquests, the Spaniards learned of a remote city with such vast wealth, the people ate from gold dishes and drank from gold cups, and the settlement itself was said to be enclosed within golden walls that soared over the surrounding treetops. According to the natives, the city attained its wealth not by mining, but as the result of incredible abilities. For it was said that every man, woman and child wielded the power to turn any solid substance into gold with a few spoken words and a simple touch of the hand.

"At first, the Spaniards regarded these stories as deceit aimed at distracting them from the region; however, as they moved from village to village, they found remarkable consistency between each tale. Finally, through torture, the Europeans exacted enough credible information to target the city's location and began drawing plans for an assault.

"Without supplies to risk wandering the jungle on a rumor, the Spanish general selected 100 conquistadors to find the city and subdue its inhabitants, at which point, scouts would return to invite the remaining troops along. So one morning they gathered their rations and set out in search of this city, despite the warnings from the local natives, who claimed all would be transformed into solid gold the moment they drew their weapons.

"Months passed without any sign of the scouts, and after a year's time, the general assumed the company of 100 dead. Vexed by the mystery surrounding his missing conquistadors and still fixated on the prospect of a city with such astonishing wealth, the general himself gathered a mass of 500 conquistadors and set out into the Amazonian rain forest on the trail of the missing Spanish soldiers.

"For weeks they made the hard journey through the jungle, suffering all brands of hardship along the way. Nearly a quarter of the company fell ill with malaria and either died quickly or were left behind at makeshift camps where they inevitably died all the same. Finally, after three months, the general and his conquistadors stumbled upon the first sign of civilization. It was a statue entangled with green vines and it lay flat upon the jungle floor. After stripping away the vegetation, the men realized the statue was crafted of solid gold, but it was not this that gave them pause. For the figure depicted a man in the midst of great suffering, with a wailing mouth and eyes made wide from terror.

"That night, they made camp near the gold statue, and while the general and his commanders drew strategies, grumbling spread evenly among the soldiers, who spoke openly about the possibility that the statue might once have lived as a fleshly man. Aware of fear's propensity for conjuring mutiny, the general immediately ordered such talk forbidden and cemented this command by violently executing the first man to break it.

"Over the next several days, the Spaniards pressed ahead, and as they did, they continued to encounter more and more gold statues. Like the first, these also depicted humans, their bodies contorted in obvious misery, faces wild with torment and anguish. And with each discovery, the soldiers grew increasingly fretful. And in that alien territory, a powerful uneasiness settled among the whole of the company, so that even the general began to entertain the notion of abandoning the quest and returning with a few of the statues in tow as validation of his efforts.

"And then the company stumbled upon such a terrifying sight, all fell mute before it. For situated within the jungle flora all around them were brightly gleaming golden statues depicting the missing conquistadors who had come before them. As if concussed by such a vision, some of the soldiers fell to their knees, while others cried out with crazed language about gods, curses and evil spirits. As the dread and terror slurked its way through the company, a chaos ensued and when the commanders fought to regain order, some of the soldiers broke ranks and raised their swords and gunpowder weapons against them. Finally, at the behest of his commanders, the general agreed to abandon his quest and the Spaniards turned away, fleeing the jungle in favor of the eastern shores.

"When they finally arrived, the soldiers spread word of the augury they'd encountered, and soon all agreed the jungle played host to such devilry, all future expeditions should be planned carefully to avoid the territory surrounding the city of gold. And so it went for 100 years.

"But devilry and magic had played no role in the story at all. In actuality, the Europeans had fallen prey to a grand lie. When the original company of 100 Spaniards first encountered the human statues, they too contemplated retreat but abandoned such thought for fear of execution at the order of their general. So despite their unease, the men pressed forward. A week later, they finally breached the jungle and their eyes fell upon the city, its perimeter without walls, or sentries, women tending gardens, children running and playing freely about.

"Driven mad by anxiety, the conquistadors fell upon the inhabitants, slashing with their swords and firing pistols into the backs of the fleeing natives. Without obstruction or intervention, they killed and looted, as the natives' simple weapons glanced off the Spaniards' thick armored breastplates.

"At last, the city's warriors gathered in great masses and engaged the conquistadors, firing arrows into their necks and overwhelming them with greater numbers. Still, against such superior armor and weaponry, the city's inhabitants endured countless casualties, and as they slay the last of the strange raiders, the sad and victorious natives looked about to see the vast majority of their brothers and sisters bleeding in the streets.

"Over the next several days, the natives mourned their losses and cleared the dead. But even as they tended to these sorrowful duties, their chiefdom drew plans to evade what all agreed to be an inevitable second wave of white marauders.

"And so, the chiefdom decided to tap the city's greatest resources to invest in a cunning subterfuge. For indeed these natives were extraordinarily rich in gold, and though its warriors were few, the city played host to an exceptional community of artisans, who spent the next year meticulously crafting gold statues to depict the Spanish conquistadors, and these they placed about the jungle to act as silent wards that would conjure such panic as to exceed the lust and ambition of the white men, who did indeed flee and remain absent for 100 years time."

At last, she stopped talking. She put the cigarette to her lips and lit it with a fresh match. She drew from it and exhaled a fresh fog of smoke.

"What was the point?" Claire asked. "I mean, what was his point?"

Karen shrugged.

"To coerce the soldiers away from fighting one another? To bask in their admiration? Who's to say why he does any of the things he does?" She smoked and shook her head and looked into Claire's eyes. "But I would suggest he does few things without reason."

They both drank from their glasses and then Karen continued.

"Anyway, the next day, we moved on, weaving through the jungle for many miles until we finally came to some sort of little village. Demetri ordered us off the trucks and told us to wait while the soldiers rounded up subjects by gunpoint. These were men and women, confused and terrified. Some ran. These they shot in the back."

She stopped for a moment, her face showing sickness but her eyes devoid of tears, as if there were simply no more to give for this particular memory.

"We took their vitals, looked them over, paying special attention for disease of any sort. After a few hours, the fit ones were forced onto the trucks with their hands bound. The rest were set free and the soldiers proceeded to order all the village's 100 or so inhabitants back inside their huts. At that point, we took our seats on the trucks and watched as the soldiers unloaded fuel canisters, which they emptied throughout the village."

Claire put her hand over her mouth, while Karen smoked and exhaled.

"Then Demetri ordered the men to set fire to the entire village and that's exactly what they did. And when the natives fled the fires, the soldiers picked them off one by one with their rifles until they were all dead. And then they drove us all back to this place and told us never to speak of what we saw."

Claire wiped tears from her eyes. She put her hand on Karen's shoulder.

"The ones you took, Karen. Are they the test subjects? Are they the people in Level Four?"

Karen shrugged.

"I don't know. Probably. Yes, I think so."

She put her hand over the top of Claire's.

"I've never been to Level Four. How can I say who is or isn't there? Is Krystoph sitting in a bar somewhere drinking sherry and talking with his colleagues? Or, is he down there too? When my term is finally over, will I really go home?" She leaned closer. "Will you?"

Claire sat back in her chair. She brought her glass of wine to her lips and pulled it away without drinking.

"So, you think I should take my chance to escape tomorrow?"

Karen shrugged.

"I would if I had the opportunity." She smoked and exhaled. "Maybe you won't get a chance. Maybe they'll shoot you dead if you try. Maybe you'll starve to death in the jungle. Maybe you'll find help somewhere. I don't know. But I invite you to look at this place, Claire. I mean really look at what's going on. The guards, the guns. They're barely pretending anymore."

Claire shook her head.

"Even if I could somehow slip away, I don't even know what continent we're on. And if I do get away and end up in the jungle, I'm no survivalist."

Karen smoked the last of her cigarette and stamped it out in the ashtray. She looked at Claire and gave a soft, gentle smile.

"It was only a thought."

She lowered the radio's volume and took a drink of wine.

"Let's talk about something else."

But before they could even try, the guard pounded his fist against the door. He entered and the two women said their goodbyes. Then they were separate, both led back to their quarters under escort.

Hours later, as they lay alone in their rooms, they both thought of life's interruptions and the consolation of little moments. And though they would each think of one another often in the days to follow, neither would see the other again.

Chapter 14

In the morning, she awoke to a beautiful silence, the real world crystallizing slowly as she lifted from her dreams. Soon, a hard knocking shattered it all apart, and her heart picked up as reality seized her mind. She put on her robe and answered the door. A soldier stood before her, his face unfamiliar and very young.

"You have one hour," he said, before turning his back.

She shut the door and hurried to the bathroom for a quick shower. Without delay, she dried and dressed her body in clothing that seemed appropriate enough for a diversity of outcomes. As the soldier pounded the door, she quickly applied enough makeup to give her pallid face a touch of life. Then she left the room and joined him in the hallway.

They made their way through the appropriate passages and elevators until they arrived topside, where they met more soldiers, who guided her out of the facility and into the open air. High away in the pale blue sky, the sun flared brightly, its forgotten warmth so nourishing to her ivory skin. She looked at it for an instant, and it seemed to look back, a floral wind kicking up to celebrate the reunion.

"Hello," said Dominic Betancur. He wore safari gear and he approached wearing the smile of a lunatic. "Please, join me in the lead vehicle."

She nodded politely and followed him, Romero watching them the whole way before climbing into a separate truck.

They left the compound and drove out into the surrounding flats. Claire studied the landscape through the open window, the grasses low and wispy, the horizon mostly bare. After two hours of this, they crossed into a strange and wasted land, with black skeletal trees that stuck from the ground like the curled ends of burned matchsticks.

Claire glanced out her window at the desolate scrub and contemplated the scant chance of life in all that dirt and sparsity. But before she got far, a family of little rabbits shot out from a distant bur shrub, their tiny footwork kicking up faint puffs of white sand that rose up in the clear air and then vanished, like little explosions of powder on some enormous expression of still life.

Dominic smiled.

"I've seen amazing things in this area," he said. "Mother Nature finds a way."

By the time the great wall of jungle flora appeared on the horizon, the sun had pulled near the earth. As its burn dulled, all makes of orange light shot through the flowing treetops, while great birds circled like giant insects above them. Together, the birds moved in perfect agreement, congealing into enormous black halos that swelled and undulated in some sort of ancient unanimity, which seemed sinister to Claire at such as distance for reasons that were beyond her will to understand.

As they approached, the wild thicket seemed to grow before their eyes, and soon they saw the dark gape that tunneled into it. They followed the road forward, the trucks like motorized toys before the flora's girth. With a bump, the vehicles pierced the jungle's edge, a thick darkness embracing them, a sudden swell of insect chatter and hooting animals booming out from every direction.

As they pressed further, their headlights bored into the obscurity, the fog concealing what lie ahead, as it tumbled over the uneven road. Every so often, animals would bolt across the path, their eyes like bright little fireballs, glinting and glimmering and then quickly disappearing into the smothering black.

Big, bulging tree roots stuck out of the road like python snakes, and as the tires thumped over them, Claire's hand clutched the door handle and then Dominic's knee by mistake. He smiled and leaned toward her, his nostrils taking an audible sniff of her hair.

"Don't worry," he said. "We're well-equipped for this terrain."

She moved away from him with care and settled in her seat. His demeanor seemed much the same despite her detachment, and after a while, he closed his eyes and fell asleep. They pressed on into the jungle, traveling in silence for hours. She tried to stay alert, but her eyelids took on more and more weight, and soon she fell asleep beside him, the jostling carriages doing little to disturb the depth of her slumber.

In her dreams, she saw her little mother all dressed in black alone beside a casket. As Claire watched from above, the old woman wrung her withered hands and wept, as she looked upon the face of her dead husband. Claire called out, louder and louder, but her mother could not hear. And after a while, she collapsed and died and turned to ash beneath her clothing, such a vision jerking Claire awake in her seat, the sun flaring considerately outside the window glass.

She immediately noticed the changed terrain. They'd exited the jungle and fell upon a paved road, which ran neatly along a picturesque coastline, where rolling waves spilled over a jagged, rocky shore. Dominic slept beside her, his mouth agape, saliva seeping out its corners. She nudged him and his eyes popped open.

"Have we arrived?" he asked.

"I don't think so," she said.

He sat up and ran his hands through his hair.

"Oh, good," he said, as he peered out the windows. "It won't be long now."

They drove another two hours before she saw the buildings stick up over the horizon and then another hour before the little city manifested around them. Soon, they joined traffic and traffic jams, and the soldiers held guns out the windows until the cars scurried to the side and let them pass. The vehicles rumbled through the streets, like armored trucks pregnant with gold bars, and people fled the roads and gathered upon the sidewalks, as if something presidential had mysteriously joined their ranks.

They continued through the streets, slowing at intersections only for a moment before rushing through red lights, and then they finally arrived at their destination: a pair of lofty twin ivory pillars that provided luxury accommodations for some of the wealthiest of the region. The trucks wheeled around the backside of the buildings and descended into an underground parking facility, then they finally came to a stop, and the engines fell silent. Dominic opened his door and stretched his legs.

"That was quite a trip," he said, as he rubbed his lower back. He snapped his fingers at one of the soldiers, who quickly approached Claire and helped her from the vehicle. A short, well-dressed bald man came scurrying from the elevator, his tiny eyes peering out a pair of round, designer eyeglasses.

"Mr. Betancur, I'm so happy to see you've arrived," he said. He offered a tiny, feminine-looking hand and it disappeared within Dominic's.

"Hello, Paul. I trust everything is arranged?"

"Yes, sir. We've seen to all your requirements."

"Good."

Dominic turned to Claire.

"Romero will escort you to your room, where you'll have an opportunity to freshen up. We'll reconnect later for dinner and some entertainment." He smiled and took her hand. "I'm looking forward to our evening together."

He raised her hand to his lips and kissed it. Then he turned and followed Paul to the elevator with five soldiers in tow.

"This way, Ms. Foley," Romero said, as the lone remaining soldier fell in at his side. The three approached a second elevator and took it to the lobby floor. After a few seconds, the door opened to show the lobby mostly empty, save for two tanned businessmen who looked upon the three of them with audacious curiosity. When they approached the front desk, Romero gave Dominic's name, which brought a keycard and several submissive smiles, and then the three took the elevator up several stories, where they found Claire's room.

"Mr. Lopez will remain outside your door for your protection," Romero said before turning to take the elevator back to wherever he was going. Claire eyed the soldier for a moment and then shut the door.

She turned to assess the room, the walls tan, bedding burgundy, the whole setup as beautiful as any she'd ever seen. She walked over to the sink and filled a cup of water. She drank it down and refilled it again, repeating this twice more and then dropping the cup into the sink. She approached the bed and collapsed upon it, immediately falling into a dreamless sleep. In what seemed like only a few minutes' time, someone began rapping the door, but when she awoke to see the clock, she realized she had been asleep for more than three hours.

"Ms. Foley," Romero called from outside.

She sat up and glanced about the room. The woman in the mirror looked at her through nervous eyes. She straightened her posture and adjusted her expression until the reflection gained her approval. Then she crossed the room and opened the door.

"Yes?"

Romero straightened when he saw her.

"Mr. Betancur has arranged dinner reservations for seven o'clock." He looked her over from head to toe.

"You'll find suitable attire in your closet. I'll wait outside while you prepare and then I'll escort you to his car."

Claire nodded and shut the door.

Over the next hour, she showered and prepared her hair and makeup, hands working in an automated sort of way, an expressionless face staring back from the mirror as she worked. The form-fitting black dress they'd selected on her behalf fit remarkably, as if they'd crept in and tailored it around her body as she slept. When she'd finished, she looked well-suited to the role she might play on this particular evening, in this particular setting for this particular man. And when she opened the door to greet Romero and his associate, both men seemed a little startled by what they saw.

"This way," Romero said. The three crossed the hall and entered the elevator, a staggering silence ushering them along. In the lobby, they found Dominic waiting, a broad smile stretching across his face at the sight of Claire in her new dress.

"You look outstanding," he said, as he clasped his hands together. "I picked this out myself and what a job I did."

She forced a smile.

"Where are we going?"

He shook his head while clicking his tongue against the roof of his mouth.

"Everything is a surprise this evening." He smiled and put his hands over her bare shoulders. "Relax, you're off the clock. Enjoy yourself."

They left the hotel in a limousine, two of the soldiers with them, each dressed in dark suits.

Outside Claire's window, the little city brimmed with electricity, vibrant neon signs glowing warm and brightly amid a diversity of human beings. Lured by every imaginable trapping, people entered and exited strange-looking venues, some of these places bold and obvious along the street, others low and hidden down narrow steps that burrowed below the city's surface.

As the limo worked through traffic, she saw all manner of buskers doing all manner of tricks, their inverted hats beside them, gathering up bills and coins of varying denominations. People gathered around the performers with clapping hands and big, affected eyes, their attention swayed only by the prostitutes, who whispered sweet promises in ear after ear while tickling with gentle hands the insides of thighs.

They approached an intersection and idled before a single red stoplight, which dangled from a wire hanging loosely across the road. As they waited, Claire surveyed the neighboring vehicles, cab drivers beeping their horns at crossing pedestrians, smart cars like toys next to monstrous trucks, which rumbled and shook, as they belched dark smoke from their rears.

Soon, the light turned green and the limo pressed forward with the rest of traffic. For a time, they cooperated with the flow, moving slowly and stopping, as the vehicles choked the streets. At last, Dominic summoned the driver with the intercom.

"Somchai, go ahead and take the outer roads," he said.

"Sir?" said the driver.

"It's perfectly alright, Somchai. Go ahead now."

The driver hooked a quick left down a dark, narrow street and accelerated past the guttersnipe, which eyed the gleaming black vehicle through wild, bloodshot eyes. Dominic looked at Claire.

"The city is well protected on its interior," he said. "On the outer streets, however, things are more uncertain. Most know better than to molest this vehicle. On the other hand, there are some degenerates who are either desperate or ignorant enough to make a mistake."

He put a hand on her knee.

"You needn't worry, though. This vehicle is impervious to gunfire and I can have a hundred well-armed men at my disposal in a matter of minutes."

She looked down at his hand and then up to his face.

"That's good, I suppose."

He smiled and nodded.

"Indeed."

He removed his hand and sat back in his seat, while the limo navigated a series of turns that led them away from traffic. Soon the lighting turned faint and the roads grew choppy, as they entered shanty neighborhoods, where shadowy figures scuttled about in the darkness. Finally, they pushed through these discouraging areas and emerged on a lonely road, which ran a circle around the unlit edges of the city. Outside, a great pale moon hung low and heavy over the barren landscape, where scattered vegetation stuck up sharply from the dry, dusty ground.

"Lower the window," Dominic said to one of the soldiers.

"I'm not sure that's a good idea, sir," the soldier replied.

Dominic lowered his eyebrows.

"It's a fine idea."

The soldier nodded.

"I'm sorry, sir. Of course."

He lowered the window and a flood of warm air filtered its way into the vehicle. A pungent floral aroma permeated their nostrils, though Claire could not identify its source out in the thin, pale light. One of the soldiers sneezed repeatedly into a handkerchief.

"I'm sorry."

Dominic watched the man as he attempted to gather himself.

"Perhaps we should shut the windows," Claire said.

Dominic frowned.

"That won't be necessary."

He summoned the driver through the intercom.

"Somchai, please pull over for a moment."

The limousine crept to a halt, while the soldier's face contorted oddly against another fearsome sneeze.

"Please join Somchai up front," said Dominic.

The soldier nodded.

"Of course."

He opened the door and exited, leaving Dominic and the remaining soldier alone with Claire.

"Was that absolutely necessary?" Claire asked as the vehicle pulled forward.

Dominic shrugged.

"Very few things are absolutely necessary," said Dominic. "In any case, the fresh air invigorates me. Don't you find it invigorating?"

She shrugged.

"It's fine, yes."

They drove on, the vehicle jerking occasionally against the old broken road, its passengers clutching the seats to steady their jostled bodies. Finally, the limo made a sharp turn and pushed back into civilization, where strange, ambiguous faces peered out from the dark edges of the road. Claire watched as tall shadows stretched out from the city's center, which glittered with all makes of lighting that were welcome and missed. Soon, her body began to relax at the illusion of safety, though in her heart she recognized it as such.

When they arrived at their first destination, a very excited-looking Asian man met them on the street. He addressed Dominic in French, his demeanor humble and polite. They exchanged pleasantries and then they entered the restaurant where they were seated amid others of similar stature.

Claire settled in her seat.

"This is the premier dining venue within 500 miles," Dominic said, his eyebrows resting high upon his forehead.

Claire offered a smile.

"It looks it."

Dominic nodded.

"Well, in this case, looks are not deceiving."

They sat in silence for a moment and then a tall, thin waiter approached the table.

"How are you this evening?" he asked. Dominic put a finger up and replied in French.

"Oui," the waiter said. He turned and walked away.

"Do you speak French?" Dominic asked Claire.

"No," she lied.

Soon their table overflowed with an array of foods, over which not a single one she had a say. She ate sparingly while taking notice of the restaurant staff, their faces painted with disgust, Dominic seeming oblivious to this along with many other things.

"Wealth has its privileges," he said, as he forced a slab of liver into his cheeks. "People seek it like children to fireflies. Their arms flailing, eyes tracing a glimmer here, a glimmer there."

Claire stirred her food with an odd-looking fork.

"But is that what they really want?" Dominic asked. He waited for a response. "No," he continued. "It is most certainly not."

Claire dropped her fork and looked up.

"What is it, then, that people want?" She asked flatly.

Dominic smiled.

"I'd like to know your opinion."

"Happiness," she said. "People want to be happy."

He smirked as if he'd pulled the string on an elaborate trap.

"People say they want to be happy, but it's not true. Not even remotely." He leaned back in his chair and folded his hands on his lap. "They know the things that would make them happy: a new job, exercise, reading, eating better, spending more time with their children, things they write on pieces of paper, things they can only manage for a day or two. But they don't follow through with any of them. Instead, every day, they take specific steps to promote unhappiness, because happiness is not what they really want."

Claire leaned back in her chair.

"What do they really want then?"

"Stimulation, of course," he said. "This is the only thing anyone really wants. It's what drives husbands and wives into the arms of others, what makes people drink, smoke. It's why people eat fast food, play sports, play video games, read, drive fast, jump out of airplanes, buy new clothes. My goodness, it's even why people get angry."

112

Claire rubbed her eye.

"Why they get angry?"

"Of course," he said, as he folded his hands together. "Anger is the perfect form of stimulation because it makes people feel powerful. It's an antidote to anxiety, to fear. It allows you to say the things you've always wanted to say to those people of whom you're most afraid. You stand up for yourself, put people in their rightly deserved places. It's an artificial form of power. It creates drive."

He withdrew a cigarette and lit it, the staff taking notice without interfering.

"It's also about the only form of stimulation you can easily generate yourself," he said. "It's really no problem. Just think about that specific something or someone, and you're there."

Claire leaned forward, the gravity of the argument dissolving her angst.

"I think most people view anger as toxic," she said. "Few would equate it with happiness."

Dominic grinned.

"But that's the point," he said. "People don't want to be happy. Why else would a person toss and turn in bed at night embracing feelings of jealousy and rage? These things happen. They say, well I can't control my thoughts. Of course, that's not true. The other thoughts are boring. The angry thoughts are stimulating. That's why they're so addictive."

He sat up.

"Let me paint the picture," he said, as he furrowed his brow. "You wake up in the morning feeling sad, helpless. What can you do about it? Not much most of the time. But within minutes, you can find your feet by conjuring up a good bit of anger. Before you know it, you're walking with a confidence, a swagger. You're stimulated. It's easy. Wake up sad or depressed? Get angry about something. People do it all the time without knowing it. Every day, they read the news, looking for stories that will set them off. They want it. They scan headlines searching for it. They want to be mad at someone. At the world."

Claire shook her head.

"That's not what I want."

Dominic pointed at her.

"Exactly. The world could use more like you. Or, better yet, more of you."

He smoked his cigarette and tilted his chin upward to exhale.

113

"But, sadly, you will die, just like the rest of us. But you will leave children behind, yes?"

She said nothing.

"Oh, that's right, you have no children. What a pity."

He brought his cigarette to his lips and then stopped short.

"When people such as you die, it is a tragedy for humankind. And this, you will change through your research. You will remove the expiration date from human life and give humanity the gift of endless longevity."

She peered at him through caving eyelids.

"Humanity? You mean if my research yields a cure for aging, you would share it with humanity? Or would you keep it for certain people? People with money? People with power?"

He shook his head slowly.

"The gift of eternal or even extended life is not for the masses. It's not like clean water or medicine, which anyone should be entitled to. This thing we talk about must be kept from the ordinary, the people who would waste it, abuse it to taint the world with more of themselves, exhaust its resources and for what?"

Claire furrowed her brows.

"Kept for whom?"

"For those who have spent their lives contributing with their minds, people we need more of."

She took up her fork and stirred her cold food.

"Think about it," he said. "How much different might this world be if we had someone such as Einstein for even just another 30 years? Instead, we get hordes of ignorant people, mass-producing with six, seven, nine children. It's a downward spiral. The worst of us growing in numbers. The best of us becoming rarer and rarer by the decade."

He smoked again and then crushed his cigarette out on an empty plate.

"That sounds like passive intellectual genocide," she said. "Would you have administered polio vaccines based on a person's I.Q.?"

"Don't be ridiculous," he said. "This is the only practical way to employ our coming discovery."

She stirred faster.

"Just think about it, Claire. You're far smarter than I. This world is already too small for its current burden. What you suggest is to increase that burden. You speak of endless life. A world where people never age, where they live without disease, without diabetes, without pancreatic cancer or heart disease."

He withdrew another cigarette and set it afire.

"What comes next is starvation, land wars, laws over procreation. Who can have children, when, and how many? Society is forever changed. We lose everything."

He put his fist down on the table and the silverware rattled.

"No. We preserve our way of life by withholding this thing. We crack Pandora's Box just slightly to siphon its gifts, without unleashing a plague upon the world. Without ending it entirely."

He sucked his cigarette and watched her.

"Dominic," she said flatly. "I could debate you. But what's the point? Why do you even care what I think? I know you will do whatever you will, with or without my approval. I know I have no choice but to fulfill my obligation and make this thing you want. And I know it's only meant for those who can procure it through means of money or power. I know all these things and yet I still have no choice but to do as you wish. Why waste your time preaching this nonsense to me? What does it matter what I think?"

He pursed his lips and summoned the waiter, who delivered a check and quickly walked away.

"In time, I believe you will see things as I do," he said, as he placed five hundred American dollars on the table. "You are one of the brightest people we've ever had at our facility, and I want you to consider staying on after your term has expired."

Her eyes trickled upward to meet his.

"I'm only interested in getting back to my mother and my life."

He gave a polite smile.

"If that is what you wish, that is what you will have. But again, I believe you may feel differently in time."

With that, he stood.

"Let's move on, now. I've made other arrangements for the evening."

They left the restaurant just as they arrived, the two sitting next to each other in the limousine, the soldiers across from them, their eyes vacant, minds seemingly elsewhere. When they reached their next destination, a short, bald man raced to open the car door.

"Mr. Betancur, it is our privilege to have you this evening," he said, without acknowledging Claire. "We have some of our finest ladies performing tonight. I hope you enjoy the show."

Dominic shook the man's hand and they followed him through the door. Inside, a crowd of well-dressed people stood shoulder to shoulder before a large, empty stage. He placed them at a center table and gave a polite bow as he left. Claire evaluated the room. It was large and dark and only slightly illuminated by low bursts of orange incandescent lamps that glowed here and there, turning the guests into featureless silhouettes that spoke to one another in all manners of foreign tongue.

"I'd like to visit the bar," Claire said. "Is that o.k.?"

"Of course," Dominic said with a smile.

She stood and crossed the room, weaving through a crowd of well-dressed men, their necks whipping back toward her, as if towed by some exotic gravity.

She lured the bartender over and ordered a drink. When it came, she sipped from it lovingly, the alcohol sifting through her vasculature, warming her body. She saw a man in an expensive suit eying her from down the bar, his jaw square, a boyish smirk bleeding from the corner of his lips. She finished her drink and raised her hand to the bartender, but before she could summon him, the lights winked out, and the place erupted in noise.

She turned her body with all the rest, as splashes of red light soaked the stage. The first performer strutted forward, the thumping speakers at pace with every step.

The girl wore a black, strappy corset, her breasts spilling over the top like great jiggling boulders. The crowd gasped as she approached the chrome pole, which jutted from the stage floor like an ill-placed support column. In an instant, she scaled the thing and wrapped her legs around the cold metal, her long black hair spilling downward as she leaned back, the line of her cleavage square to the crowd. As her fans applauded, she traveled the pole with a practiced sexuality that seemed new and fresh and just for you. When it was over, she left the stage to an explosion of whistles and cheers.

A train of performers followed, each more talented than the last, each costume more colorful, more revealing. As the girls played their roles, energy built and flowed through the room, the men driven to the brink by the brazen display of sexual confidence, some of the girls winking shyly, others flexing and stomping the floor.

Finally, a beautiful red-headed girl took the stage. Last and most anticipated, she drew a prolonged introduction from the announcer and a ruckus from the crowd. As the lights flickered pink, she took the stage as if it were built just for her, drawing another girl forward by a leash affixed to a vinyl neck collar. The room became feverous as she teased and tempted the young thing with tickles from a feather and sharp lashes from a leather flogging whip. Soon, she was rid of the younger girl, banishing her from the

116

stage with a stern slap to the face. Then she commanded everything: the stage, the crowd, time.

When it was over, the lights picked up a bit, and many of the guests filtered out. Claire stood up on her high heels and wobbled a little, her mind swimming under the influence of several cocktails. A strong hand took her arm and steadied her.

"Are you alright?" Dominic asked.

"Yes," Claire said, as she stripped her arm away. "Thank you."

"Did you enjoy the show? Burlesque is the premier attraction here, I'm afraid. Other than gambling, that is."

"It was fine," she said. "Very entertaining."

He started to say something, but before he could, one of the soldiers appeared and whispered into his ear. Dominic nodded and turned toward Claire.

"I'm afraid I must leave you for a short time," he said. "Lopez will escort you back to the hotel, where we'll be attending a party. I'll meet you there in a couple of hours."

He smiled and walked away. Lopez held out his arm and the two left the building. Outside, a handful of young men moved busily between the exiting patrons, each one handing out fliers, which advertised another more lascivious venue. Claire took one of the fliers and saw it featured a blurry, photocopied image of a fat woman blindfolded and bound. She looked at Lopez, who snatched the paper away and crumpled it. One of the young men stepped forward but withdrew when Lopez opened his jacket to show his gun.

"Let's go," said Lopez, as the limousine pulled forward, his voice low and mealy as if he whispered through a metallic fan.

He opened the door and Claire stooped down to see the sneezy soldier waiting within. She adjusted her dress and slid inside. Someone shouted something to Lopez, who turned and withdrew his pistol. The crowd eyed him lazily, few showing any signs of interest, much less concern. After a few moments more, Lopez sat down within the vehicle and closed the door.

"Everything alright?" Claire asked.

Lopez gave an affirmative nod, as he slipped the gun back into its holster. The limo pulled out into the street and moved through the city streets, which had thinned out considerably since their arrival. Twenty minutes later, they pulled up to the hotel.

The moment she stepped out the limousine, a gray-haired doorman approached and asked her name.

"Claire Foley," she said.

Lopez exited the limo and reached into his jacket pocket, removing two one-hundred-dollar bills that looked as bright and new as the day there were made.

"Escort her to the party," he said.

The old man nodded and saw her inside, where he passed her over to an elevator attendant. This was a tall, square-looking man with thick eyebrows which had begun to meander. Without saying a word, he escorted her to the elevator and waited for the shimmering gold doors to slide apart.

"The party is on the roof," he said through his brambly beard.

"Do I have time to visit my room?" She asked, but he didn't answer.

They rode together, neither talking, the elevator soaring upward without the slightest hint, save for the gentle swimming in her stomach once it reached the top.

The second the elevator doors opened, anxiety flooded her chest. The rooftop was filled with wealthy, well-dressed men, escorted by exquisite-looking women who looked as if they'd been grown in a lab. Tall, buxom and beautiful, they all wore colorful party masks with fluffy feathers jutting up from one side. As she stepped out the elevator, a man approached and looked her over.

"I think this one," he said, and he presented a gold mask accented with a pretty little red feather.

Without speaking, she took the mask and put it on, feeling both ridiculous and relieved all in one moment. She left the man and approached the bar.

"Champaign or something stronger?" the young bartender said, as if sensing her unease.

"A martini," she said.

While she waited, she scanned her surroundings. Men huddled together and shook hands, while their dates stood quietly, their flawless little faces looking vapid and bored.

"Ever been to one of these things?" the bartender asked, as he served her drink.

"No."

"There's an orgy at the end."

She smiled at him, but he just turned and walked away.

"Ah, there you are," Dominic said, as he approached through the crowd. He wore a fresh tailored suit and as he approached, his cologne stung her eyes.

"I hope you haven't been waiting long," he said, as he took her hand.

118

"Just a few minutes."

"Please," he said, "let me introduce you to a handful of acquaintances. Some of these people are worth much in the way of amusement, I assure you."

They approached an old, fat man with a deep purple scar on the side of his neck and a sparse layer of thin gray hair strung horizontally across his freckled head. Claire felt her lip curling spontaneously at the sight of this creature, but the beautiful young girl clutching his arm seemed oblivious to any defects.

"Jean Paul," Dominic said loudly, as the old man grinned in delight. "Let me introduce you to my good friend Claire."

"Enchanted," Jean Paul said with a slight accent that was difficult to place. "What a lovely girl you are. Dominic is fortunate to have such a beauty for company this evening."

Claire accepted his outstretched hand and he placed a moist kiss on top.

"Jean Paul is an investor, but that's not what makes him interesting," Dominic said. "He is also a particularly accomplished explorer, who's been to places most people have never seen."

Claire raised her eyebrows in a forced demonstration of interest.

"This is true," Jean Paul said. "I enjoy traveling very much and have met many astonishing people on my journeys."

Dominic looked at Claire and smiled.

"You see, Jean Paul has no interest in things that lure many travelers: history, architecture, culture and whatnot."

Claire nodded.

"What does attract you?" she asked.

"Why the cuisines, my dear," he said with a grin. "Or more specifically, the rich oddities which some cultures ingest for sustenance and ritual alike."

Claire pinched her eyebrows together.

"You see, Jean Paul has a unique appetite for things you and I might find repugnant," Dominic said. "Please, Jean Paul, share."

"Yes, Dominic is correct. I have eaten things you might consider odd; however, to the people who eat them on a regular basis, they are like your hamburgers and French fries." He took a sip of his drink and peered at her thoughtfully. "For example, in Europe, as you may know, they enjoy blood pudding, which is comprised largely of coagulated blood drawn from pigs, cattle, sheep or what have you: earthy, meaty like iron. In Asia, they have bat paste, where a live bat is forced into a vat of boiling milk until it becomes malleable enough to be mashed into an edible pulp. Elsewhere, balut, hasma, jellied moose nose, countless dishes consisting of fried or boiled rats, hornets, spiders, roaches and other arthropods."

Claire put a hand to her stomach.

"Ah, a common reaction, my dear," Jean Paul said. "However, had you tasted some of this, you would assuredly change your opinion. Some are quite tasty once you get past the textures. In fact, I've adopted many to my usual menu. Casu marzu, for instance, which is made when the rind of a whole Pecorino cheese is removed to give flies an opportunity to inject their larvae. As the maggots feed, the acid from their digestive tracts works to break down the fat in the cheese, leaving a particularly unique flavor. Currently, this cheese is banned by the European Union due to ridiculous health concerns, so it must be procured on the black market; however, it is a treat worth pursuing, I can assure you."

Claire looked at Dominic who smiled with sincere amusement.

"Tell her what else you've added to your personal menu, Jean Paul."

A wry little grin shot across the old man's face.

"It's alright?" he asked Dominic, who nodded and put his hand out. "Please."

Claire furrowed her brows as Jean Paul cleared his throat.

"Well, you see my dear, throughout my life, one of my largest curiosities has centered on the consumption of human beings, themselves, by other human beings. So I made a point to explore regions of the world where this was said to still occur. More often than not, these turned out to be falsehoods; however, occasionally, I found success."

He squinted and licked his lips.

"The way it was prepared by natives left it stringy and tough and somewhat sour; but since then, I've found if you soak the meat in milk prior to consumption, the flavor is much better."

Claire moved a little closer to Dominic.

"You eat people?"

Jean Paul smiled.

"No one you know, my dear." The old man chuckled and put his arm around his date's slender waist. "Money brings privileges."

An awkward silence fell upon the circle before Dominic finally spoke.

"Well, we should mingle elsewhere," he said. "Jean Paul, as always, thank you for entertaining us."

Jean Paul nodded and held out his hand.

"It was a pleasure."

Claire placed a reluctant hand atop the old man's wrinkled fingers, and he pushed another warm, moist kiss against her knuckles.

"Nice to meet you," she said, and then they were off to meet other guests, who all seemed perfectly comfortable describing their own unique lifestyles and habits.

By the end of the night, Claire's mind was reeling.

"Have you not been entertained?" Dominic asked with a little smirk.

"It's certainly been something."

As if from thin air, Lopez approached and whispered something into Dominic's ear. He frowned and set his drink on a table.

"I'm sorry to say I must leave you again," he said, and then the two walked away.

Claire watched them weave through the crowd which had thinned considerably in the last hour; and then they both disappeared behind a big black door. She swallowed the last of her martini and returned to the bar.

"Where has everyone gone?" she asked the bartender.

"To the after-party in the suite below," he said. "The elevator attendant will take you there at your request."

She looked around at the sparse crowd and saw Jean Paul grinning at her from across the room.

"Maybe I'll have a look."

She ordered another drink and headed toward the elevator. The attendant asked her floor, and when she told him, his eyebrows lifted. Seconds later, the doors opened. He gave a gracious nod and she stepped out into a beautifully decorated hallway that stretched out beneath dim lighting. Quickly, a very large security guard rushed forward and asked her intentions.

"I was told there was an after-party on this floor?"

"Yes," he said politely. "Just down the hallway and through those doors."

She nodded and proceeded the rest of the way, but as she approached the doors, something stopped her. It was noise, strange, muffled noise, the origin of which her mind could not resolve. She looked over her shoulder toward the security guard, but he only smiled and nodded.

Without responding, she turned back toward the doors and took hold of the knobs. With a sudden jerk, she pulled them open to reveal a mob of nude men and women engaged in an astounding array of fleshly acts. She froze in the doorway and watched as women engaged in oral obligations, while men took them from behind. Only inches away from them, men wrestled together, their bodies entangled in a twitching diversity of lurid homosexual

121

acts. In one far corner, three men had their way with a woman who appeared to be drugged. A few feet from them, a very young girl lay unconscious, her makeup smeared, arms covered with human bite marks.

The center of the room was like one mass of skin, mouths, genitals and writhing legs. Men and women switched partners indiscriminately without regard for age or gender, each moving from body to body without making eye contact with its host. And all the while, some just sat in chairs watching it all, cigarettes dangling from their fingers, serious looks on their faces.

At last, Claire drew the eyes of some of the men and a few stood, their naked bodies glossy with sweat, faces hungry, like animals at the sight of unspoiled meat.

Without thinking, she fled down the hallway and slipped past the security guard who was busy reading a newspaper. He opened his mouth to speak, but before a single word dropped from his lips, she had successfully summoned the elevator and made her escape.

An hour later, she sat at the rooftop bar sipping a martini, while the bartender talked about this and that. She was beginning to think Dominic would not return at all, but just as she contemplated an escape, a man arrived with a message.

"Mr. Betancur wanted to me to apologize for leaving you unattended for so long and would like you to join him for a drink in his apartment suite three floors down."

Having delivered his message, the man turned abruptly and walked away.

Claire finished her drink and said goodbye to the bartender.

"Goodbye to you," he said with a smile that brought a unique appeal to his ordinary face.

"Can you tell me which apartment suite is Mr. Betancur's?" she asked.

"Three floors down," he said, as he wiped the bar.

"Yes, but which one?"

"No," he said. "He occupies the whole floor."

When she met the elevator attendant this time, he greeted her with a familiar smile.

"You, again?"

"Me, again."

"Mr. Betancur's floor?" he asked.

She nodded and he pressed the floor and crossed his hands.

When the doors opened, Lopez stood before her.

"This way," he said.

They crossed through a hallway, the walls pale, elegant paintings placed here and there. When they reached the end of the hall, they stood before a large steel door. Lopez approached a keypad to the right of it and tapped in a series of numerical codes, the buttons glowing green with every tap. When he finished, a soft click went off and the door popped open. Lopez took a large step back and turned his palm upward.

"Please," he said.

Claire nodded respectfully and entered, closing the door behind her.

Inside, it was all white leather and tasteful extravagance, a tiny fire burning within a massive fireplace, a candle in every direction.

"Have a seat," Dominic said from behind a little wet bar situated in the far corner.

She put her head down and crossed the room, his eyes tracing her every step, studying her as she smoothed the backside of her dress to sit. He finished whatever it was he'd been doing and approached her, a single glass of scotch in his hand. He looked as if he'd just come from the party, the belt gone from his black slacks, the tie from his white shirt, two or three buttons undone to reveal the upper portion of his chest. He sat beside her and leaned back, his knees spread open as if he'd known her long enough to expect anything and everything without asking.

"Would you like a drink?" he asked, as he sipped his scotch.

"Yes, thank you."

He lowered his eyebrows and swallowed, a shallow hiss escaping from his damp lips.

"Help yourself."

She smiled as if he were joking, but his demeanor remained unchanged. She lifted to her feet and made her way over to the bar. He watched her the way, noting the ticks of her high heels against the white tile.

She surveyed the liquors: everything you could imagine and some she'd never seen before. Without thinking much about it, she made a martini and splashed a pair of olives inside. She returned with her drink in hand, while he took in all her subtle movements through lazy eyes. In her absence, he had moved to the center of the couch, and his face flashed a cunning little smirk that made him look somewhat malevolent. She sat beside him and sipped her drink.

"You are very beautiful, do you know that?" he said, his words afflicted by drunkenness. "I find you very attractive."

He rested his arm over the couch behind her and leaned in closer, his fingers lightly touching the ends of her long hair.

"I've been thinking of this moment all night," he said, as he moved in for a kiss.

She lowered her head and turned away.

He moved back and dropped his eyebrows.

"Is there a problem?" he asked, as he withdrew a pack of cigarettes from his pocket.

She shook her head.

"It's nothing to do with you, Dominic, but I have no interest in a romantic relationship with anyone at the moment. As I said before, my only interest is to fulfill my duties and return to my life."

He held a very beautiful lighter up to his cigarette and lit it over a pulsing blue flame.

"Who said anything about romance?" he said, as he exhaled a cloud of white smoke.

She eyed him carefully.

"I'm only looking for a bit of fun for the evening, nothing more."

She looked at her drink.

"Even still."

His face hardened and he stood up. She watched him cross to the other side of the room and take a seat in a chair.

"Let me tell you a story," he said. He paused to suck from his cigarette, his eyes lowered to the floor, eyebrows squinted as if he were deep in thought. He exhaled and scratched the dark whiskers which had grown noticeable this late in the evening. "Once, there was this girl, a dancer here in the city."

He drew from his cigarette once more, a bright orange kernel flaring and then fading. He took it away from his mouth and continued, while flittering streams of white smoke escaped his lips.

"She was a beautiful girl. Long blond hair, endless legs, a mouth that seemed to be always wet, always pink and wet."

He raised his cigarette and took another deep, long pull, his eyes studying her face, its beauty marred by fear despite her best efforts. He smiled as he inhaled, thin wisps of smoke escaping upward along the sides of his sucking cheeks. Finally, he took the cigarette from his lips and turned away.

"When she first came here, she was a clueless cunt, nothing more," he continued. "I took her in because these types arouse my interest." He turned his hand over toward her as if to make an example, his eyes drifting upward as if he struggled to remember. He put the glass of scotch to his lips and took two large swallows. Then he wiped his mouth with his sleeve and placed the glass on the table beside him.

"She was like my pet for a while." He looked toward her, his eyes dark in the low, amber light, shadows hovering over them, making him seem inhuman, demonic.

"These types," he said, gesturing toward her again with a flip of the hand. "They are willing for anything, even if they think otherwise. Their lives before: gray to them, oppressive. When they come to me, they are like rutting animals, asses up in the air, their scent so obvious. I have them however I want them, and they go willingly, begging for me to degrade and humiliate them, loving it."

He smiled to himself, as he flicked ashes into a ceramic tray. Claire shifted in her seat, her eyes on the door, on anything in the room that might pass for a weapon.

"This girl I speak of, she was very kindhearted, but as I said, she had no clue. It took me no time to adopt her for my purposes, and soon she recognized her fate."

He shook his head and ashed in the ceramic tray once more, his back turned toward her, eyes scanning the room, appreciating his great wealth.

"Ultimately, I bored of her," he went on. "However, I decided to maintain ownership of her, so I instructed her as such and put her in a small apartment downtown, under guard of course."

He put his cigarette out in the tray and turned to face Claire.

"A time or two, she made attempts to free herself; however, these were met with brutal discipline that left her scarred and useless to any man save a pimp."

He lifted his eyebrows and offered an empathetic frown.

"Sadly, these events drove the girl to cut through her wrists with a large shard from a broken bathroom mirror."

His eyes drifted to the floor for a moment while he thought. Then they trickled upward and bored forth, the pupils seeming to swell according to his will.

"You see, she knew it was her only way out, and so she took it."

He shook his head slowly.

"There was simply no other way."

A harsh knocking slammed against the front door, and Claire jumped in her seat. Dominic smiled and stood, dusting his slacks and then making his way across the room. He called through the door, and Lopez gave an earnest response. Dominic opened the door and stepped into the hallway, closing Claire inside.

Immediately, she took to her feet and scampered to the kitchen. She opened drawers in search of knives, but she only found forks, spoons, butter knives and chopsticks. She slammed the drawers closed and ran down the hallway, checking door after door to find every one locked. Finally, she put her hand around a doorknob and gave it a successful turn. The door opened to reveal a closet packed with heavy coats and a stack of cardboard boxes.

She looked over her shoulder to make sure she was still alone, then she tore one of the boxes open and put a hand over her mouth. Inside, there were pictures of women, their lifeless bodies sprawled awkwardly upon cement floors, wrists tied together, knife wounds decorating their skin, their vacant eyes staring off into nowhere, mouths agape.

She heard the soft thwack of the front door unsealing and lost hold of the box, the photos flittering in the air and drifting in all directions. As the soles of his shoes clapped the tile entryway, she fell to her knees and grabbed the pictures in bunches, pushing them into the box and closing it shut.

She jumped to her feet, but the shifting weight inside the box threw it off balance, and it slipped through her hands and crashed to the floor. His footsteps grew louder, thumping the tile with a growing urgency, like big wooden hammers pounding a hollow drum.

In a panic, she bent over and gathered it all up, pushing it awkwardly into the closet and closing the door just as his tall, broad silhouette filled the space at the end of the hall.

"I need to use the bathroom," she said, her eyes darting softly between his shadowed face and the carpeted floor.

He approached her without speaking and took her arm with an unforgiving hand.

"This way," he said, as he led her back up the hallway and into the living room. He released her and pointed to a door in the far corner of the room. "Fix your makeup while you're in there."

She hurried to the bathroom and closed herself inside. She opened every drawer but found only cotton swabs, linens and decorative soaps. She closed the last one and studied the mirror. A ragged, shaken woman looked back, her tears polluted with mascara, eyes bleeding ink. Soon she was sobbing, her hands on the countertop, body shaking.

A fist smashed against the door and she flinched at its force.

"Don't take all night," he said from outside.

"I'll be right out," she said with a quivering voice not her own.

As his footsteps faded, she straightened her face until the girl in the mirror looked more like the one from a few hours before. Finally, she put her makeup bag back inside her purse and opened the bathroom door.

Outside, he sat on the couch with his back to her, a fresh cigarette dangling from his hand.

"Come join me," he said.

She moved slowly toward him, taking a seat on the other side of the couch.

"Now, now," he said, as he patted the space immediately next to him. "Slide closer."

She swallowed hard and slid over, his left arm engulfing her slight body. He smelled of cigarettes and too much cologne, and the stink of it nearly gagged her. He placed his hand over the top of her head and pressed her face against his chest.

He began massaging her scalp, and as he did, his fingers gathered up bunches of her hair and twisted it into a firm handle.

"Unbutton me," he whispered, as he exhaled a cloud of cigarette smoke.

"No," she said, turning her head away.

In a rage, he yanked her upward, nearly tearing the skin from her skull. She let out a shrill cry and tears welled in the corners of her eyes.

"You don't ever tell me no," he whispered into her ear. "Do you understand?"

When she didn't respond, he leaned in and took her earlobe between his teeth. She shrieked as he clamped down. He chewed the flesh until she thought she might pass out from the pain. Then he finally released and spit blood onto the lap of her dress.

"Do you understand now?" he whispered into her ear.

"Yes."

He re-gripped her hair and brought her closer.

"Wait," she said. "Please, just let me have a drink first. Just one drink."

He paused for a moment and then released her.

"Make it quick."

She got to her feet and turned to go, but before she'd made even a single step, he had her by the wrist.

"Get me one too."

He drank his glass empty and pushed it into her hand. She took it and made her way to the bar.

127

While he sat smoking, she looked about for knives without success. And then from the corner of her eye, she saw something metal give off a glittering sparkle of refracted light. She turned to see a corkscrew sitting atop the marble counter.

She looked over to Dominic, but he was busy with his cigarette, his lips moving along with whatever stream of thought sifted through his drunken mind. Without hesitation, she took up the corkscrew and slipped it under her skirt, twining the coiled metal tip in the string of her underwear, where it crossed over the top of her left thigh. She filled his glass with scotch and returned to the couch.

She handed him the glass, and he took it without looking, a little wrinkled smirk on his face. With a measured haste, she sat next to him, pulling her skirt upward in bunches to hide the bulging corkscrew handle. He placed his cigarette in the ashtray and downed his entire drink in three large swallows.

Chills climbed her spine as she watched him drink, his throat bulging grotesquely as it consumed. When he'd drained the glass dry, he set it on the table and wiped the slick from his mouth. He turned and smiled, his bold eyes hungry and showing obvious signs of intoxication.

"Where were we?" he said, as he palmed the back of her head and gathered up a bunch of her hair once more.

He forced her down again, and this time she offered no resistance. But before he knew what was happening, she'd taken hold of him with all her strength, her fingers rooting in around his vulnerability, her grip like a vice.

Wails of agony escaped his throat as she clamped down harder. He released her hair and pried against her hand, but as he lunged forward, she withdrew the corkscrew with her other hand and plunged it into the side of his neck.

The shiny metal sunk into the fleshy tissue, a string of dark purple blood bowing upward and splashing against the white tile floor.

He put both hands to his throat to stop up the bleeding, but it boiled out between his fingers as he gurgled up words. Claire scrambled to her feet and froze, the corkscrew still dangling from her hand, the coils congested with gore. Dominic staggered to his feet and stumbled toward her, his eyes flaring wildly, face painted with a medley of fear, blood and rage.

He came at her full bore and put his fingers around her neck, but the moment his hands left the wound, a red waterfall escaped, and he dropped to the ground, his handsome face pallid, eyes uninhabited.

Claire looked down at his lifeless body, half expecting him to spring back up to his feet. She kicked at him, the toe of her high heel shoe digging

128

into his ribs without conjuring any sort of response. Once convinced, she turned her attention toward the door, approaching it cautiously, her body trembling and heaving with great exasperated breaths.

In the corner, a security monitor showed the goings-on in the exterior hallway lobby. She watched Lopez pacing around outside, his hand in his pocket, a drowsy look on his face. Without hesitation, she worked the locks on the door and opened it. Lopez turned abruptly, his body straightening to prepare for the sight of his boss. But instead, he saw only Claire, her dress and skin saturated in blood.

"Please," she said, her eyes welling up with tears. "There's been an accident."

Lopez hurried forward and looked inside the apartment, his face paling at the sight of Dominic Betancur. He reached into his jacket, but before he could grasp the butt of the gun, Claire drove the corkscrew into the back of his neck.

This time, her aim was exact, and Lopez collapsed to the ground as if his soul had been plucked free. She stood over him for several seconds, the corkscrew handle sticking out the back of his spine as if it powered an enormous wind-up toy. She removed her shoes and scampered to the elevator. She pressed the button and waited, her heart thumping wildly as if it wanted out. Within seconds the door opened, and the bearded elevator operator greeted her with a look of great worry.

"Please," she said, her palms turned upward. "Mr. Betancur needs your help."

Without thinking, the man fled the elevator and sprinted for the apartment. As he did, Claire took his place and furiously tapped the ground floor button. As if beckoned by some noiseless tone, the operator stopped and turned.

"Hey!" He bellowed, the depth of his voice rugged and frightening. "What are you doing?"

Claire frantically pressed the button several times more, as the thud of his boot heels grew louder and louder.

"Get out of there!"

At last, the doors flashed out of their hiding places and raced toward one another; but before they met, the burly operator thrust his hand between. The doors met his arm and relented, the entryway opening enough for him to squeeze between, his big body swelling before her, eyes red with rage.

A rush of fear washed over her, as the furious man moved forward and took her by the arms, his massive hands enveloping them whole, so his fingers touched on the other side. Without thinking, she let out a soft little cry and brought her knee upward in a sharp forward angle. The hard bony kneecap struck true enough to draw a slobbering yowl that filled the elevator and hurt her ears.

As if all the oxygen had vanished, the operator collapsed onto the ground and clutched at his genitals, his face contorted, tears welling in the corners of his eyes. The elevator doors flared out again, this time stopping around the man's legs and withdrawing once more. In a panic, Claire stomped her heel into his shins, until he finally pulled them toward his chest and made room for the doors.

Immediately, she pressed the button to summon the doors back again, but they remained withdrawn, while the operator crawled to his knees.

"You fucking bitch," he gasped. "I'll kill you!"

Finally, the doors appeared again, and when the operator saw this, he staggered to his feet and limped forward, one hand stretched out, fingers clutching the air.

Claire held her hands to her mouth as the man encroached, his image growing slender between the closing elevator doors. Convinced he would interrupt them once more, she positioned herself to offer whatever defense she could muster, but just before his hand could slip between, the elevator sealed itself shut and began its descent.

As she drew closer to the lobby floor, she looked at her dress, which now resembled a costume from a horror film. When the elevator opened, a well-dressed old couple stood before her, their jaws agape at such an unexpected vision. She stepped between them and into the lobby, where gasps spread from person to person like a virus.

Through the hush, Romero rushed forward and took her by the arm.

"You're not going anywhere," he said, as he held his off hand to an earpiece that barked instructions in low tones.

"Help me!" Claire yelled to the people in the lobby, but all seemed too shocked to move. "Please, help me, for God's sake!"

Finally, a large man in a cowboy hat stepped forward and blocked Romero's path.

"Hold it right there," he said. "Where are you taking this woman?"

Romero looked the man over.

"This is none of your concern. I advise you to stand aside."

A fire took life in the large man's eyes, and he cocked his hat back and pointed a thick finger at Romero.

"You're not taking her anywhere until we figure out what in the hell's going on."

A crowd started to form around the three, and this seemed to make Romero nervous. He looked from side-to-side and then released Claire's arm. The large man held out a hand, but before she could take it, Romero drove his empty palm into the front of the man's neck, knocking his hat backward and choking the breath from his throat.

The crowd gave a collective gasp, as the large man fell to his knees. Without hesitation, Claire turned and made a run for the exit, but just before she could grab the door handle, Romero had her arm again."

"You're not going anywhere," he whispered into her ear. "You'll pay for what you've done."

With that, he turned to face the lobby, but before he could focus his eyes, a large fist collided with his nose, and a crunching noise racketed across the room. Instantly, Romero lost consciousness and fell forward, his face landing hard against the floor.

Tooth fragments shot out and skipped across the tile, settling just in front of the old couple from the elevator, their faces advertising horror and disgust. The large man hovered over his fallen adversary, his left hand still clutching his throat, whistling, wheezing breaths passing between his purple lips.

"Are you alright?" a woman asked.

"I'm fine," he whispered. "Someone call the authorities."

As people gathered around him, he looked for the girl.

"Where's that woman?" he said to no one in particular.

Everyone looked around, but no one had an answer, and no one knew what to say when the authorities finally arrived.

Chapter 15

Outside in the daytime streets, the people moved about in great hoards, their sweating limbs clutching meager commodities, small children begging for money and snatching things from people's hands. Entitled by norm, they all moved against one another with a practiced sort of panic, shoulders banging hard against other shoulders without drawing even a grunt or a glance in return. Through this swimming mass, riders would pass, their motor scooters moving a few feet and then beeping, a few feet more and then the same.

Amongst all the congestion, Claire moved about, her presence seemingly unnoticed despite the blood on her dress and the white of her skin. As she slithered between bodies, the street people shouted to one another with offers of fruits, newly plucked poultry and jewelry that left green marks on the skin. The chaos gave welcome cover, and she used it for all its worth before finally ducking into a small tavern that could serve no more than eight at a time.

Inside, a little man stood behind the bar polishing glass mugs, his face too old to wager an age. He glanced up at the bloody mess in the doorway light before him, his expression unchanged by such a kink in his day. Unfazed and unmoved, he pointed a thumb to the back and then returned to his duties. She hurried past him into a bathroom and shut the door.

Within the tiny room, she found a hole in the floor and a bucket of water, no mirror or paper or window from which to flee. She removed her dress and mushed it up into a wad, the smell of Dominic's blood mingling with the foul stink from the hole. She plunged the wad of cloth into the bucket of water and wrung it full. She withdrew the dripping mass and scrubbed it against her flesh, grinding the dried flecks of burgundy loose until her skin looked reasonably clean.

She heard a gentle knock at the door and stiffened. She took the knob and pulled the door open a crack. The old man stood before her, the same disinterested look on his face, some dirty clothes in his hands. He shoved them through the crack and then walked away. She dressed quickly and splashed water on her face. She checked the mirror but saw only wall. She toed the creaking wood floor and pushed her head out into the room, no one there except the old man. He rubbed his dirty rag against the glass mugs, a strange and quiet tune on the back of his throat.

"Hello," she said.

He stopped his work and turned.

"American?" he asked.

She nodded.

He sighed and fled his post. He approached the front door and shut it. He locked it.

"One night," he said. "In the morning you go."

He showed her a room in the upstairs, a tiny, old-looking thing. Dusty.

"Thank you," she said.

"One night," he said, holding a crooked finger up to make plain his point.

"Yes," she said. "I understand."

He turned and walked down the stairs, his footsteps slow, the boards crying softly with each careful step.

She looked about the room. There was a little soiled army cot, a window, a bedpan and not much else. She shut the door and opened the window, the rumbling chaos outside so noisy and yet seemingly distant. She collapsed onto the cot, falling into sleep's embrace deep and suddenly, the breeze filtering through a pair of torn little white curtains that bloomed up silently as the room breathed the air.

Within the fog of her dreams, they all came, the dearest of her darlings, the few that were. She saw her mother, with her gray, coarse hair and tiny frail hands. A real woman, so somber and sweet, and still going despite so obvious her right to quit.

She saw her father, his body younger, his smile broad, only kindness and understanding within his familiar blue eyes. No sign of vacancy or haze.

She saw Alfred, his wild hair and shy little smiles. The smell of pipe smoke on his jacket. The tenderness of his words.

And Nathan. She saw Nathan. And heard his voice and felt his touch. Their power enough to stymie the real world and keep her asleep forever and always, swimming freely in this bleary and harmless in-between place.

A hard racket awoke her. Knuckles on the door.

She sat up and waited while the sharp world crystallized around her. It was dark in the room, the night awake and full-bore.

More knocking.

She stood up on her cold feet and approached the door. She opened it a crack. The old man stood before her, in his hands a bowl of soup, writhing coils of steam escaping its surface.

"Thank you," she said, as he passed it over.

He turned without answering and descended the stairs.

She sat on the cot and stirred the soup, chunks of unfamiliar meats and vegetables boiling up from the murky broth. She gathered a spoonful and brought it to her mouth. Something spoiled lurked within the salty brine. She chewed, even so, a sourness in every bite, a growing vigor with every swallow.

When she'd finished the bowl, she set it aside and ventured downstairs. The steps bent and sunk beneath her feet, filling the darkness with a chorus of squeaks and moans and whines. When she reached the bottom step, she saw a burst of candlelight in one far corner of the room where the old man sat near the window eating his soup.

She held to the bottom step for a moment and then proceeded to the bathroom without looking over again. Once inside, she shut the door. She attended to her business and stood up. She opened the door and looked around. There he sat the same as before. She began walking upstairs.

"Stop," he said.

She stopped.

"Please," he said.

She crept back down and looked over. He gestured to the seat across him. She approached and sat, several minutes passing without words between them.

"I know who you run from," he said finally. So much gravel in his old voice.

She sat silently while he dug up solids from the broth and chewed them with a slow elderly jaw. He lifted the bowl to his mouth and sucked down the liquid. She yawned against her will, but he didn't seem to notice.

"These people," he said. "You cannot run." He ran a sleeve across his lips until they were dry. "They find you."

He reached over and collected a half-smoked cigar from the table. He lit the thing with a match, tangles of white smoke adrift in the space above their heads.

"You go back in the morning."

She rubbed her tired face.

"I won't."

He smoked. His eyes looked tired.

"You have people?"

She looked at him and he looked at her.

"You go back."

She bent her head and cried.

"How do you know these people?" she whispered, as little salty tears slipped within her speaking mouth.

He smoked his cigar and ashed in a charred little wooden bowl.

"They built this place."

She looked up.

"Your bar?"

He shook his head slowly.

"The city."

She leaned back in her chair and they met at the eye.

"This whole place is theirs?" she asked.

He crooked his head as if confused, his eyes pale enough to be blind.

"Everything is theirs."

The wind picked up outside, it's invisible fingers strumming the trees and aluminum rooftops like instruments, a slow whining chorus funneling through the streets.

She firmed her mouth.

"Not everything."

He smoked his cigar and dumped the ashy tip in his little bowl.

"All but death," he said. "This we still own."

The wind whirred and moaned as it pushed its way into the voids of the world. She leaned forward and made a gesture for his cigar. He passed it over without hesitation, his expression unchanged by this and all else. She brought it to her mouth and smoked, the rush so sudden and sickeningly good. She exhaled and passed the thing back.

"Someone should stop them."

Now the rain came, the old window shutters clapping sharply outside, the smell of wet earth sifting in through the open window.

"You go sleep now," he said.

135

He smoked and exhaled.

"You go at first light."

She stood up and looked him over while he smoked.

"Thank you."

He nodded without looking up, his eyes fixed on the table, each one tired and cloudy and slightly flaring with every puff of his cigar. She walked away without speaking and climbed the steps. She entered the little room and shut the door. Outside, the rain dropped hard and heavy, splashing in great pools of water, where cigarette butts gathered up like little boats in the gutters along the muddy streets.

She lay upon the cot and tried to think, but soon she was adrift again within a gentle slumber, with all her monsters locked up in little boxes and her dreams running free and unfettered, like little children in the summer breeze.

Chapter 16

When the morning broke, she threw her legs over the bed and stood without thinking. Outside, a rumble of activity had begun, despite the pale light and early hour. She approached the window and looked out to see people assembling along the streets to sell, beg or steal, just as they had done all the days before. She turned away and opened the door. She ventured downstairs and looked around. The place sat empty and quiet. She crossed the room and disabled the heavy locks on the front door. She pulled the thing open and the light knifed into the dark room. She turned back and gave a last look at the little bar, old and meager and aromatic with the scent of rotting wood. She stepped outside and shut the door behind her.

The streets were loud with the clamor of strange languages and motor scooters, which buzzed and beeped as they made their way amid the congestion. She followed the covered wooden walkway a short distance and then stepped out into the street, where a small white sun bathed everything in a growing heat. Out in the open, people moved about in a whir of confused patterns, their bodies trading sweat as they brushed against one another. She pushed into the mob, doing her best to navigate through all the elbows and shoulders, which clacked hard against her body, leaving little unseen injuries that might take on blue and purple complexions in the hours to come.

At last, she emerged from the writhing mass of bodies and stepped onto the walkway opposite the one from which she'd come. This path led directly to the hotel and she walked it with steady, deliberate steps, despite the loathing within her mind. Soon, she stood before the front of the building, where people came and went through a revolving glass door that spun amid a bright, gold frame. She waited for the door to settle and stepped inside, making her way into the interior, where bellboys carted luggage for important-looking people dressed in important-looking clothes.

"Ms. Foley."

Claire turned sharply to see Demetri sitting in the lobby on a white chair, his legs crossed, the day's newspaper in hand. In the chair next to him sat Romero, his face discolored and heavily bandaged, his eyes aflame with hate. Demetri motioned her over with a finger. She approached.

"Are you alright?" Demetri asked.

She nodded.

"Good."

He scratched his chin and folded his newspaper. He stood up and Romero did the same.

"Shall we?"

He held his hand out toward the door. She nodded and all three crossed the lobby. Outside, a big black car waited, its windows tinted, the rear doors already ajar. They left the hotel and Demetri guided her into the vehicle with a gentle hand. She took a place within the vast leather interior and waited, while the two men settled in beside her, their thick legs pressing tightly against her hips.

At Demetri's instruction, the car pulled out into traffic and made its way through the streets, where it pushed past everything from smart cars to limousines to mules, mopeds, rickshaws and nearly every other form of primitive transportation. They rode the way in silence, save for the dry squeal from Romero's broken nose, which whistled with every breath, like a ripe tea kettle ready to burst. Every now and again, Claire felt the weight of the man's heavy stare, but she kept her face pointed forward just the same.

After a short time, they rumbled out of the urban sprawl and into the countryside, where vast fields of tall grass swayed in the hot, flowing breeze. As the roads evolved from concrete to gravel to mud, the car began to struggle for traction, and after threatening to dive into the ditches several times, it finally came to a stop at the order of Demetri.

"Please remain seated," he told Claire, as he opened the door and exited.

When he was gone, she slid away from Romero and pressed herself against the door. She peered out the window, while Romero watched her through wide, bulging eyes.

"I'm going to kill you," he said.

She kept her eyes fixed on the outside world, where three green military trucks approached from the edge of the horizon.

"Do you hear me?" Romero asked. "I'm going to slit your throat open."

Claire said nothing.

"Look at me." He snatched her wrist and squeezed.

The door opened and Romero turned her loose.

"Please exit the vehicle," Demetri said. "Both of you."

Claire swallowed hard and stepped outside.

"Wait here," Demetri said, as he walked to the other side of the vehicle. He took Romero by the arm and led him several feet away. Claire watched as he spoke into Romero's ear, his gestures giving no hint to what he might be saying or how he might be saying it. She turned and looked toward the trucks, which steadily increased in size as they motored forward. The wind kicked up and she brushed the hair from her face. She started to cry.

"Now, now," Demetri said as he approached. "Don't worry. You're completely safe."

He handed her a handkerchief, while Romero watched them from afar.

"Please," he said. "Take it."

She accepted the handkerchief and wiped her eyes.

"Breathe easy," he said. "We mean you no harm."

At last, the trucks arrived and stopped before them. She watched as soldiers poured out and stood at attention. Demetri motioned Romero over and he approached with some obvious reticence.

"Where are you taking me?" Claire asked.

"Back to the facility, of course," Demetri said. "Where else?"

He nodded to one of the soldiers, who gathered Claire's arm and led her to the rear of one of the trucks. He guided her up a set of metal steps and placed her on a small bench, which ran along the insides of the canvas walls. The soldier started to sit on the opposite bench, but Demetri appeared and shooed him away.

"I'll ride with her," he said.

The soldier nodded and jumped out the back. Demetri climbed aboard and approached the cab. He pounded his fist against the metal and the truck crawled forward. He sat in the opposite bench, his hands folded neatly across his lap, hers clenched into a ball upon her own. He withdrew a small notepad from his jacket pocket and began writing, his penmanship careful and slow, as if he crafted every word in flawless calligraphy. She stared blankly into his face as he worked, her head bobbing with the beat of the tires, which throbbed hard and often against the stony road beneath.

He set the pad down beside him and rolled up his sleeves. He looked at her.

"Are you comfortable?"

She sat silently, her eyes steady and unflinching.

"I'm afraid I have some troubling news."

She stared at his face.

"Your mother and father have passed," he said. "He several weeks ago, she not long after."

He watched as she choked back tears.

"According to the report we received, your father died of a lung infection due to aspiration of food. Your mother suffered a heart attack several weeks later."

She began to cry, her tears running fast and free despite all efforts to the otherwise. Demetri leaned forward and propped his forearms against his thighs.

"I'm very sorry for your loss."

He waited while she gathered herself. He looked into her wet, glittering eyes.

"You know," he said. "I like you. I actually do."

He scratched his ear.

"I don't blame you. This thing you did. I don't blame you for it. He was a pervert. A dangerous man. He was not fit to lead our project. I always knew this."

He waited for a response, but she said nothing. He leaned over and reached into a cooler that sat on the ground between them. His hand fished through the melted ice and collected a bottle of clean, cold water. He held it in front of her.

"If I pour this for you, will you drink it?"

She did not speak.

"Alright."

He opened the bottle and drank from it. Then he tossed it back inside the cooler and shut the top.

"I don't care about this," he said, as he leaned forward again. "I don't care about Betancur. I don't care what you did to him or what he did to you." He pointed a thick finger at the center of her face. "What's important is that you return to your work. That is all that matters."

She shook her head slowly.

"I won't."

Demetri flexed his jaw.

"You will."

She cracked her knuckles.

"You can't coerce me. I don't care about myself anymore."

140

He smiled and put his hands together.

"I don't have to coerce you. I only have to convince you."

He stood and moved toward the cab of the truck, his feet surfing the floor as he carefully negotiated the vehicle's shifting momentum. He pounded his fist against the metal and the truck slowly came to a stop.

Claire heard a door open and the sound of boots crushing gravel. Demetri moved to the rear of the truck and a soldier came around the corner to take his place.

"When we arrive at the facility, you'll spend two weeks in the upper level so you can recuperate," he said on his way out. "Then you'll return to your duties."

With that, he disappeared, leaving Claire and the soldier alone to ride all the savage hours that lay afore.

Chapter 17

Over the next two weeks, she roamed the first level alone, except for the staff and another faceless soldier who tailed her every move. She thought they must manufacture these men, their faces mum, expressions clone-like, never the same one twice, except for this particular individual who always seemed to linger some 50 yards behind.

Up in the top level, time went quickly, the wounds on her face growing fainter with every passing day. In the mornings, she would pass Gretchen, who sat at her desk wearing a polite little smile, the shape and contours always the same, as if she kept her face on a hanger in a closet at night and glued it on when the morning came.

Despite her best efforts, Claire very much enjoyed the food, and the sun in the courtyard and the birds that circled aimlessly above. But at night, the quiet gave rise to troubling thoughts; and after a while, she knew nothing else to occupy her mind but the research she had said she would not do.

In that place, answers seemed to come without effort, each one like a living thing that wanted out from her brain and into the world. Out into a world, where they would do indiscriminate harm or good, without intentions and with no feeling. And all these revelations conjured excitement and pride within her, and then an inevitable shame.

After ten days, she drank a bottle of wine and smashed apart the mirror in her room, taking up a piece of glass and running the edge against the flesh of her wrist. But she lacked whatever it was that allowed for such things, and this made her feel helpless and even more ashamed.

On the morning of the eleventh day, Gretchen buzzed her room.

"Ms. Foley, please visit the courtyard. You have a visitor."

She dressed and applied her makeup before the sad reflection of a girl she once knew. She left the room and made her way past Gretchen, the soldier tight on her trail, as she made her way down the curved hall, around the empty cafeteria and up the stairs. Small and steep were the steps on these stairs, which ascended up, up and up, before finally spilling out into a concrete deck that overlooked the courtyard. She approached the metal rails and placed her hands on top. The air was warm and sweet, and she filled her lungs greedily as if she might not get another chance.

"Claire."

She looked down to see Alfred smiling up at her.

Without speaking, she fled her perch, shoes clicking the concrete stairs as she scrambled toward him, eyes wet with tears. The old man held a book in his hands, and this he dropped to the ground as he opened his arms to receive her. They embraced with a thud, his glasses bent crooked, hat knocked to the dirt. She wept and he shushed her, and they held one another for as long as they needed.

"I thought I'd never see you again," she said, as they took a seat on a bench.

Birds clamored about in the treetops above as he held her hand.

"I was worried of that as well."

She wiped her eyes.

"Are you ok?" she asked.

"Yes. I'm fine. How are you?"

She shook her head and looked around. The soldier stood atop the concrete deck watching them through a set of pointy eyes.

"Terrible. I've seen terrible things."

He frowned.

"I'm so sorry, my dear. I fear we may be in store for more."

She looked at him, tears welling.

"I don't know what to do, Alfred."

He looked up at the soldier.

"I don't know that we have many options, I'm afraid."

He let go of her hand and acquired his pipe from his jacket pocket. He glanced at her for a moment, and she gave her blessing with a nod. He loaded it up with tobacco and set it afire, the familiar smell erupting up and around her. An unexpected comfort.

He lifted his hat and scratched his head.

"I want more than anything for you to find your way out of this," he said. "I don't care about myself or anyone else."

They sat quietly for a moment, the birds behaving as birds behave, the wind gently sifting through the high up leaves above them.

"Have you seen Nathan?" she asked.

He smoked thoughtfully, his eyes looking off into the distance.

"They took him away. We were in the cafeteria. He kept talking to someone. He was always talking, and they were always warning him to stop. But he kept talking. Always talking. A soldier told him to stop and he outright refused, and they gathered him up and dragged him away, and that was the last I saw him."

She lowered her head.

"When was this?"

"Nine months ago."

They sat without speaking for several minutes, each trapped in the invisible spotlight that was the soldier's glare.

"There's no way out of here," she said.

Alfred smoked his pipe and exhaled.

"You have a brilliant mind, but even you can't see around every corner."

She looked at him.

"What are you doing up here, Alfred?"

He looked at her for as long as he could, before his eyes trickled away and held firm to something far away.

"I'm told to urge you back to work," he said.

She shook her head slowly and looked off.

"I doubt they care what you say. They only want to remind me they can hurt you if I don't."

Alfred nodded slowly.

"Yes, I believe you're right."

They sat together silently as ominous thoughts wove tangles within their tired minds. Alfred smoked his pipe and watched the white smoke coil up and climb the still air, his chin tilting to trace its movements, revealing bruises around his neck. She reached out and traced them with a gentle touch.

"Oh, Alfred. I'm so sorry."

He collected her hand and held it in his.

"Do you believe things happen for a reason?"

"No," she whispered.

He nodded once.

"And when people offer examples in their lives that appear to prove it so?"

She looked away at the pale green grass, each blade fat and full and samely-cut.

"It's not really proof."

He smoked his pipe and exhaled.

"Explain it to me, if you will."

She rubbed her head as if it hurt.

"It's human nature to survive, to reach toward better things," she said. "When people suffer hardships, they inevitably move on with their lives, and some good things are apt to occur. When these good things happen, the person credits the hardship for them to award meaning and justify its existence. But even though a hardship can fork a life into another direction, it's not fate or planned. It's only human nature."

Alfred looked at her.

"How so?"

"I hate these sorts of conversations, Alfred. What's the point?"

"Please," he said. "Just humor me. Tell me what you really think."

She squirmed about on the bench, her face pinched slightly as if she feared judgment.

"What I really think," she said. "Fine."

She cleared her throat and straightened her back.

"A person has no choice but to make the best of things," she said. "It's human nature. The person continues to breathe, even after the hardship. And as time passes, the person is likely to encounter some new positive, a new job, a new relationship, the birth of a child. Of course, since this other thing would not have resulted without the original hardship, the person inevitably credits the hardship. To excuse its existence. To answer the question: why has this happened to me? And so the person is apt to say: well, this bright, shiny thing in my life would not have occurred without that hardship or tragedy. If not for my breakup, I would not have met this person. If not for being fired, I would not have found this job. But it's really just a person's natural tendency to move forward that brought the new good thing. There was no reason behind the hardship. It just happens, and the person moves on to encounter some new positive along his or her timeline."

"You sound as if you've answered this question before."

She shrugged.

"It confuses me, really. Why people choose to see it otherwise. If you have the strength to make something good out of something bad, why surrender the credit? If things work out for the best, it's because you make it so. Not because of some devised plan."

He smoked and exhaled.

"I feel I could offer a good defense against that way of thought, but I won't waste our time with debate. Instead, I'll adapt my words to your

145

perspective by saying this to you: that things can happen for a reason, and your refusal to see it as such is due to your attribution of the cause."

She turned to face him.

"I knew a man once who endured a great injustice," he said. "He lost a young child to a poisoning sponsored by some type of corporate negligence. Some pollution. I cannot remember the details. What I do remember is the corporation used its resources to prevent justice. And this drove the man into rage and sorrow, as it would any caring person.

"But instead of throwing his hands up, he chose to give the tragedy meaning by using his personal wealth to provide for other young children in need. He founded organizations to see to their well-being, and those organizations continue to provide, even though he's been dead now for many years."

He held up his finger.

"You see, that tragedy did have meaning, but not because it was preordained. It had meaning because he chose to make it so."

She looked down.

"I understand what you're saying, Alfred. I do. But it's not possible. Not here. Not for us."

"Why not?" he asked.

She started to cry.

"Because we are never going to leave this place."

He took a sip from his pipe and then cleared his lungs.

"That doesn't matter, my dear." She turned to face him, and he looked into her eyes. So young to look so tired, and much, much harder than he remembered.

"You know what they want?" he asked.

She nodded.

"And you know how they would use it? How it will affect the world? What it will do to people? Today's people and tomorrow's people, for generations on end? How it will change the course of everything?"

She nodded and he took her hand.

"They chose you for a reason, Claire. And when they did, this inevitably set a course in motion. A course which now we are bound to. And they, as well. A course which none of us can undo or rewrite. One which must play out. But even though this course may appear to fall in line with their wishes, it still remains open-ended, despite their efforts to make it appear otherwise."

146

He lifted his hand and pointed at the soldier, who straightened his body in response.

"It is for their reasons you are here, my dear. And, yes, it was their choice to bring you here and not yours. But it is still within you to decide what that choice will ultimately mean. For them, for me, for yourself. For everyone. It is still up to you to write the ultimate reason for this. For everything that's happened and for everyone involved. If you can find a way."

She looked up at the soldier, who gripped his rifle and flexed his jaw.

"What if there is no way?"

"You will find a way when you accept your fate and not before."

He turned over his pipe and tapped it over his palm, spilling the contents out onto the ground.

"That I'm going to die here."

Alfred shrugged.

"The possibility of escape constrains your mind. It is part of their manipulation. Hopeful people are more easily controlled, but the volume must be managed. Too much hope leaves a person emboldened and resistant. Too little leaves them disabled and useless. But just the right amount of hope subjugates them. They cradle it like a dying ember, and they'll do anything to keep the wind from extinguishing it. They'll serve."

He removed his glasses and rubbed the pinch marks on his nose.

"Resignation," she whispered.

He nodded.

"It starts there."

She breathed in the air and slowly released it, the smell of flowers sweet within her nose.

"Then what?" she asked.

He pushed his glasses back in place and blinked until the world went clear again.

"You have to get angry in the face of bad situations. It's the most effective way to escape the bridles of despair."

They sat for a while longer, the birds chiming playfully in the trees. Careless and beautiful and exempt from the troubles beneath them.

"What if there is no way?"

He gave his pipe one last tap and slipped it back within his coat pocket.

"Whoever is winning at the moment will always seem invincible."

He stood up and she joined him, his old eyes looking up into hers and hers looking down into his.

"I want to give you something."

He reached into his jacket pocket and withdrew his lucky penny. She shook her head.

"No Alfred, I can't. It's much too valuable."

He smiled faintly.

"I want you to have it." He reached out and took her hand. "It will bring you luck."

She opened her fingers and he placed it gently into her palm.

"I don't believe in luck," she whispered.

He closed her hand around the coin.

"It's bad luck not to believe in luck."

He smiled.

"I'm so very glad to have met you, Claire."

She reached out and took him in.

"I am too."

They held on for a few moments longer, until the soldier tapped his rifle against the steel railing, and then they surrendered each other to their fates, the two leaving the courtyard forever and without looking back, for it did not seem the thing to do.

Chapter 18

She spent the weeks that followed in the third level, moving between the lab and her quarters, a very large guard shadowing her the way entire. Everywhere she went, this man followed, a gun in his belt, a vacant expression on his stony face. While she worked, he studied her through a pair of bulbous gray eyes. When she used the bathroom, he tapped his boot outside the stall. Soon, she grew accustomed to this quiet man, his movements and manners like a white noise to her everyday routine.

What she could not grow accustomed to, however, was the reaction of her colleagues, who would scatter like cockroaches when she approached them in the halls. Once friendly, now fearful, these people moved past hurriedly, their faces pointed down as if her gaze might convert their supple bodies to stone.

The cafeteria now off-limits, she received her meals in a cold, empty room, where she sat alone at a table eating in silence before a very broad two-way mirror. This thing she tried to ignore, her eyes and mind fixed on her work, even as she chewed the bland meals that came cold and runny on flimsy aluminum trays.

Stripped of pleasure and amusement, her life was now bleak and routine. And yet, despite such gloom, her mind flourished, and soon, she'd put together a new serum, with new attributes that would demand new subjects and new trials.

When all was right, she informed the guard who brought the information to the appropriate parties. And on the very next day, she was summoned through another maze of doors and pathways into a small room, where she found Demetri waiting at a table, two thin manila folders placed flat beneath his chin.

"Please sit," he said, as she entered.

She approached and sat, the two situated directly in front of one another, a wide steel table between them.

"I've been informed we're ready for trials."

"Yes," she said.

"Before we begin, I want to make sure you understand the implications of these trials."

He lifted a folder from the table and held it in his hands.

"You've thoroughly read the results of the previous trials?" he asked.

"Of course."

"Good. Then you understand why we'd like things to go differently this time."

"Yes."

He opened the file and removed a sheet of paper.

"Subjects demonstrate immediate effects upon injection," he read. "Visual evidence of skin regeneration within one hour. Evidence of organ rejuvenation within two hours. Marked improvement of muscle strength and physical vitality within 24 hours. Etcetera, etcetera."

He removed several photographs from the back of the file.

"And then."

He slid the photos across the table.

"Please, have a look."

She collected the photos and went through them: a medley of agonized faces, ungoverned hair growth throughout entire bodies, flesh riddled with grotesque tumors and lesions. Death.

She swallowed hard, as he watched the images tear through her.

"You haven't seen these, correct?"

She placed the images face down on the table.

"You know I haven't."

He nodded.

"Is it different to see their faces? Once it is no longer just data on a report?"

"Yes," she said.

He leaned forward. He rested his forearms on the table.

"Does it make you doubt your work?"

She looked at him, his black, depthless eyes like boiling wells of oil.

"No."

He smiled.

"Good."

He set the folder aside and took hold of the second one. He thumbed it open.

"On to the second order of business."

He removed a sheet of paper and scanned it.

"Your stint here is ending," he said. "Tomorrow, you'll be leaving the facility."

She sat quietly, despite her heart.

"I'm appointed to provide the terms of the dissolution agreement as it's written here."

He cleared his throat.

"Tomorrow morning, you will travel off-site under the protection of our personnel. Once you've arrived at the withdrawal point, you'll board a plane, which will take you to your intermediate destination. This will be a hotel in one of three geographic locations to be determined by the on-board security staff. There, you will stay for three months, at which point, you will receive commercial airline tickets to a primary city within the continental United States. From there, you'll be responsible for your own travel."

He looked up from the paper.

"Is that clear?"

She nodded. He looked at the paper.

"For your contributions to The Xactilias Project, your compensation will be three million American dollars. These funds will be deposited in a Swiss banking account made available to you. All relevant information will be transferred along with your plane tickets at the conclusion of your three-month stay in the intermediate location."

He slipped the papers back within the folder and set it flat on the table.

"Now," he said," as part of your dissolution, you'll be required to agree to numerous non-disclosure agreements. I'm sure you can imagine the details of these. Regardless of what they say, you should understand that you'll be legally required to forfeit your earnings should you disclose any aspects of your activity here or the actual existence of this facility and The Xactilias Project itself. Do you understand?"

She nodded.

"Speak," he said flatly.

"I understand."

He looked at her hard and long.

"Do you really understand?"

"Completely."

151

He nodded once.

"Good."

He collected both files and stood.

"That's very good."

He turned and walked toward the door.

"You'll wait here for the time being," he said, as he pulled it open. "Soon someone will come to guide you to the trial room, where you'll administer the injections."

She turned.

"Me?"

He smiled.

"Yes. You should be honored."

She shook her head.

"Anyone can do it. Why me?"

He pinched his eyebrows together.

"Don't worry. It will be your final contribution to the project."

She started to speak, but before she could, he opened the door and stepped from the room. She turned and looked at the photos, each one still face-down on the table. He'd left them intentionally, she thought. Another game. All of it a game. Just a game. Right?

She looked around the room, her mind fighting off all the what-ifs that squirmed within her head. She thought of her mother and her father, of Alfred and all his words. Of Nathan. His face, his voice, his smile. Was he alive? What if he was? Nothing to do about it either way.

The photos sat before her, each one silently beckoning to be seen once more. She gathered them up and shuffled through the faces. Her fault. Her doing. Her legacy.

Someone pounded the door.

She stood and turned as it opened to reveal another faceless soldier.

"Ms. Foley," he said. "If you'll please come with me, I'll escort you to the trial room."

She nodded and followed him through the door and down the hallway, his belt jingling with an assortment of metallic objects, the likes of which she had never seen. They moved through the usual pattern of deliberate confusion. In one door, out another, sometimes back through the same doors and down the same hallways. They passed through rooms filled with unfamiliar people, places that seemed like classrooms, where men and women sat straight and attentive at little individual desks, pale, unhappy expressions on their faces, men spitting out lectures, while the others scribbled notes on bright orange legal pads.

Minutes later, they moved down a very long hallway, where the soldier finally stopped at one door in particular and gestured her toward it. Without looking at his face, she worked the handle and entered a room. Inside, she found three women dressed in lab coats and goggles. Behind them stood two armed soldiers of equal size and stature.

"Welcome," one of the women said. "We're ready to begin."

Another woman collected a metal tray, which held a tourniquet, a pair of latex gloves, a surgical mask and a syringe.

She advanced toward Claire and held out the tray.

"You'll need to wear a mask."

Claire took the mask and slipped it on, her breath warm and wet against her face.

"The subject is in the adjoining room," the woman said, as she handed the tray to Claire. Then she turned away and rejoined the other two women.

Claire looked to her left, where she saw a closed steel door. She gave a quick glance around her and nodded. One of the women approached the door and punched a series of codes into a panel positioned beside it. The door made a shushing sound as it released, and the woman pulled it open with much effort. She gestured with a nod and Claire moved forward.

She entered the room and looked around. She lowered her mask.

The old man sat on an exam table, a sad little look on his face, his torso shirtless, old flesh sagging in all the ways old flesh sags.

"Hello, my dear."

She approached him, tears welling in the edges of her eyes.

"Hello, Alfred."

He held out his hand and she accepted it. He smiled.

"I understand," he said. "Know that I understand."

His feet dangled above the floor, his slight body looking old and tired and long without food.

Claire glanced over her shoulder at the soldiers. They stood on either side of the entryway looking very much like replicas of one another, faces stony and without soul, eyes wide and closely watching, guns firmly in hand.

She set the tray to the side and turned to face the old man.

"I want you to know that I care for you. I truly do. I care for you very much."

He put the palm of his hand against her cheek.

"I feel the same."

She raised her hand and cupped it over his. They looked into each other's eyes for a moment. Then she finally let go and took up the gloves. She stretched them over her hands until they were snug. She collected the tourniquet and quickly wrapped it around his arm.

At her request, he gripped his hand into a fist several times, until his thin veins bulged up enough to paint a target.

"What will happen if it works?" he asked.

She raised her eyebrows.

"Your body will replenish itself. You'll begin to heal."

He nodded once.

"I'll grow younger?"

She looked at his face. So old and wrinkled. So beautiful and just right. She swallowed.

"Yes."

He looked at his arm for a moment, and then his eyes shot upward.

"Will it work?"

She started to cry.

"I don't know."

The soldiers gripped their rifles.

"Well," he said, but after that, nothing came.

She soaked a cotton ball with alcohol and ran it over a vein, gray hairs spreading flat against his delicate skin.

"I'm so sorry, Alfred."

He gave her a hard look.

"Never apologize for correct actions."

With that, he gave one last smile before squinting his eyes and turning his head.

She looked down at the metal tray and the syringe, its contents thick and murky and yellowish-green. She took the thing up and tapped it once, the soldiers leaning forward with interest as if they expected something more than a simple injection. An instant transformation perhaps. Or maybe an attempt at escape.

Instead, they saw her level the needle over the old man's arm for only a moment. And then before either soldier could move a single boot, she turned the thing upward and plunged it into her flesh.

Alfred whipped around to see the outcome, a heartbroken look upon his face.

"No," he whispered, but before anything more, the two soldiers raced forward, their faces lit up with panic and fear.

Without knowing what else to do, one slammed the butt of his rifle against the back of Claire's head, knocking her to the ground.

Quickly, the other subdued him, as Alfred collapsed to the floor and cradled her bleeding head.

Immediately, the door popped open and Demetri entered, his face stony, a pistol in his hand. He surveyed the room and all its inhabitants. He raised the gun to the soldiers and spoke.

"Move away from him," he said. The soldier let go of his associate and backed away.

The man opened his mouth to say something, but before he could say a word, Demetri fired into his face, the cracking pop of the firearm deafening every ear in the room.

He took a step forward and leveled the pistol at Alfred who sat weeping over the girl.

"You are responsible for this."

The old man looked up.

"You are the one who is responsible. Only you."

Demetri held the gun in place, the barrel set square at Alfred's forehead. He eyed the room, people moving here and about, a mess of blood and disruption, chaos and misrule.

"You will be the one held responsible."

He lowered the gun as more people entered the room and swarmed around Claire.

"Tend to her injury and confine her," Demetri told them.

"What about him?" the remaining soldier asked softly.

Demetri looked Alfred over, a young man's hate bubbling within the old man's eyes.

"Take him to Level Four."

Chapter 19

In the beginning, they gave her water, but it didn't take long to see the error in this. For water provoked something from within. Something remarkable and terrifying and so obviously new to the ordinary world.

In a stupor, she ripped her straps away like tissue and tossed the doctors and nurses like dolls. Screams fired through the room as she moved upon each one, chairs and tables bouncing off walls, chunks of glass splashing against the floor. They rushed into corners and huddled against her encroachment, tranquilizer darts dangling from her flesh, like oddly placed jewelry, each one brushed away with ease.

After six fatalities and two shattered walls, they finally lured her into a reinforced room, comprised of steel walls and bullet-proof ballistic glass. This held her for eight minutes, and then they cleared the entire third level to make room for the weaponized gas. They fired off canisters, effectively clouding the halls, the masked soldiers creeping into the smoggy murk, the whole of them armed with every manner of non-lethal weaponry, loud red sirens blaring from all directions.

As each one passed through the gloom, he was forced to step over his broken associates, their yawning faces pallid, limbs bent in all the wrong ways. Finally, after 12 hours, they found her at the bottom of an elevator shaft, her body pressed against the ground in an awkward sprawl, limbs lying weakly by her side.

For the next 72 hours, she received no water, while they pricked samples from her body, within each, a secret perhaps, though none could find the reason why.

"You're a very special person," Demetri told her, as she sat fastened to a chair. "Not only have you happened upon an amazing discovery, you appear to have a unique genetic architecture that brings forth its gift."

156

She stared at the floor, her lips cracked, mind thinking only of water. He pulled up a chair and sat before her, their faces only a foot apart.

"Unfortunately, we had to run through multiple subjects to ascertain this."

She stared at the floor.

"Can you guess what happened to them?"

He grasped her chin and raised her head.

"Look at me."

She steadied her eyes.

"Yes," he whispered. "All dead."

He released his hold and her chin bounced against her sternum.

"In most horrible fashions, I'm afraid to say."

He molded his expression into one of false concern.

"Boils on the skin. Bleeding from the eyes. Screaming, writhing. You can imagine it, I'm sure."

He shook his head slowly and ticked his tongue against the roof of his mouth.

"And every one begging for death, which we would have gladly given if not for the science. You see, we had to know if the process might pass. To see if they might rejuvenate. Such was the confidence my superiors had in you. But, sadly, they had placed this confidence in the wrong person. An astounding person, to this I will certainly admit. But still a failure all the same."

He stood up and dusted his slacks.

"And now they'll dissect you to determine why you are able to tolerate your failed concoction. Until then I'm told to keep you breathing. Such is my role with The Xactilias Project. To follow orders, while maintaining order and security against threats. And now, you are no threat. And so, what can I do but follow my orders?"

He stood there a few moments longer, his eyes assessing this tragic figure, incarcerated within her weakened state.

"You have very little time to save yourself," he said.

She used what she had to raise her head, but he had already turned to go.

"What do you mean?" she whispered.

He approached the door without regarding her. He gave it a couple of hard knocks and it opened almost instantly to reveal two hulking guards.

"Watch her closely," he told them. "Even at night."

The door closed and darkness claimed the room.

157

A day later, she slew the two guards and made her escape, withdrawing into a sanitized jungle of rooms and hallways, where she drank from gushing water faucets until her belly was too full to stand another drop.

Chapter 20

On the first day, they came with bullets. The soldiers spread among the shadows in practiced formations, fanning the halls. They kicked in doors and infested rooms, their foreheads speckled with beads of sweat, hearts thumping hard against their bony enclosures.

With every step, broken bits of glass crunched beneath their heavy boots, these sounds like thunder within her sucking ears.

They popped off shots at the slightest disturbance. Glass shattered. Electronics sparked. Burning plastics gave rise to white smoke. Through this noxious fog they crept, the pollution filtering up and through their noses and into their burning lungs.

One of the soldiers came across a damaged door and summoned others with his hand. They crowded around it, their weapons raised. A captain fell in behind them. He waited a few seconds before giving the signal. The lead soldier kicked in the door and the rest poured into the room, guns darting about, looking for something at which to fire.

"Clear," one of the men said.

The captain entered, his face old and scarred and very rugged. He stood with his hands on his hips while the men swept the room.

"Sir," a soldier said from behind.

The captain turned. The soldier held in his hand an empty bottle of water.

"It was sitting on the floor," he said.

The captain took it and looked it over.

"Christ," he murmured.

"Target!" Someone shouted from outside. Gunshots followed and the captain ordered the men back out into the hall.

"Move, move, move," he said, and the soldiers did move, leaving the captain behind in the room alone.

The old man drew his pistol and watched through the entryway as his men raced by in pursuit of their target. A swell of gunfire bloomed up and then diminished, before giving way to screams and boot clatter. The captain listened as the boot steps grew louder. Then he saw a blur of soldiers race by the entryway. He opened his mouth to gain order, but before he could speak, a very large vending machine flew past the entryway on the heels of the fleeing men.

A thunderous explosion of broken metal stung the old man's ears. He swallowed hard and crept forward, his pistol grip wet within his trembling hand. He approached the entryway and peered around the corner. The men lay scattered throughout the hallway, each one broken in a uniquely awful way. Some lay face down, others face up. Some lay inexplicably, with their legs above their heads. Still, others lay crushed beneath the vending machine, their arms and legs poking out the sides as if they wore an intricate costume, their bodies, safe and whole inside.

The captain turned his head the other direction and saw her standing at the end of the hall. He raised his pistol and aimed, his back pressed firmly against the jamb of the door.

"Surrender," he said, but his words did not carry.

She eyed him from afar, and he did his best not to cower.

"Leave," she said.

He looked her over. A slight thing, so small on the outside.

"I can't," he said.

She waited while he moved out into the hall.

"Where are you going to go?" he asked. "They'll never let you out of here."

She shook her head slowly.

"I have no intention of leaving."

He swallowed the void in his mouth and raised his pistol.

"Be quick," he said, and he fired toward her. His eyes open out of habit only, and in spite of the terror closing upon him.

On the second day, they killed all the lighting and the facility went black. Once again, the soldiers permeated the halls and rooms, night-vision goggles painting everything in a bright green hue. This time, they kept no radio communication, the evidence pointing toward enhanced hearing on the part of the target. In retrospect, this realization should have been married to another. That other senses might too have been augmented, one particularly relevant considering the circumstances. But this notion crystallized much too

160

late for those involved. And soon, the lights illuminated once more to reveal a fresh tapestry of death, but not the artist behind the work.

On the third day, they pondered extreme tactics once considered off the table. Within the compound existed a broad spectrum of radical weaponry, including an extensive collection of weaponized chemical agents. There were vesicants that blistered away skin, blood agents, skin necrotizers, choking agents, nerve agents and numerous other appalling concoctions dreamt up by past residents of the compound. Ultimately, they kept these locked away for fear of rendering the facility useless. There was also no way to know if chemical agents would even make a difference on this creature. Most, in fact, agreed they wouldn't. So on the orders of Demetri, they opted for a passive approach, clearing the facility of any trace of moisture and waiting for her body to run dry.

In groups of two, the soldiers filtered through each room like a scavenging army of cat burglars, gathering up everything from water bottles and soda cans to dairy creamer and saline solution. Once they'd carefully swept the entire third level, they turned the heaters up to coax the sweat from her pores. They then holed up together in a fourth-level bunker behind two 25-ton doors, sizable enough to withstand a 30-megaton nuclear blast.

Three days later, it was time to hunt. Demetri released a scout team, which dispersed throughout the third level in search of what, exactly, they could not know. At this point, she'd gone days without drinking and would certainly be diminished. The soldiers cherished this notion, for it improved morale, at least until they began stumbling over the many bodies which littered the hallway floors.

"Focus," someone whispered, as they crept over at least a dozen broken men.

As they neared a corner, they caught the scent of melted rubber. The men exchanged hand signals and scattered into strategic positions along the walls. A captain urged a soldier forward. He peered around the edge of a wall and scanned the area. He gave an all-clear sign and the other soldiers spilled around the corner.

They stood still for a moment evaluating the scene before them. The hall had been charred black by a flamethrower. The incendiary weapon now lay on the floor amid gummy blobs of melted paint that had drained down the walls and gathered, like big pools of noxious molasses. Nearby, they saw the weapon's former handler, his crisped body looking up at each passerby with big black eye sockets and a broad skeleton smile. The stench of petrol mingled indelicately with the aroma of smoldering meat, causing some of the soldiers to fold over and void their stomachs.

They gathered themselves and moved on in an automated sort of way, their faces stony, despite these grim discoveries and others like them. Every several steps, the group would stop and send a good, reliable man into a room, where he would probe every dark corner, while the others gathered into a knot amid the entryway. This they repeated for hours, pausing occasionally to suck from their canteens and urinate in dry toilet bowls.

After a while, their focus softened somewhat, perhaps from repetition, perhaps from fatigue. Now they entered rooms in a hurry and exited just as fast.

"Focus," said the party's captain, as he snatched the two-way radio from his belt. He held it to his ear and started to speak, but before he could, they all heard something jangle in one of the rooms ahead. The men scattered apart and pressed their bodies against the walls. They glanced back at the captain, who gestured them ahead.

The soldiers moved forward, each taking a strategic position behind another. Now the good, reliable man approached the door. He glanced over his shoulder to make sure everyone had their positions. Then he nodded once and steadied himself. With one, sudden strike, he drove his boot into the door. It flung open and he raced forward a few steps, panning his gun from left to right.

"Clear," he said.

The men filtered into the room one by one, their weapons up despite his claim. The captain entered and put his hands on his hips, while the others made damn well sure the room was clear.

"This is a fool's errand," the captain said, but before anyone could agree, one of the soldiers shrieked gibberish.

They turned toward him, his eyes bright and wild and looking above them. They turned their heads upward, where she clutched the ceiling like a great spider.

"Shoot!" The captain yelled, but his words were lost in a bedlam of gunfire.

She dropped among them and spun like a top, her legs and arms whipping frantically until every last man lie busted and bleeding on the floor.

As the soldiers lie moaning, she scampered out the door and down the hallway, her bare feet tapping lightly against the cold tile as she rounded corner after corner. Finally, she stopped and bent over, her breath somewhat labored, muscles cramping beneath the skin. She heard the faint sound of boot clicks in the distance and stood straight. She saw a door and approached it. She raised her leg to kick it open, but her foot punched a hole through the metal. She pulled it back through and wrapped her hand around the knob. She gave it a twist and the thing crumbled apart in her hand. She took a deep breath and gave the door a gentle tap with an open palm. It separated from the hinges and sailed across the room.

She stepped inside and looked around, her eyes cataloging every item in a single glance. She moved forward and opened all the drawers with a delicate touch. Inside, she found little to work with, papers, staplers and other office junk. She felt the pains of thirst and stumbled backward, her knees erupting in pain as she reclaimed her footing.

A soft cry leaked from her mouth and a young soldier entered the room. He aimed his rifle and popped off a few shots, the bullets tapping her flesh and flattening like coins. She looked at her stomach to inspect the damage, but everything looked just right. She raised her head and met him at the eye. He took a step back and lifted his rifle for another try. But before he could draw the trigger, she had a stapler in her hand.

Seconds later, a group of soldiers saw him stagger before them in the hallway, a stapler-sized void in the middle of his stomach. He looked at them with his hands held upward, his mouth open, eyes wide and white. He opened his mouth to speak, but there was nothing left to say. So he closed his eyes and let his body splatter forward, his face bouncing audibly against the cold, hard tile.

The soldiers stood frozen, their faces advertising fear. As they surveyed the body from afar, she stepped out into the hall. She watched them, her hands clutching, hair looking wild atop her slight feminine frame. They raised their rifles, the five of them, and when they did, she turned to run. The sound of gunfire claimed the hallway, and then the pattering pings of bullets deflecting from her body. She raced away from them and turned a corner, but they kept firing anyway, the wall before them growing dark with little black holes.

She fled the noise, her quick strides eating up considerable ground. Soon, she was alone again, weaving her way through room after room and corridor after corridor until she stumbled into one of the facility's many laboratories and shut the door behind her.

She took a knee and sucked the air, her breathing labored, mouth impossibly dry. She stood up and staggered toward one of the sinks. She turned both handles and waited, but nothing came. There were four other sinks and she tried them all in turn, but none would yield a single drop, and so she sat on the floor and wept dryly, until fatigue overtook her, and everything went black.

Now, she entered a world of her own making. A wet, lush world with a watercolor sky of orange and pink and blue. There were old trees in this world, with woody shafts that soared up into that watercolor sky, where they erupted into great leafy awnings, which flowed and flittered in a breeze that was soft and warm and kind. Far below these awnings, little streams hurried along, tumbling around the natural rubble on their way to a vast fresh-water ocean, where the fauna lapped hungrily and danced in the rushing tides.

Claire moved about this world quietly, her bare feet crushing a lavish salad of grass and flowers. She saw skinny little waterfalls that started in high away places and trickled noisily down shelves of clean, white rock. She hurried upon one and plunged her cupped hands into the falling liquid, feeding her mouth with gulp after gulp of clear, cold water, until her belly was too full to stand another drop. Then she followed the noisy little brook to the ocean, where all the little animals romped about like very young things.

She approached them with a sense of belonging. But when they saw her, the creatures shrieked and scattered and ran back up into the wood, leaving her alone and wanting and plagued by returning thirst.

She awoke with her face against the floor, a vicious pain against her cheek. Something was jerking her arms backward. It was a soldier trying to work a zip tie around her wrists. For a moment, it all seemed like part of the dream, and she let it continue, like some impartial onlooker without any stake. Then a cold clarity seized her mind, and she ripped her hands free and spun around.

The soldier stumbled backward and raised his hands as if to proclaim his innocence from this and all else. He had placed his gun on the floor, and when his eyes flicked toward it, hers followed. They both lunged toward the weapon with great panicked gestures that left them grappling with one another on the ground. They tumbled across the floor, each one gouging at the other with fists and fingernails and elbows and teeth.

The soldier had training, and he used it to his advantage. Soon, he was behind her with his arm around her neck and his legs vised around her waist. She battled for freedom, but her strength had mostly passed. As she struggled, he clamped down harder, choking the blood from her brain. Things grew foggy almost at once. She writhed about, without making much difference. Then she finally went still and closed her eyes.

As he strengthened his hold, she summoned the last remaining energy from all over her ruined body. From her hips, her legs, her ears, her toes. With a sudden movement, she seized his arm and pulled with all she had left.

The bone snapped and he gave a soft whimper, as she freed herself and moved away. While she regained her breath, the soldier held his arm like a cracked vase, his mouth slobbering down over an unseemly bend. Finally, he looked up at her and she at him. Then they both looked to the gun once more and began a second attempt.

He scrambled forward and collected the gun with his working hand. He turned and aimed, but she'd already closed the space between them. With an upward thrust, she knocked the barrel off its mark, and bullets sprayed into the ceiling tile. He turned the gun sideways and used it to push her backward until she was flat against the wall. His eyes grew dark and wide as he pushed the weapon against her throat.

"Die," he whispered, as he pressed against her softened flesh.

She dug her fingernails into his cheeks, but this only seemed to harden his resolve.

"Die you bitch," he said louder. "Just die."

Her body grew limp beneath his hands, and a brief look of satisfaction claimed his face. But before he could finish her, he felt a hard strike between his legs. He did not let go, even as she withdrew her knee for another blow. Flecks of white light infested her vision, but she conjured the strength for one more effort. She brought her knee upward once more, and his face turned purple as he struggled against the pain.

Finally, the agony spread throughout his abdomen and took away his breath. His grip softened and she tore away, as he crumpled into a heap before her.

She coughed and spat, the blood returning to her head, and with it, her mind. She looked down at the gun, harmless in its quiet. Asleep. She stepped forward, the soldier's impotent fingers clutching at her leg and then slipping away. She approached the weapon and bent down. She lifted it and looked it over, evaluated it.

"Please," he whispered, and nothing more.

She turned and aimed. She fired.

Now boot steps came thumping down the hall.

She limped toward the soldier, his arms sprawled out, eyes studying vacantly the ceiling above. She fondled his belt and found something. It was a canteen. She unsnapped it from its holster and took its weight. A group of soldiers appeared in the doorway, their eyes bright, guns up.

She flipped the canteen open and brought it to her lips.

"Fire!" Someone shouted. "Shoot her now!"

The soldiers opened fire and her body twitched like it had touched something electric. Holes appeared in the canteen and water oozed out. She fell backward against the ground, but the soldiers kept firing nonetheless until their guns ran empty and her clothes were tattered to bits.

They watched and waited, some of the soldiers reloading, others still pulling the triggers on their empty weapons. One of the soldiers ordered a subordinate to approach the woman. The young man swallowed and gave a nod. He injected a new clip into his gun and put a bullet in the chamber.

He entered the room, his eyes bouncing between the woman and the dead soldier to her left. The woman lay sprawled with one leg crossed over the other, her delicate arms splayed out to her sides. Her face was concealed by her hair, the strands wet and stringy and matted in blood.

Blood, he thought. There's blood.

"There's blood," he said to the others, and this brought him comfort for a moment.

"Confirm the kill," his superior said. This man held a toothpick in one side of his mouth, and he shifted it to the other side every time he spoke.

The young soldier nodded without looking back. He poked the woman in the stomach with the barrel of his rifle. He waited.

"She's not moving."

"For Christ's sake," the superior said, and he stormed into the room and raised his weapon. He fired into her chest, a bright spark painting the wall with short-lived human shadows. A shrill ping stung their ears, as the bullet deflected off her skin and struck the young soldier in the face. The young man stood there for a moment, eyes wild, mouth agape. Then he splattered to the floor in an awkward heap, his superior watching all this with a sort of mute, paralytic wonder that persisted even as the young woman rose to her feet.

She stood before him, her body heaving with every breath. He looked into her eyes, the pupils large and piercing, a scorching rage within. He tried to raise his weapon, but she'd already plucked it from his hands. She turned it around and fired into his belly, the bullets going in and through and out the other side. Blood boiled out from his wounds and rained onto the floor below. He looked down and touched the hole in his stomach. Then he fell backward onto the floor, the toothpick standing erect from between his gritting teeth.

When he fell, his absence revealed to her the rest of the soldiers still lingering in the entryway. They had their guns up, but none had fired. She looked at them and they looked back, their winking eyes peering through the sights of their weapons, collectively focused on all the usual kill points. She looked down at the gun in her hands as if she'd noticed it for the first time. Then she tossed it aside and watched it skip across the floor.

"Put your hands behind your back and kneel," one of the soldiers said, his voice coming out all broken and wrong.

She turned her head to regard him.

"You should leave," she whispered.

The men gripped their rifles.

"It's your last chance," said the same soldier.

She inhaled the air, a taste of gunpowder on the back of her throat.

"Please," she said. "Just leave."

They all stood as before, their weapons fixed on her.

"Stop," a voice called out from down the hall. "Fall back."

The soldiers withdrew from the entryway, their faces showing obvious hints of relief. She waited for a moment as the sound of their boot clicks grew faint. Then she approached the doorway and peered around the corner.

At the far end of the hall, Romero stood alone and unarmed.

"Please," he said. "It's time to talk."

She remained as before, her body needlessly concealed behind a wall.

"Alright," she said.

He nodded once.

"We need to get you out of here. It's best for everyone."

She looked him over, her brain assessing everything from his expression to his posture to the way he breathed the air.

"How?" she asked.

He took a step forward and clasped his hands behind his back.

"I'm ordered to escort you to the top level and off the premises. If you'll allow it."

She looked him over. He'd shed his fatigues for oversized business slacks and a white button-down shirt. These fit his thick, muscled body poorly, making him look somewhat meek and nonthreatening. All of it window dressing that failed its purpose, for he still harbored the same virulent look in his eyes.

He took another step forward.

"We will provide a vehicle and rations," he continued. "There will be no interference from topside personnel. We only ask that you go without further incident. Once you do, you will be responsible for yourself and will receive neither assistance nor obstruction. Do you agree?"

167

She stepped out into the hall.

"Yes."

He paused for a moment as if he still had more to say, some practiced script perhaps, with agile responses for every conceivable reaction.

She entered the hallway.

"Now?"

Romero nodded and approached her.

"Follow me."

He passed by her without making eye contact, his shoulder brushing the sleeve of her blood-soaked shirt. She watched him without moving, her eyes evaluating every action. He stopped.

"Are you coming?" he asked without looking back.

"Yes."

He continued down the hall, his stride even and unhurried, as if he strolled without company on the most ordinary of days. When they reached the end of the hallway, he unlocked a door. The lights bloomed to life automatically as they entered the room. Then they gently failed to nothing as the two exited through yet another door. They repeated this sequence a half dozen more times before finally arriving at another hallway, which featured a pair of large stainless-steel elevator doors at one far end. He glanced back at her without really looking.

"We'll take the elevator to the top level."

She gave a nod and the two continued forward. When they reached the end of the hall, Romero tapped a series of codes into a wall panel and the doors separated to reveal a very small man. Claire took Romero in her arms and held him between herself and the stranger.

"Please," the old man said. "I'm here to help."

Claire looked him over. He was about five feet tall and Asian. He wore a white short-sleeved shirt and a wide striped tie better suited for another decade.

"Here," he said, as he held out a pair of clean hospital scrubs in her size. "Please take these."

She waited a moment and then tossed Romero aside, his shoulder crashing hard against the wall.

"Who are you?" she asked.

"Me?" he said. "No one. I'm not anyone."

He pushed the clothing at her.

"Please," he said, his small eyes like black dots behind the thick lenses of his glasses.

"Take them," Romero said, as he rubbed his shoulder.

She collected the articles from the little man and held them against her chest. Romero approached a door and unlocked it.

"Please take a moment to freshen up and change your clothing," he said.

She approached the doorway and peered inside to see an empty broom closet with a box of wet wipes centered on the floor.

"You'll have to make do," said Romero, who sheltered a tinge of contempt within his softened eyes.

Claire went inside without closing the door. The two men turned away to afford privacy, while she stripped off her clothing and scrubbed her body. Minutes later she returned looking fresh and new, save for the clots of gore interlacing the tangles in her hair.

"Shall we?" Romero asked.

She nodded and the three entered the elevator in turn. The little Asian man took the space between the two others, his face camouflaging poorly the terror infesting his soul. Romero tapped the wall panel and the elevator doors sealed. They soared upward, the three of them, Claire's face looking pretty and serene, as if she were gifted with a madness that left her ignorant of worry.

When they reached the top level, the doors opened to reveal Gretchen, her giant body looking larger than ever.

"Hello, Ms. Foley," she said, her face bright and sunny as if she were back in the lobby greeting newcomers on their very first day. "Romero and I will escort you to the exterior of the facility now."

Claire stepped out from the elevator and looked up at the feminine monstrosity.

"Shall we?" Gretchen asked, her voice bright and crisp as ever. But her face did not correspond.

"No," Claire said. "We shall not."

The great woman's smile faltered.

"I'm sorry?"

Claire moved suddenly, collecting Gretchen's arm and spinning her around.

"What are you doing?" Romero shouted, as the little Asian man receded against the elevator wall.

Gretchen screamed as Claire wrenched her arm upward.

"Stop!" Said Romero.

Claire eyed him from behind Gretchen's gigantic frame.

"Get back into the elevator," she said calmly.

Romero's face hardened.

"Go to hell."

She narrowed her eyes and forced Gretchen into him, the two tumbling awkwardly into the elevator and onto the floor. She stepped inside and pulled them apart. She laid her palm over Romero's face and clamped her fingers around his cheeks. She lifted him into the air until his toes dangled from the ground.

"Take me to Level Four," she said.

He wrapped both hands around her arm and writhed about, like a rodent caught in a predator's jaws.

"Never," he said hoarsely.

She stepped forward and pinned him against the elevator wall.

"Take me to Level Four," she said louder.

"I'll do it," said the Asian man.

She looked at him and released Romero.

"Then do it."

Gretchen had gathered herself into a sitting position against a wall, and the little man stepped over her legs on his way to the keypad.

"Don't," she said. "Please God don't."

"They'll kill you," Romero told him. "They'll kill us all."

Claire kicked Romero in the face, and he fell unconscious. She looked at Gretchen, who cowered like an enormous child.

"Go ahead," she told the Asian man.

He nodded once and raised his quivering hand to the panel.

"Will you let me go?" he asked, as he began typing.

"No," she said. "I suspect not."

The doors closed.

Chapter 21

Seconds raced away as the elevator sunk low into the facility's understructure. Claire's eyes darted nervously as she counted the floors.

"This isn't right."

She took the Asian up by his collar.

"I said Level Four."

The little man winced his eyes.

"Yes, Level Four," he said. "It's deep. There are layers of concrete and steel."

She dropped him and faced the doors.

"You're a fool," Gretchen told the little man, but he gave her no attention.

"Shut up," said Claire.

The elevator hummed, while its contents waited. Romero began stirring, a low animal groan escaping his mouth. He rubbed his head and looked around, his mind working hard to make sense of what his eyes gave it. He blinked over and over while the others watched him.

"What have you done?" he whispered to the Asian.

The elevator hum fell silent as it settled to a stop. At last, the doors separated and revealed a long, narrow room covered with polished onyx tile. The four peered out curiously from inside the metal box. The long room was dimly lit and mostly featureless, save for a bright silver door ensconced within the opposite wall and no less than 100 feet away.

Claire crept to the edge of the elevator and saw the room had no floor, but instead, a 300-foot drop to what appeared to be a collection of moving gears and metallic parts, which droned and murmured like the inner workings of some immense clock. She turned to Romero.

"What is this place?

Romero shrugged.

"I've never been here before." He looked at the Asian man." But he has."

Claire approached the little man.

"What is this place?"

The Asian fell backward against the corner of the elevator and put his hands out.

"I don't know," he said. "I've only been to the testing areas, and they make up a fraction of the entire level."

She turned and eyed the shiny metallic door across the void.

"How do we get over there?"

Romero looked at the Asian and shook his head.

"There's a retractable walkway," the little man said.

Claire plucked him up by his shirt collar and set him before the wall panel.

"Withdraw it."

The Asian tapped the panel and waited, while a thin metal platform sprouted from beneath the silver door and raced with great speed toward the elevator. It affixed itself with a high-pitch clench and the entire thing illuminated from the elevator to the door. Claire stepped out and looked back.

"Let's go."

The others stood up and followed, their eyes peering into the low, where all the whirring mechanisms spun, spiraled and rotated together, like a roiling ocean of serrated metal. When they reached the other side, the Asian tapped another wall panel and the bright silver door opened from the bottom to the top.

With great haste, the Asian man dove forward through the entry, as if fleeing an imminent explosion. By instinct, the others looked back to see the metal platform release its hold on the elevator and shoot backward toward them. Claire forced Romero through the passage and the two found footing on the other side. They turned to see Gretchen stumbling behind, the walking bridge swift in its cold, uncaring pursuit.

Within her simple, terrified mind, swift calculations of distance and speed were at work, and her face advertised the disappointing results.

"Help me!" She demanded as the platform exceeded her.

Claire and Romero leaned forward and watched, as the great woman tumbled into the low, where she was consumed by the grinding machinery, which revolved crimson for a time and then not at all.

Claire turned to assault the little Asian man, but two dozen ample-eyed faces gave her pause. She looked about the room. Men and women of all ages and nationalities watched her with terrified expressions. They wore short-sleeved t-shirts with ties and khaki pants, and they sat at small metal desks, peering out from behind computer monitors, like typical worker drones at any Fortune 500 operation.

"Can I help you?" a man asked. He stepped from behind his desk and eyed her from head to toe. He was short and thin, and he wore thick, black-rimmed glasses on his tiny nose. Claire glanced over her shoulder at Romero, but he said nothing.

"What is this place?" she asked the man.

"Level Four," he said. "I'm sorry. Do you have clearance to be here?"

Claire started to tell the man she didn't need clearance to be there, but before she could, siren blasts filled the room and red flashing lights illuminated the walls.

"Evac!" Someone yelled, and the people fled their desks and scattered about. Claire stumbled backward and watched as the men and women rushed to the far side of the room and jumped through tiny vacuum chutes positioned along the wall. With "shoomp" after "shoomp," the vacuums sucked them all down and away until the room was empty, save for the desks and the computers and some papers, which flittered in the air like the loosed feathers of shot birds.

Claire addressed the Asian man.

"Take me to the testing area."

The man stumbled to his feet. He nodded without looking at her.

"This way."

The Asian rushed toward yet another door, while Claire ushered Romero along with a forceful hand. They waited for the little man to do his thing, as the blaring sirens bored deeper into their skulls.

"Hurry up, for God's sake," said Romero, hands flush over his aching ears.

At last, the door opened, and they all funneled through. The Asian quickly shut the door, and the quiet eased over them.

On the other side, they found a bright, white hallway that stretched at least 100 yards before terminating at yet another door. On either side of the hallway, there were a number of evenly separated, black tinted glassed panels. Claire approached one and cupped a hand over her eyes, but even she could not see inside.

"What's in there?"

The Asian furrowed his brow.

"Show me," Claire said.

173

The man cleared his throat and approached one of the glass panes. He flipped open a small wall panel and applied his thumb. The panel turned green and offered a soft tone. The Asian man stepped back and waited, while the glass slowly grew transparent to reveal what couldn't be anything else but a holding cell.

Inside, a gaunt young man sat alone on a bed, his dark skin laced with tribal tattoos that rippled awkwardly over his protruding ribs. He looked up and out through the glass, his eyes dark and receded within his sunken orbital sockets. He watched Claire put her hand against the glass, and then he lay down on the bed and turned away. Claire looked toward the others, her eyes awash with tears and rage.

"What is this?"

The Asian man stared at the floor.

"Answer me."

"It's the testing floor," Romero said. "He's a subject."

Claire looked down the hallway and counted out four dozen dark windows.

"How many more of these rooms are there?"

She took the Asian up in her hands.

"How many?"

The little man remained mute.

"Many more," Romero said. "More than you can count."

Claire dropped the Asian and turned toward Romero, who met her at the eye without blinking.

"You should have left when you had the chance," he said. "You're a fool."

She extended her arms and gathered him up by his head, his mouth mumbling a litany of curses, while his feet kicked the air. She held him high for a moment and squeezed until he wept blood. Then she tossed him down the hallway with such violence, his bones shattered apart beneath the skin.

The Asian man cried out and fell backward onto the floor.

"Please," he said. "I'm a good person. No one here has any choice."

She stood above him, her chest expanding with heavy breath.

"I want you to find someone for me."

He looked up at her.

"Can you do that?"

"Maybe," he said. "Yes."

She took him up by his arm and set him on his feet.

"This way," he said.

174

She followed him down the hallway, the two stepping around Romero's body, while his dead eyes gawked up with frozen surprise. As they passed all the dark windows, Claire considered the faces on the other side. Were Nathan and Alfred among them? Were they still alive?

"Here," the Asian man said. He pointed to a door.

"Where does it lead?"

"System access," he said. "I can use it to probe the database for subject profiles."

She nodded.

"Do it."

He tapped a wall panel and the door opened vertically from the ground. Claire held the man back.

"I'll go first."

She entered the room and found two soldiers standing before her. They aimed their weapons and watched her nervously.

"You're free to leave the facility," one said. "Please do so."

She approached them and they retreated a few steps.

"You should go," she said.

They exchanged looks and took another step backward.

"Where is your prisoner?" the other soldier asked.

The Asian peered around the corner and the soldier's face lit up. He aimed his rifle at the little man's forehead and squeezed the trigger, the bullet flaming forth and piercing the air on its way to its target. Claire moved suddenly and the metal squashed against her flesh. The Asian man vanished from the entryway, as the other soldier opened fire in his direction.

Claire quickly closed the distance and dealt with the men.

"You can come out," she said.

The little man glanced around the corner.

"It's alright?"

"Yes."

He entered the room and surveyed the dead soldiers.

"You have to take me with you," he said. "When this is over."

She shoved him toward a computer panel.

"We'll see."

He turned toward the computer and fired it to life.

"What's the name?"

"Nathan Clark."

His fingers tapped the keyboard and the system did its thing.

"Deceased."

175

Claire fell silent.

"I'm so sorry," said the Asian.

She turned away and crushed the tears against her eyes.

"Is there another?" asked the little man. "I'm sorry, but we must hurry."

She straightened her posture and faced him.

"Alfred Fernsby."

The Asian tapped the appropriate characters and waited with great hope.

"Asset."

Claire spun the man around and held him by the shoulders.

"What does it mean?"

"He's alive," he said. "He's still alive."

Claire released him and enjoyed the moment.

"Please," said the man. "We must hurry."

Claire looked at him.

"Where is he?"

"Not here."

"Then where?"

The Asian manipulated the computer.

"I don't know."

Claire held his shoulders.

"Find him."

The Asian put his hands up.

"I can't. He's been transferred."

"Transferred where?"

The Asian shrugged.

"Another facility? I don't know."

Claire pushed him away and took several steps back.

"What other facility?"

"I don't know."

She placed a hand against her head.

"How many of these places are there?"

He shrugged.

"I don't know. A dozen. More perhaps."

She fell silent while the significance of his statement permeated her brain. For the past several weeks, she'd defended herself against killers, and in the process became one herself. Each night, she would hole up in a dark nook and weep at the loss of her soul. At the troubling satisfaction of her change.

And she raged against the entity that had corrupted her. And within the fertility of this grief, a purpose took root. She would destroy those who had destroyed her. She would destroy The Xactilias Project and all those responsible for it. But that seemed impossible now.

"We must leave," said the little man.

She looked around the room.

"I'm not leaving until all these people are free."

He shook his head.

"That's impossible."

She put a hand to his face.

"You're going to die. Here today or sometime later, far away from this place. Do you think they won't find you? What will a few weeks or months be worth? With all you've done, what would it matter?"

He looked at the floor and wept.

"I have a family."

She pulled his chin upward.

"Then protect their safety by dying here today. And honor them by saving these people."

His weeping ceased and his face hardened.

"Ok."

She stepped back from him.

"What can we do?"

He collected his thoughts.

"I can free them, but they'll never let them leave the facility."

She looked at the computer panel.

"Can we access the intercom?"

"Yes."

"Do it."

He turned and tapped buttons furiously.

"They control everything from a mainframe, but I can override it for a moment. It won't last long. They'll regain control within a minute or so."

"A minute is all I need."

He worked through the process and stopped.

"As soon as I hit this button, speak into the microphone here. Are you ready?"

She nodded.

"Go."

She put her lips to the microphone.

"Demetri," she said. "Listen to me. I'm coming to kill you. I'm coming to kill all of you unless you do as I say. I'm releasing all the subjects. Send escorts to safely move them out and off the facility. Provide visual evidence of your cooperation and I'll leave. You can have your facility. You can have your life. This is the only way."

She nodded at the little man and he shut off the intercom.

"Can we access the security cameras?" she asked.

"Only if they allow us to."

She nodded.

"How do we release the people?"

"I can do it from here."

She looked at the time.

"Wait five minutes and then do it."

They waited and watched, while the clocks seemed to resist time. And then the moment arrived, and the Asian did his duty.

"What's your name?" she asked the Asian.

"Cho."

She shook his hand.

"Claire."

They waited for a moment.

"Alright, Cho, bring up the security footage."

He did so and they watched, as hundreds of staggering bodies crept from the openings of their cells. At first, they all moved cautiously, their eyes wide and wild and unbelieving. Soon, however, they found confidence in their growing numbers and at last became a hoard that flowed collectively like a great liquid mass. As the liquid moved forward, the doors opened automatically to allow passage from room to room.

"They're letting them go," Cho said. "It worked."

Claire watched silently as the people moved forward.

"Wait," said Cho. "Look."

He pointed to another monitor, which showed a group of armed soldiers exiting the elevator. They summoned the walkway and crossed it, their weapons raised.

"What are they doing?" Claire whispered.

She turned to Cho.

"Pull up the intercom."

Quickly, he tapped the buttons.

"We're locked out," he said.

178

They both turned back to the monitors and watched as the two parties moved toward one another on separate security monitors. In the people's faces, they saw hope and fear in a tangled, ungiving struggle, with each emotion exchanging advantage over and over, and over and over again.

At last, the soldiers settled at the neck of the bottle and waited, while the people collected in the room on the other side.

"I've got to stop this," Claire said.

She raced toward the door.

"Wait," said Cho. "Look."

Claire raised her face to the monitors and stopped. The door had opened, and the people had begun to leak through.

"What's happening?" she whispered.

"I think they're letting them go."

She joined Cho and watched as the soldiers coaxed the mob forward, their faces offering expressions of kindness and decency. Cautiously, the people moved, their arms clutching at one another in reassuring embrace, despite age, religion, race or foolish barriers otherwise. Soon, the soldiers had them divided into groups of six, which they took in turn up the elevator and out onto the top level.

Hours passed before they'd finally cleared the bottom level, and now Claire and Cho watched as the people were fed and watered in the first-floor cafeteria. A separate security monitor showed the exterior of the facility, where the soldiers prepared a number of buses. After a time, they led the people outside and placed them on the vehicles. Then Claire and Cho watched as the buses pulled away.

"Where will they take them?" Claire asked.

"Back to their villages perhaps," Cho said. "We can hope."

They watched the monitors for a while longer, but there was nothing left to see.

"What now?" asked Cho.

"Now, we make sure they don't bring them back."

"How?"

She approached a faucet and released a pillar of running water. He watched while she stooped and drank.

"What are you going to do?"

She rose up and ran a sleeve over her mouth.

"I'm going to make sure there's nothing left to come back to."

"But you said you'd leave."

"Not just yet."

He rubbed his head.

"You lied?"

"I made a tactical misrepresentation," she said without looking at him.

She rubbed her hands together as if preparing for an act of great athleticism.

"Which way, Cho?"

He pointed to the door.

"Only one way."

She looked at it and then at him.

"Good luck to you."

He nodded.

"And to you."

With that she struck out, obliterating the door with a single outstretched palm and making her way through a half dozen hallways more. Finally, she arrived at a monstrous steel door that looked like the entrance to a great vault. Forty feet high and several more thick, the door blocked a passage wide enough for a dump truck. Claire balled her fist and pounded the structure. The great door jazzled around its edges as vibrations shocked its surface. She took a step back and waited for what? She did not know.

Again and again, she struck the steel, punching and kicking, until she'd forged a two-foot-deep cavity in the center. She jabbed in the edges until the hole could accommodate her entire body. Then she began pounding again. An hour later, she breached the other side, the steel bowing and exploding outward with an obscene noise that reverberated for a long while before drowning in the vastness of the room. She stepped out from the tunnel and dusted her pants.

"Impressive," said Demetri.

He stood alone in the giant room, save for a single man sitting beside him in a small metal chair. She approached them slowly, crossing between a glittering collection of computer panels and video screens. The man wriggled against constraints, his hands strapped behind him, mouth stretched open by a tightly wound gag.

"Please," Demetri said. "Join us."

Claire rushed forward.

"Let him go."

Demetri jabbed the barrel of his pistol into the back of Nathan's ear.

"Not just yet."

Claire's fists hung at her sides like tiny mallets. Demetri watched her, his face calm and still.

"Sit."

Another steel chair sat in the center of the big round room. Claire acknowledged it with a glance and made another movement toward Demetri.

"Now, now," Demetri said. He collected a handful of Nathan's hair and dug the gun deeper into his skull. Nathan winced, and a soft whine leaked through the red cloth gag in his mouth.

"Sit," said Demetri.

Her eyes flashed seven kinds of hell.

"If you hurt him, I'll kill you."

Demetri nodded.

"I have no doubt. Now please sit."

She approached the chair and gave it a thorough look. She took it up in her hands and spun it around. Then she placed it on the floor and sat.

"Very good," said Demetri. He withdrew the pistol from behind Nathan's head and lowered it to his side. "Let's discuss our options."

Six soldiers entered the room, their weapons spraying red laser targets at the back of Claire's head. Demetri raised his hand to ward them away and the men receded back through the entryway.

"Now," he continued. "Before we settle on a common solution to our impasse, I'm obliged to ask that you reconsider your position."

She squinted as if he'd spoken mumbled nonsense.

"What the hell are you talking about?"

He put his hand up.

"Please," he said. "Just listen. I want you to reconsider cooperating with our project. I know that may sound repugnant to you, but there are sound reasons why this makes sense from your point of view."

Her hands gathered into fists.

"You're crazy."

"Please," he said. "Hear me out. First, I want you to think about all the lives you can save. Not just the people living in the world today, but generations of people. Millions of people. Hundreds of millions. Countless generations of lives for countless hundreds of years."

He raised his hand and turned his palm upward as if to take the weight of some invisible object.

"On the other hand, by choosing not to work with us, you condemn these people to death. You, in effect, become their assassin. Millions of lives, endless suffering, all because of one singular decision you made from a selfish desire. A vendetta."

She watched him, her eyes hot.

181

"For tens of thousands of years, humans have toiled and suffered against disease and death. You can modify the course of all humanity and put an end to this. All with a simple choice. You can change the course of history. Of our planet. Think of all the things we can accomplish. Imagine what can happen when all the world's brightest minds vacate their studies of human health in favor of other more progressive interests. Think of how technologies and human understanding would leap. You can fast forward history a hundred years at least and save countless lives all at the same time."

He stopped his talking and gave a little smirk.

"Whose words are you speaking, Demetri? Because I think you'd have me dead if given the chance."

He shrugged.

"As I said, I'm obliged to ask that you reconsider your position. My feelings on the matter are of no consequence."

She looked straight into the depths of his black eyes without blinking. She stood.

"Even if every word you've said is true, why would I need anything from you? I can do all this myself."

His face hardened and he shook his head.

"No one can do anything substantial without this organization's consent. For two hundred years, this has been so, and it shall continue for two hundred more. The world as you know it exists at our pleasure. It is allowed to exist because of its obedience. When it becomes fractious, corrections can be made quite easily. Disease, catastrophic events, war, all these are quite useful at shaping the collective minds of the public. This is the way it has always been. We are not new. The world's most influential leaders work for us, as does your neighborhood garbage man."

He jabbed his pistol into Nathan's ear.

"As does he."

He raised the pistol and fired into her belly, the bullet tearing a hole in her clothing and deflecting away and into the ceiling.

"As do you," he said with a smile.

She looked down and explored the hole with her finger. The soldiers had gathered on the other side of the entryway, and now they watched with wet, narrow eyes.

"I decline your offer," she said. She held her open hands to her side. "Now what?"

Demetri put the gun to the side of Nathan's head.

"Now, you step over there." He gestured with a nod to a very large red circle painted on the floor.

"What is it?" she asked.

"Evacuated tube transport," he said. "A high-velocity, airless, frictionless transportation system that uses vacuum to move people and items. This particular one is used to remove unwanted materials. Mostly waste. In this case, you."

She looked at Nathan, his face leaking sweat, the gag cutting deep between his lips, his eyes showing sadness and fear."

"And you'll release him."

Demetri frowned.

"Of course," he said. "Why would I want to be on your bad side?"

She looked back at the soldiers

She and Nathan locked eyes for a brief moment, and somewhere within that brief moment, they seemed to say goodbye.

"Alright, Demetri."

She crossed the room and stood within the red circle. Demetri looked toward the soldiers and summoned one forward with a nod. This man lowered his weapon and approached.

"Kill this man if she moves."

The soldier agreed to his instructions and centered his weapon at Nathan's forehead. Demetri lowered his gun and turned. On the far side of the room, a curved computer panel sat before an expansive video screen. Demetri approached it and twisted whatever levers and buttons controlled the device.

Claire looked up as a transparent glass tube descended from the ceiling and enclosed her. She pressed her palms against the circular prison and looked out at all the watchers.

"Look at him, Demetri," she pointed at Nathan through the glass. "You will not live through this if he doesn't."

Demetri smiled.

"Then I have nothing to fear."

He tapped his finger against one last button and the floor opened beneath her. She heard a piercing squeal and felt the flesh pull away from her bones, her eyes bulging out from her skull and straining against the fleshy tethers within her head. Then she was gone, sucked down and away beneath the floor.

The floor closed and the red circle reformed. The soldiers crept forward and scattered around it. They aimed their weapons downward and waited until the evacuation light turned from red to green. A soldier gave an all-clear signal and Demetri nodded. He eyed Nathan, as he withdrew a knife from his pocket.

"And now she's gone," Demetri said.

Nathan mumbled something though his gag, as Demetri approached.

"But for how long?" he said. "That is the question."

He slipped behind Nathan and flipped open the blade.

Nathan's mumbling grew louder, the gag growing dark with slobber.

"Just another moment," Demetri said, while he positioned the blade between Nathan's wrists and sliced upward. The zip tie fell apart and he brought his hands around to remove the gag.

"Yes, indeed," Nathan said as he rubbed his wrists. "Not very long, I would guess."

He stood and stretched his back.

"Very well done, Demetri."

He held out his hand and Demetri passed over the pistol.

"What next?" Demetri asked.

"Well, let's see," Nathan said, as he approached the computer panel. He looked around the room and pursed his lips. "Disruption Protocol, I suppose."

Demetri frowned.

"They won't like it."

Nathan shrugged.

"They'll like the alternative a lot less."

Demetri nodded.

"I'll initiate the process."

He summoned three of the soldiers and they left the room, while Nathan eyed the green evacuation light with a lazy, apathetic gaze.

Chapter 22

For what seemed like a long while, Claire tumbled about inside the tube, her knees and elbows thwacking against its walls, ears crackling within her throbbing head. She felt herself sucked forward through at least a dozen curvatures and elbows, though even her eyes could not make sense from all the tumble and darkness. At last, she transcended the blackness, as the tube brought her away from the facility and into the blinding sunlight.

Now, she traveled far and out from the compound, away and away through the transparent tube, her body holding together in places that would have surely broken otherwise her miracle state. And finally and abruptly, the motion stilled, and the tube opened up and evacuated its contents into a great muddy bog.

She splashed down in a flailing fit of motion, the sucking mud sticky to her flesh and reeking of spoilage. She struggled to the surface and reclaimed her breath, her eyes consuming the surroundings in search of threat.

On the banks, she saw nothing but rows of bristly trees and sparse vegetation. Within the bog, however, she swam amongst butchery and carnage in the form of shattered bone, which permeated every inch of the mud like small bits of white, crumbly rock. She receded from this vision in a panic, her legs kicking skull fragments away as she stumbled up and onto the hard shore.

Shrieks of horror escaped her mouth, as she climbed the high banks and rolled herself over the top. She stood up and looked down upon the all human remains, while big bubbles of mud boiled up and exploded gritty wet splatters outward into the air.

With a very real weakness, she collapsed onto the ground, where she lay on her back weeping at the happy blue sky. This went on for a good while and then something stronger took place of the grief. This something was not like the other, but instead, a white-hot burn that felt good and powerful and right.

She stood up and found the facility, small and concrete and far away in the distance. Her fists balled up against her hips and her mouth roared until the trees bent forward and surrendered the bulk of their leaves. Birds cried and fled up into the heavens, soaring high in their panic above the ridiculous, chaotic world.

She ran. The dry earth shattering beneath her feet and turning the air orange and brown in her wake. Tears streamed from her face, as she devoured the land, teeth gritted white and bright against her dirt-stained face.

As she gobbled up the miles, big ravines appeared before her, their starving mouths open for the swallow. These she cleared without much effort, the compound growing ever larger in the nearing distance. Soon, she was within a mile, her eyes able to make out the smallest details of the compound's architecture. And something else.

She stopped and watched, as a swarm of black helicopters erupted into the air, like great prehistoric insects over a monolithic, concrete hive. She cupped a hand over her eyes to block away the sunlight, while the helicopters took altitude and moved off into the horizon.

She took a step forward and stopped again, as something erupted deep within the facility. The structure buckled for a moment and then split around the center, brilliant white light spraying out all the little cracks. Then everything went quiet, as the facility disintegrated beneath a great pillar of fire that soared upward into the heavens and flowered into astonishing plumes of orange and yellow and red.

She stood small upon the earth before the monstrous flower, all the colorful happenings reflected in her big, wet eyes. Then a sudden concussive blast traveled through and past her, disintegrating the trees and the land and even the birds in their places high away.

Chapter 23

(One year later)

Alfred Fernsby sat at his desk doodling complex patterns on a white sheet of paper, his mind off and ambling, despite the accuracy of his hand. The wall clock offered promises of lunch, but he'd lost track of the hour, along with an amounting number of other things. Someone knocked on the door and opened it without asking.

"Alfred," a young woman said.

The old man looked up, his eyes looking as lost as his mind.

"Yes?"

The slight looking woman entered. She wore sophisticated business clothing that did little to offset her young age.

"Will you not come to lunch with the rest of us?"

Alfred frowned.

"No, thank you. I have so much work to do." He opened a drawer and withdrew a bulging paper sack. "Besides, I spent a good ten minutes creating the perfect sandwich and I wouldn't want to leave it for waste."

The young woman smiled.

"Alright."

She turned and opened the door.

"But I'm going to keep asking."

She gave an even brighter smile that brought her innocence seeping past her beauty. Then she was gone.

Alfred stood and crossed the room. He approached the door and stuck his head out to look around. No one at their desks. He shut the door and returned to his seat. He opened the paper sack and withdrew a sad little peanut butter sandwich that looked as if it had been sat on. He opened the plastic bag and took a small bite. He chewed the tastelessness without thought, his eyes transfixed on a speck of dust at the corner of his desk.

Time passed gently without his awareness, and soon the workday came to an end. He checked his watch and sighed. He collected a few papers and shoved them into a briefcase. He stood and rubbed the pain in his lower back, before crossing the room and opening the door. He paused to look back at his office and all its spacious audacity. Then he shut off the light and closed the door.

Outside, the city boiled with furious movement. Young businessmen and women walked the sidewalks without regard for one another, each one feigning aloneness despite the obvious otherwise. Each one safe within his or her isolation. No one talking much.

Alfred watched them from the steps of the building, his face lacking expression. The building's security guard noticed him with some concern.

"Are you alright, sir?"

Alfred looked up at the man.

"Yes. I'm fine. Thank you."

He stepped out and let the crowd take him in its current, his eyes studying the ground as he went. He walked two blocks and stopped before a small pub. He went inside and took a seat at the bar next to a young man and girl, who barely seemed to notice him over their groping. The bartender approached.

"What can I get you?"

Alfred ordered a scotch and the bartender brought it. He lifted it to his lips and tilted the glass, but before he could draw a single sip, the young girl bumped his elbow hard with her purse.

"I'm sorry," the girl said unconvincingly.

"Oh, it's alright," Alfred said, as he dabbed the liquor splatters from his jacket.

The two returned to mauling each other, while the bartender slid another drink beneath Alfred's nose.

"Take that shit outside," he told the young couple.
The two flashed a look and fled out into the world.

"Sorry about that," said the bartender. "These fuckin kids nowadays, am I right?"

Alfred started to respond, but something on the television caught his eye.

"Can you please step aside some?

The bartender looked over his shoulder.

"What, the news?"

"Please," Alfred said. "Just for a moment."

The bartender shrugged and walked away.

Alfred looked at the television, where a young female news anchor spoke mutely, while captioned subtitles interpreted the silence. He leaned closer and adjusted his glasses to clarify the words.

"The worldwide hunt continues for the suspected terrorist responsible for last year's catastrophic explosion in southeast Asia."

Alfred's mind went numb as Claire's face appeared on the screen.

"Claire Foley is wanted for playing a major role in the destruction of a multimillion-dollar research facility last October. According to authorities, the facility was dedicated to disease research and had made considerable progress toward potential cures for a variety of afflictions including cancer. A former researcher at the facility, Foley is suspected of having ties to a bioterrorist network known as Bloc 9. Authorities say the group has been responsible for a number of attacks targeting everything from military facilities to hospitals. At the urging of the President, Congress recently passed a funding measure allocating billions of dollars to support efforts to identify and eliminate Bloc 9 agents. According to military experts, Foley currently stands as one of three primary targets, although the total number of suspects could exceed thousands in varying locations throughout the world."

Alfred looked around the room. Others had also been reading and their faces showed fear and rage.

"It's only a matter of time before they target something over here," one man said.

Others agreed.

"A cancer research facility," a woman said. "These people are evil."

Everyone nodded.

"This is the President's fault," another man said.

"That's ridiculous," said another man. "He just put billions of dollars toward stopping them."

"He had no choice," the first man said. "He should have done something sooner."

Alfred downed his drink with a single swallow and placed his money beneath the glass. Then he stood and left, while the argument swelled behind him.

Outside, the crowd had thinned substantially, leaving him to walk quietly and alone the rest of the way home. It was only a short walk to his apartment, but that didn't seem to matter to his tired legs, which ached and throbbed beneath the knees. He climbed the steps and opened the door. A young couple stood at the elevator, their infant daughter clutching her father's great voluminous hand.

"Hello, Alfred," the woman said with a soft smile. "How was your day?"

"Oh, fine," the old man said, returning her smile. "And how is this little bird?"

The young girl nestled her face into the woman's long coat.

"She's just shy," the mother said.

"Oh, I understand."

He fished a candy from his pockets and held it up.

"Is it ok?"

The father nodded.

"Of course, Alfred." He knelt. "Penny, Alfred has a piece of candy for you."

The little thing cast a quick eye at the old man's hand and then returned to her sanctuary.

"I'll take it," said the mother.

Alfred passed it over, as the elevator doors opened. The four stepped inside and pressed their buttons.

"I don't know how you keep it up, Alfred," said the man. "I'm ready to retire and I'm 30."

Alfred smiled politely.

"Oh, I wouldn't know what to do without my work."

The young woman put her hand on his shoulder.

"You're an inspiration."

Alfred smiled.

"Thank you."

They rode the rest of the way in silence, and then the doors opened to allow the family off.

"Please, let us know if you ever need anything, Alfred," said the woman.

"Oh, I will. Thank you."

"It's no trouble, really," she said, as the doors shut them away.

Alfred nodded with a smile through the dwindling crease in the shutting doors. Then he celebrated his solitude with a frown.

When the doors opened on his floor, he exited the elevator and walked the hall. He stopped before a wall. There was a painting. One he'd seen dozens of times before. The brush strokes made a man in a landscape of blues that

190

floated atop a textured backdrop of milky nothingness that could have been the past or a budding storm or a million little mistakes or nothing in particular at all. For this old man, it was something uncertain, and he didn't feel much like figuring it out. Not on this evening.

He turned away from the hanging and approached his front door. He looked down at the doormat and rubbed his feet against the big white welcome, which sunk deep within the brown gristle of the fibrous rug. He held his key to the doorknob and pushed it through.

He went inside and closed the door.

He made his little dinner that night. The same frozen meal he had the night before and all the long nights before that. It didn't bother him. He was beyond bother these days. When he finished eating, he tossed the paper tray into the garbage and climbed into bed without brushing his teeth. He slept. He woke. He went to the bathroom and urinated. He stopped in the midnight. He looked into the mirrored glass and a little old man looked back.

"You get to take what this world gives you," he told the sorry figure. "It's not always what you want. But you have to make do. You make fucking do. If you can't make do, I have no time for you. There are so many who'd make do with far less. This is all you get. You get no more. It should be enough."

He left the reflection to consider its failures and went back to bed, his legs wrestling the covers, mind resisting the pull of sleep.

Hours later, the morning came violently though his window shades, like a noisy child stirred by the wonder of light and day. He flipped his legs over his bedside. He stood and walked to the bathroom. He arranged his hair as best he could. He packed his lunch mechanically. He left his home.

Outside, the people moved about in groggy droves without much regard for the others beside them. He watched from the front of his apartment building for several minutes and then finally joined the swarm with a sigh. He walked with them for a while and finally broke off in front of his office building. The security guard offered a nod, which Alfred did not return. He entered the building and rode the elevator in silence, while others chattered loudly around him.

When he finally reached the right floor, he crossed by his coworkers without looking up and entered his office and shut the door behind him.

The early hours passed slowly while he fiddled with a project. His mind wandered this way and that despite his best efforts to bridle it. After a while, he pushed the work aside and read the newspaper.

Someone knocked on the door and opened it without asking.

"Alfred," a young woman said.

"Yes?"

A woman entered. The same from all the days before.

"We're heading to lunch. Will you join us today?"

Alfred shuffled some papers and looked up.

"No, thank you, dear," he said. "I'm just so behind on everything."

She gave a sad little smile.

"Alright."

She turned.

"I'm going to keep asking."

She left and shut the door behind her.

Alfred stood and crossed the room. He approached the door and stuck his head out to look around. No one at their desks. He shut the door and returned to his desk. He opened a drawer and removed a paper sack. He removed his peanut butter sandwich and unraveled it from its cellophane coat. He took a bite and chewed thoughtlessly.

A knock at the door.

"Yes?" Alfred said through a mouthful of food.

The door opened and Demetri stepped through.

"Hello, Mr. Fernsby."

Alfred straightened in his chair and swallowed awkwardly.

"Please, don't get up."

Demetri passed through the entryway. He removed a pair of black leather gloves from his hands without breaking eye contact. Alfred watched him cross the room, the old man's eyes throwing forth hate without any effort toward the otherwise.

"Now, now," Demetri said, as he sat in a small chair across from Alfred's desk. "Let's keep this civil."

"What do you want?" Alfred asked.

"I just came to see how things are going." He offered a polite smile. "How are you liking it here?"

Alfred pushed his food to the side and folded his hands.

"It's fine."

Demetri nodded.

"That's nice."

They watched each other for several moments without speaking, Demetri's face casual, as if he sat across his oldest friend.

"You should really show more appreciation," he said. "We pulled some major strings to get you hired here. Viox Genomics is a first-rate organization. You belong here like a mule at a wedding party."

Alfred shrugged.

"I'm happy to resign my position."

Demetri smiled.

"No, no. We prefer to keep you rich and happy."

Alfred leaned back in his chair.

"You think that will make a difference?"

Demetri shrugged.

"Someone does."

"But not you."

"I think it's completely unnecessary."

"And why is that?"

"Because whether you're living or dead, she's not coming."

Alfred narrowed his eyes.

"I disagree."

Demetri leaned forward and propped his forearms on his thighs.

"Your affection for her clouds your reason," he said. "She is not coming. Not ever."

Alfred shook his head.

"If you really believed that, you'd have done away with me long ago. She's the only reason I'm still around."

Demetri shrugged.

"It's simple practicality. Everyone knows she's not coming, but even the smallest gambles can be hazardous. It's a simple decision really. What's the life of one old man? You go on living. The threat remains unprovoked, fictional as it may be in the opinions of most. Your existence balances a hypothetical equation."

Alfred smiled coolly.

"Perhaps," he said. "For now, anyway. But I'm a 72-year-old man. I don't have a lot of time left. Maybe ten years. Maybe five. Maybe three months. Then your little equation becomes imbalanced, and you'll have quite the reckoning. You and all your like."

Demetri smiled.

"I'm not here to deprive you of your fantasy," he said. "I'm here to remind you of your obligation."

He reached across the desk and took up a framed picture.

"She's quite lovely, your granddaughter." He nodded as if to agree with himself. "Quite lovely, indeed."

Alfred sat with a stone face.

"I'm aware of my situation," he said. "That is where we differ."

Demetri replaced the picture and leaned back in his chair.

"It's sad, really. Your delusion. It evokes my pity."

Alfred leaned forward.

"Save the pity for yourself."

Demetri rubbed his eye, as if weary from the argument.

"She won't come."

Alfred leaned forward.

"You think she's afraid of you? What does she have to fear?"

"Nothing," said Demetri. "Nothing to fear. Nothing to rage against. Nothing to love. Nothing for which to weep. She has nothing, because she is nothing."

Alfred chuckled.

"And what of the news reports?" Alfred asked. "Why go to the trouble if she's really perished as you say?"

Demetri lowered his eyebrows.

"Let me tell you a story."

Alfred raised his hands.

"No stories," he said flatly. "I'm bored of them."

Demetri smiled.

"As you wish."

He sat back and folded his hands together in his lap.

"I understand," he said. "I found her dazzling as anyone. Even before her transformation. Afterward, I was transfixed. The things she could do. Incredible." He pursed his lips and shook his head slowly. "But bullets are one thing. A tactical nuclear blast, quite another."

The old man's eyes narrowed.

"Yes," Demetri said. "Ten kilotons." He slapped his hands together, one over the other. "Right on top of her."

Demetri looked off for a moment in contemplation.

"I believe a ground-level exposure would mean temperatures exceeding 6,000 degrees. But, of course, you're the expert on such matters."

Alfred sat quietly, while Demetri stood and withdrew the gloves from his pockets. He slipped one onto each hand and stretched his fingers against the leather.

"I'm afraid this will be the last of our meetings."

He turned and approached the door. He stopped and looked back.

"It's better this way, Alfred. When the people are not enlightened enough to exercise intelligent control, you take it from them, not to command their lives, but to create a safe depository for the ultimate powers."

He gave a nod and opened the door.

"Someone will come," Alfred said. "If not her than someone else."

Demetri smiled.

"Against ignorance, God Himself is helpless."

With that, he left the room and closed the door behind him.

Alfred sat quietly, while the electricity ran slowly from the air. He collected his sandwich and raised it to his lips. He took a bite and chewed and chewed. He swallowed with a sickly expression and then threw the rest of the sandwich in the trash basket.

Time passed. People came and went from his office. He did his best to accommodate them, his demeanor cordial but quiet. The day dragged and dragged and dragged, but as with all places, a day at Viox Genomics must come to an end, and at last, the clock settled in the right place.

He shuffled his papers away and gathered his belongings. He pushed his chair from the desk and stood. He collected the picture of his granddaughter and appreciated all its givings. The silk ribbon in her hair. Her sweet radiant smile. The vivid enthusiasm behind her sunny blue eyes. Her dimples. He felt so much love and gratitude for her life, but these feelings mingled also with a deep sorrow for the world he and his like would leave for her and hers.

He set the framed photo on his desk and left the room.

Outside, the streets boiled with movement, young businessmen and women feigning aloneness despite the obvious otherwise. Alfred watched them from the steps of the building, his face lacking expression. The building's security guard noticed him.

"Are you alright, sir?"

Alfred looked up at the man.

"No."

He stepped out and let the crowd take him in its current, while the guard watched him through bewildered eyes.

He walked two blocks and stopped before the same pub from the day before. He went inside and ordered a drink, which he drank quickly before returning to the city streets once more.

Outside, the crowd had thinned substantially, leaving him to walk quietly and alone the rest of the way. When he arrived at his apartment, he

195

climbed the steps and opened the door to an empty lobby. He walked inside and summoned the elevator with a single outstretched finger. He entered and the doors closed. He waited while the lift pushed upward, soft instrumental music purring gently from the speakers overhead.

When the doors opened on his floor, he exited the elevator and walked the hall. He stopped before the painting and looked at the man amid the feathered landscape of varying blues. The painting hadn't changed, but now the man looked different, his body seeming very small before the backdrop of milky nothingness, which seemed bigger and more ominous than ever before.

He turned away from the hanging and approached his front door. He looked down at the doormat. He rubbed his feet against the big white welcome. But this time, something caught his eye. It looked like paper, peeking so slightly from beneath the rim of the doormat. He slid the mat aside with his boot and revealed a small white envelope. He knelt to collect it and took a quick look around to make sure he was alone.

He caressed the envelope with his hands. Something small inside. He looked around again but saw no one. He tore the envelope open and turned it over. A very old penny tumbled into his hand. He held it up and let the light dance against all its glorious imperfections. He smiled.

THE END

**The story continues in the thrilling sequel:
THE GIRL OF FLESH AND BONE,
available NOW at AMAZON!**

Read on to preview the first 8 chapters!

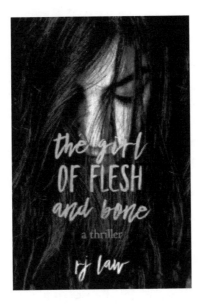

CHAPTER 1

The sun burned high and small in its place above the park, where people celebrated the budding spring with pale skin and light jackets. Where the grass had greened, children ran about, while parents gave chase, despite aching backs and grinding knees. Above in the shallow treetops, birds had gathered at last, their subtle songs light and tentative, as if they lived in doubt of their warming reality.

Below all the gentle cooing, Alfred sat straight upon a park bench, his crooked fingers tracing the roughened edges of a photograph, eyes wet behind his glasses. As the wind kicked up around him, he ran a thumb over the image of his granddaughter, sweet and young, all dimples and curls. He considered the details. The beauty. The innocence. The potential. Most of that a memory now. But, the latter? Who could predict a person's potential?

"I'm so sorry," said a voice from the side.

Alfred stared at the photo without blinking, while a great lumbering dog snorted his ankles.

"Douglas!" said the voice. "Come here!"

Alfred caressed his photograph, while a woman yanked Douglas back by his leash.

"I'm so sorry," the woman said.

Alfred wept.

"Oh, my goodness, are you alright? Do you need help?"

Alfred turned his head and looked at the woman with a scrunched-up face.

"No," he whispered. "No, I'm quite fine, thank you."

He forced a trembling smile, and the woman attempted to reciprocate.

"Are you sure?"

Alfred nodded.

"Oh, yes. I'm fine. Thank you, though."

The woman stood up and saw that Douglas was eating another dog's feces.

"No! Douglas!"

She yanked Douglas away and bent down to scold his face. Then, the two went away, leaving Alfred alone with his thoughts.

Alfred watched the two of them cross the greening grass and disappear over a hill. Then, he turned his head toward the photograph and gave a tremendous sigh.

Another light breeze swelled around him, chilling away the spring sun, as if it were the cold ghost of winter, stubbornly awake amid a ripening world of color and scent. With the breeze came a voice.

"Alfred," it said.

The old man looked up and squinted through his glasses.

"Hello," he said dryly.

A thin, sickly woman looked down at him, her face neither cruel nor kind.

"May I?" she asked.

"Please," he said, as he scooted across the bench to make room.

The woman sat and placed a small brown bag over her lap, her posture poor, jaw skin sagging.

"Thank, you for coming," she said.

Alfred stared away at a pair of young boys clumsily kicking an old soccer ball.

"Alfred?"

He continued watching the boys, his eyebrows furrowed up, as if he longed to be little again.

"Alfred, are you ok?"

As if to intentionally dismantle his nostalgia, one of the boys took a great swipe at the ball and dug a chunk of skin from the leg of the other, who collapsed in a screaming fit. As the boy's mother raced forth to treat the boy, the old man snapped to.

"Yes," he said. "Yes, of course."

The woman looked at him with concern.

"I know this is hard for you," she said. "I'm very sorry to ask it."

Alfred caressed the photograph and frowned.

"Yes," he whispered.

They sat in silence for a while, the air growing colder as the afternoon waned.

"Alfred," the woman said gently. "Can you find her or not?"

Alfred pursed his lips.

"Yes," he said. "I have it here."

He slipped his hand into his coat pocket and withdrew an envelope. The woman's eyes grew wide, as if he held a passport to another better world. She cleared her throat and inched closer.

"Please, Alfred," she said. "Give it to me."

The old man looked at his hand and blinked, as if he'd forgotten its contents already.

"Yes," he said. "I brought it for you."

The woman leaned closer and reached across his lap, snatching the envelope in a sudden and swift movement.

"I'm sorry, Alfred," she said, as she slipped the envelope into her bag. "But you understand, don't you?"

Alfred looked at the photograph and nodded.

"Yes. I understand."

He stood up like a very old man and looked around the park. Across the way, the tired mother herded her children back to their car, while the wind tickled the leaves overhead.

"You know," said Alfred, as he looked at the woman's face for the first time. "I once believed you could be who you wanted in this life. But, that was just another lie like everything else." He lowered his chin, so his eyes peered over his glasses. "There are no guarantees with her. You should know that. This could go very badly for you."

The woman shrugged.

"I have no choice. You understand, don't you?"

Alfred looked at the photo and then slid it into his coat pocket.

"Yes," he said. "I understand."

He turned and walked away, his hands in his pockets, footsteps slow and choppy. As he reached the edge of a little grassy knoll, he turned back and saw that the park bench now sat empty.

He rubbed the back of his neck and looked up at the sky, as if to regard the master, high away in his celestial nest. He closed his eyes and slipped a hand back into his pocket to caress the picture once more. Then, he turned away and walked back to the bus top.

CHAPTER 2

Claire stood in the high away parts of the parking garage, her eyes studying the streets, where people rushed about, their skirts and ties whipping around like little flags in the wind. She scanned their faces, one to the next, none peculiar, save for one man, who appeared to be drunk or insane.

She watched this man scuttle about for a while, the crowd of people parting around him, as if he were a light fixture, inconveniently secured to the street. And as they did, he shook his fist and scolded them for not seeing the truth of things, whatever that was to him.

At last, Claire saw the woman with the red umbrella and, along with her, a young girl who looked to be about 12. The two moved deliberately among the crowd, neither appearing much concerned with the vulnerability that came with open spaces. They moved quickly without rushing, the child keeping up well enough to suggest experience in such endeavors.

Claire watched them move across the intersection and make their way up the street. They approached the parking garage without looking up and stood still before the base of the building. Claire scanned the streets, her sharp eyes searching for irregularities of any kind. When she was reasonably sure that no one was tailing their movements, she picked up the paper cup and dropped it over the side of the ledge. The thing spun in its descent and then clattered on the pavement with a few hollow bongs. The woman took the child's hand without looking at the cup, and both entered the stairwell.

Claire withdrew the hood of her jacket and scratched the bristles of dark hair poking up from her shaved scalp. She sat on the hard concrete and rested against the cold brick wall, closing her eyes to better hear. Soon, she sensed footsteps clomping the stairs. She opened her eyes and watched the steel doors open to reveal the woman and young girl. She did not stand to greet them.

"Claire?" the woman asked.

Claire nodded, and the woman led the girl forward. She set the child in a little space to the side and withdrew a tattered book from her bag. She held it out, and the girl took it. As the child began reading, the woman turned to Claire.

"Have you been waiting long?"

Claire shook her head.

"Good," said the woman.

She approached and gestured to the ground.

"Is it alright if I sit?"

Claire nodded once.

"Thank you," said the woman.

She tucked her dress beneath her legs and sat upon the curbed edge of a walkway, her knees popping loudly amid the cavernous concrete structure. Claire looked her over, and the itch of her stare seemed to make the woman shiver.

"Thank you for meeting with us," she said with a daring little smile.

Claire said nothing, her eyes studying the woman, noting every facet of her appearance. She wore simple attire that had surrendered much of its color to years of wash, and her hair was pulled into a bun that did nothing to soften the wrinkles on her weathered skin.

"Your sandals," said Claire.

The woman looked at her feet.

"Yes?"

"How can you run in those?"

The woman looked at Claire and then back to her feet.

"Beggars and choosers and such."

The woman had a little brown purse, and she gathered it in her hands.

"Is it ok?"

Claire nodded, and the woman stuck her hand inside. She removed a wrinkled pack of cigarettes. She looked up again and Claire nodded.

"I'm sorry if I seem strange," said the woman, as she fingered a cigarette from the pack. "I haven't slept in two days."

She held the cigarette to her lips and raised a lighter, the little flame shivering above her erratic hand. At last, the cigarette came to life, and she inhaled deeply. Almost immediately, the woman grew calm, her breathing more relaxed, jittering hand growing steady.

"That's better," she said, as she rubbed her eye. "Now, I can think."

Claire looked over at the child.

"Who is she?"

The woman looked at Claire and then at the girl.

"Someone very special."

Claire eyed the child again. Her hair was tangled and ratted, and her clothing was much too big for her slight frame. She wore a pair of boy's work boots that looked about two sizes too large, and some of her fingernails were split, and those that weren't were filled with something black.

The woman followed her eyes to the girl.

201

"We've been on the road for some time," said the woman with a look of shame. "Things have not been easy."

"I understand," said Claire.

The woman looked at Claire's hair and clothing.

"Yes, of course. I'm sorry."

An engine murmured in the lower levels of the parking garage, like a trembling in the bowels of a giant beast. The woman spun her head in a panic, and then looked to Claire.

"Is someone coming? Should we leave?"

Claire sat without speaking, her eyes affixed to the woman.

"Why is she special?"

The burbling engine noises died away, and the woman breathed deeply. She drew from her cigarette and let the smoke trickle out the sides of her mouth. She began to cry.

"It doesn't matter," she said. "I just need you to take her to Bloc 9."

Claire narrowed her eyes.

"Take her why?"

The woman looked at the child.

"Because she is special."

Claire watched the woman watch the child.

"Why is she special? What can she do?"

"Do?" the woman asked. "Nothing. Nothing extraordinary anyway."

The child continued reading despite the slight, as if deafened by the contents of her book.

"Then what makes her special?" Claire asked.

The woman looked over her shoulders, as if to confirm that they were still alone.

"She is special, because of what she is."

Claire studied the child for a moment, as if she might glean the truth by sight.

"What is she?"

The woman swallowed hard and smoothed her dress over her knees.

"She is an asset to them."

Claire tilted her head and appraised the woman anew.

"An asset to the Project?"

The woman nodded once and swallowed the void in her throat.

"An asset and that is all," she said. "Nothing more. Not a child, not human. Just an instrument for their purposes. That is all they see when they look at her."

Dimples broke out on the woman's chin, as emotion rushed through her body. Claire waited a moment, while the woman composed herself.

"And what is she to you?" Claire asked.

The woman's eyes trickled upward and something bold shot through.

"I love her," the woman said. "I care only for her safety. That and nothing more."

Claire looked at the child again, but the girl paid no notice.

"I'm in no position to care for a child," Claire said. "I am hunted day and night. Why would you think she could be safe with me?"

The woman nodded.

"Yes, I know," she said. "I know about you. What you have done, what you can do."

She leaned forward.

"I know you are hunted. I know who hunts you. It is the same with her. Hunted day and night. Pursued always."

Claire rubbed her eye.

"Why do they want the child? At least tell me this. If you want my help, I must know."

The woman swallowed hard once more, her throat buckling audibly.

"She knows things."

Claire leaned forward.

"What does she know?"

The woman shrugged.

"I don't know," she said. "Not really, anyway."

Claire sat back against the wall.

"You know she knows something, but you don't know what it is?"

"Yes," the woman said. "I know only that it is of great value to the ones who hunt you and to the Bloc 9. They would do anything to have it, both sides. To leverage her knowledge for their purposes. Your hunters, to strengthen their grip on the world. Bloc 9, to further their goals."

"Then, why take her to Bloc 9?" asked Claire. "If they see her as a tool, how are they any different?"

The woman shook her head.

"No," she said. "They are different. They want to topple the Project. To restore power to the people. To expose the lies. But they are also human. They care for one another. They will use her, it is true. But they will also protect her. Her safety will further their cause; the same as the knowledge in her head."

They both sat quietly for a while, as the street traffic murmured below.

"And once they have the knowledge, whatever it is, what's to keep the girl alive?"

Claire glanced at the girl, but she didn't seem to be listening.

"You mean why won't they kill her after?" asked the woman. "To keep the information from the other?"

Claire nodded.

"Because they care for one another. For me. For you. For all life. They want to expose lies. That is all. They are not interested in dominating the world. They want to save it, and then deliver it to the people."

Claire shook her head.

"How do you know all this?"

The woman shrugged.

"It doesn't matter. You don't have to believe me. But you must take her. You must keep her safe and deliver her to the Bloc 9. I cannot keep her safe anymore. I cannot do what you can do."

A horn popped loudly below, and someone yelled something at another driver. Then the street sounds normalized and drifted away into the background.

Claire looked at the girl.

"What could she possibly know?" asked Claire.

"I don't know," said the woman. "She will not speak of it."

Claire turned toward the woman and noticed for the first time how wrongly her clothing fit her thin frame.

"You don't look well," she said. "Whatever it is, those won't help."

The woman held out the burning cigarette and looked it over, a daze in her eyes, as if she were staring past the object in her hands.

"It's too late for all that," she said. "Too late for everything."

Her eyes flicked toward Claire.

"Except for this," she gestured toward the girl. "This is all that is left."

Claire watched as a tear fled the woman's eye and raced down the swell of her cheek bone. She looked at the girl, who continued to read quietly, her demeanor unaffected by these words and seemingly all else.

"I'm sorry," said Claire.

The woman shrugged.

"It's alright," she said. "Everything is acceptable as long as she is safe."

They sat for a moment without speaking, as if they had stirred some wrong thing up into the air. At last, the woman sucked from the cigarette and looked away.

"Why won't she talk?" asked Claire at last. "Is something wrong with her?"

The girl looked up, a rage flaring up within her brown eyes.

"There's nothing wrong with me," she said. "What's wrong with you?"

"Hush, Mila," said the woman. She looked at Claire and sighed. "I'm sorry. She is angry about this. She doesn't understand the dangers around us. She doesn't know these people as we do. She doesn't understand why this has to happen."

The girl stood up and threw down her book.

"You just want to get rid of me," she said to the woman. "Just go. I don't care."

She walked several steps away and sat on the concrete with her back turned.

Claire watched as the woman crushed out her cigarette and stood. She approached the girl and placed a loving hand on her shoulder.

"I'm sorry," she said. "I don't want this. I love you so much. You must understand. I don't want to say goodbye. Not today. Not ever."

Claire watched them both silently, her head slightly acrook, as if to better evaluate every gesture from a slightly irregular perspective.

"Just go," Mila whispered. "Just go."

The woman turned and wiped her eyes, her expression buckling from a great internal harm. Beneath them, the street traffic cut through the moment indelicately, like machinery screeching through an unspoiled forest.

"Come," Claire said at last. "Let's discuss the details of this. I need to know exactly where we are going. Exactly what we will be walking into. I need to know everything exactly."

The woman looked up and forced her lips into a smile.

"Thank you."

She left the girl to speak to Claire in low tones that would not be overheard. And, they talked for what seemed like a long while, until it was finally time to part ways and say their goodbyes. And, when they said their goodbyes, the girl did not look at the woman's face. Nor did she return the woman's embrace, nor affirmations of love. And, when they left the woman, she was waving goodbye, her body looking too old for its age, eyes drowning in waters of sorrow. And, when the girl looked back, she did so without waving, through eyes that were cold and dry.

CHAPTER 3

The ticket agent assessed the crowd from behind the window glass of her booth. The lids of her eyes hung halfway, as she watched the people contend for position, each one shrewdly jockeying for space with a shoulder or an elbow or the slightest of steps. At last, she flipped the sign to affirm her readiness, and the first traveler came forward.

One after one, the rest followed, each passing over money in exchange for his or her boarding pass. And each time, the ticket agent made a smooth and seamless exchange, her wondering mind disentangled from the moment, her automatic greeting ten thousand times practiced.

After thirty or forty exchanges, she noticed the two men, maybe eight, maybe ten turns back in the line. And, once she saw them, she couldn't stop looking, despite strong intentions toward the otherwise.

There was something weighty in their presence, these two men, despite their casual expressions, despite their ordinary clothes. As she contemplated the root of this, a chill filtered its way up her back, and she stopped to elevate the setting on the space heater kept within the little ticket booth.

Finally, the two men came forward, one exceptionally large and unkempt, like someone who'd just woken up. The other, just a man, save for his eyes, which shot forth like little daggers, a natural thing or a purposeful gesture, she couldn't say for sure.

"Nebraska," the large man said, as he pushed forward his identification.

The ticket agent collected the ID and looked it over. There was a picture and a name that fit miserably the figure before her. She nodded, and he paid for his ticket. Now the second man came, his eyes bright and vivid, as if they were lit up from the inside.

He smiled and declared the same destination, and the ticket agent quickly processed the transaction.

The matter complete, she watched the men walk toward the train, her eyes transfixed, the remaining people irritable and awaiting attention as the line enlarged behind them.

As they boarded the train, the two men passed over their tickets and moved on to their compartment coach. Once inside, the larger man sat and released a great sigh.

"I'm gonna get some sleep," he said. "This day needs to end."

He turned over his hand and examined his knuckles, as the other man sat down beside him. They were bloodied and bruised, and a dime-sized hunk of flesh dangled apart the rest. He gripped his hand into a fist and relaxed.

"The hell you sitting right next to me for?" he said. "Get on the other damn side, leave me some room to stretch out."

The other man crossed his legs.

"We're riding with someone."

The large man shook his head.

"God dammit."

They waited a while, but no one came.

"Fuck it," said the large man, and he began to take off his boots. "I'm getting comfortable."

Before he had leveraged the first one free, a young girl entered the compartment. She was slim and pretty with long blond hair that bounced about in large elaborate curls.

The large man quickly forced his foot back into his boot.

"Welcome," he said, raising up halfway. "Please."

He gestured toward the seat across from them.

The girl appraised the two men, her attractive face polluted with discontentment, as if she'd just bitten into a rotten apple. She paused in the entryway for an awkward amount of time, and then, having accepted her predicament, took the seat across from the two men.

"My name's Len," said the big one, as he plopped back into his seat. "This here's Matt."

The girl looked from one to the other.

"I'm Becky. Nice to meet you."

Her quiet little words leaked out with involuntary inflections, as if they rattled over bumpy ground. Len grinned at this, but Mathew barely looked up from the newspaper he read.

"You can relax," said Len. "We won't bite you."

The girl smiled politely and placed her leather bag atop her lap. She removed a magazine, positioning it to block the heat of Len's stare.

After some time, the train whistle shrieked, and the locomotive lurched forward. All three sat quietly for the next hour, while the urban landscape gave way to open pastures, where cows chewed the grass and contemplated their places in the world.

Len watched all this through the window glass, his large booted foot thumping the floor.

"This place looks like hell," he said at last. "Just grass and dirt and filthy animals."

He waited a moment, but no one replied.

"So, what's your story?"

The girl swallowed hard and lowered her magazine.

"Me?"

She had long lovely eyelashes that blinked bashfully over her big round eyes, and the fear within them made Len aroused.

"Yeah, you," he said with a broad grin. "Tell me something about yourself. Help pass the time."

The girl's eyes flicked over to Mathew, but he paid no attention.

"I don't have a story," she said.

Len lowered his brow.

"Everybody's got a story. Even kids got stories. Most have lots."

She shrugged.

"Well, I don't."

She watched as his face grew soft and passive, but his boot tapped faster the floor.

"Aw," he said, his voice gentle as cool cotton sheets. "Just tell me something. Help pass the time."

The girl set her magazine over her lap and covered it with her hands, as if to conceal some personal secret within.

"Well, ok but there's really nothing to tell," she said. "I'm a waitress. Born and raised in Cheyenne. Headed to visit my friend in Omaha. That's about it."

Len nodded.

"Damn, you weren't kidding," he said. "Not much to tell."

She shrugged again, and they all rode quietly for a while.

"That's it," Len said at last. "Let's have some drinks. That'll lighten the mood."

He reached inside his coat pocket and removed several tiny liquor bottles.

"Vodka or whiskey?" He asked the girl.

She lowered her magazine.

"Oh, I don't think so."

"C'mon," he said. "Matt will join us. Isn't that right?"

Mathew looked up.

"Sure, why not?"

Len passed over two little bottles of whiskey, and the girl watched as Mathew twisted one open and downed it in two swallows.

"Well?" asked Len.

The girl glanced outside as another expanse of nothingness whirred by.

"Oh, I suppose one won't hurt."

Two hours later, the girl had downed three little bottles of vodka, and Len didn't seem all that bad. During that time, he had listened patiently while she spoke of her childhood in Wyoming, the cruel winters and empty spaces, the longing for something else.

"Damn, do you ever shut up?" he finally asked, a little smile poking out from one side of his mouth.

The girl sat back and crossed her arms.

"Ok, fine, you go. Tell me your story."

He shrugged.

"I ain't got a story."

She gave a condescending smirk.

"Oh, come on, I know you've just been sitting there waiting to talk."

He leaned back in his seat.

"My life ain't that interesting."

She looked over to Mathew, his eyes still trained on his newspaper, even after he'd emptied two little bottles of whiskey.

"He doesn't talk much does he?"

Len chuckled.

"He just doesn't want to interfere with this thing we got going."

The girl rolled her eyes.

"Ok, ok," Len said. "I guess I can tell you a story if that will hold your attention."

"Good," the girl said. "I'm getting bored over here."

Len cleared his throat and leaned forward, his big face growing serious and somber.

"When I was a kid, I didn't have a lot of friends," he said. "I had this stepbrother, but he and I didn't get along. His dad, my stepdad, treated him like he was the second coming, treated me like I was dirt."

The girl eyed him with interest, as she sipped from her little bottle.

"Well, every day, I'd come home from school, and I'd just run to my room and close the door, and I'd hug this little stuffed elephant that I loved more than anything."

He looked off to the side, and his mind seemed to go someplace far away.

"My stepdad couldn't stand it. Always said eight years old was too old to have stuffed animals, but my mom wouldn't let him interfere. Anyway, this went on for a while until my stepbrother's birthday come around. They planned this big party out in the backyard, and all his shitty little friends were invited."

He leaned back in his seat and rubbed his forehead like it hurt.

"Well, I tried to be friendly with all of them, but my stepbrother got them turned against me, and they kept calling me names, until I got to crying. So, I run inside to hug my elephant, like I always did, but it wasn't there. I looked all over my room, but he was gone. And then I heard all this cheering outside, so I look out the window, and you know what I saw?"

The girl had leaned forward, her face looking fresh and beautiful, eyes wide and blue.

"What?" she asked with much interest.

Len pursed his lips and his chin trembled.

"My stepdad, that sumbitch, he had gutted my elephant with a knife, filled it with candy, and hung the damn thing up like a piñata."

The girl pressed her hand firmly over her mouth, as if a fog of bugs had swelled around her face.

"I just sat there staring out the window crying, while they all took turns beating my little elephant to bits."

Tears welled in the corners of the girl's eyes, her face wrinkling up with genuine empathy.

"You poor thing," she whispered. "That really happened?"

A big smile surged across Len's face.

"Nah, I'm just yanking your chain."

He roared with laughter and smacked Mathew on the back, spilling some of his whiskey.

A great rage built within the girl's eyes.

"You are the worst person I've ever met," she said.

Matt shook his head while he read his paper.

"How can you be friends with him?" she asked.

Mathew looked up.

"He kind of grows on you after a while."

Len grinned and slapped his knee.

"I'm sorry, I'm sorry. I can't help it. That was funny."

The girl shook her head.

"I can't believe I actually felt sorry for you."

Len raised his little bottle and swallowed more whiskey.

"You wanna hear a real story?"

"No," said the girl. "I've heard enough out of you."

Len put his hand up, as if swearing before a court.

"I promise you, this one's true for certain."

The girl took another sip of alcohol and narrowed her eyes.

"Fine," she said. "If it'll help kill the time."

He nodded once and sat forward in his seat. As he began to speak, his broad face took on a seriousness that made the girl shutter on the inside.

"A long time ago, I had this roommate," he said. "Couldn't stand the guy. He was always bitching about the dishes, bitching about hairs in the sink. Annoying shit like that. Anyways, this guy, he had a girlfriend, and he comes home one day and tells me he's proposing to this girl, and that they're moving in together. So, this means I'm out, and I ain't too happy about it."

He sipped his liquor bottle and hissed at the burn.

"So, I tell him, ok fine. Do whatever. Guy just shakes his head and walks away. Later that night, I'm up drinking late, watching TV, and this guy's asleep. So, I go into his bedroom, and I take his little engagement ring out of the box."

The girl put her hand over her mouth.

"That's terrible," she whispered through her fingers. "You're terrible."

Len grinned at this.

"Shiiiiit," he said. "That ain't even the half of it. What I did next was hide the ring in my room somewhere I know he ain't never gonna look. Then, I wait until morning, and, sure enough, he comes into my room all panicked. He's like, goddammit Len, where's my ring? Gimme my ring. So, I tell him I ain't got the ring no more, cuz I lost my temper bout him kicking me out and ate the sumbitch."

Wrinkles shot across the girls pretty face, as she considered Len's words.

"You ate it?"

Len's expression turned sour.

"Shit no," he said. "I ain't dumb enough to swallow no ring. That's just what I told him."

"Why would you do that?" asked the girl.

Len looked at Mathew, who pretended to read his newspaper.

"You tell her, Matt."

Mathew looked at Len without acknowledging the girl.

"It's your story."

Len shook his head.

"Alright then," he mumbled, before refocusing his attention on the girl. "I done it so he'd dig through my shit."

The girl's face turned green. She looked at Mathew.

"This really happened?"

"You bet your ass it did," said Len. "Every day, that fucker'd wait until I had me a shit. Then, he'd fish it out the toilet and root through it with his rubber gloves, just cursing and gagging the whole way through."

Mathew put his newspaper down and looked at the girl.

"Just let that detonate in your brain for a minute."

The girl rubbed her temples, as if to wipe his words from her brain.

"You're so terrible," she said. "Did you ever give him the ring?"

Len looked a little confused.

"Nah, he gave up after a few days, and I eventually sold it to a pawn shop."

The girl shook her head.

"That's it," she said. "I'm through."

She set her little bottle down and picked up her magazine.

"Awe, c'mon," said Len." I ain't even hit on you yet."

The girl looked over her magazine, a genuine look of disgust in her round, lovely eyes. Without a word, she returned to her magazine, but whatever had been in those eyes had stirred up something malicious in Len.

"That's alright," he said. "I don't drink from dirty puddles anyway."

The girl lowered her magazine.

"What did you say?"

Len leaned forward, his eyes looking black and cold.

"I said I don't fuck whores."

Mathew folded his newspaper and set it neatly across his lap.

"That's enough, Len."

The girl looked at Mathew and then Len.

"I'm getting security."

She lifted from her seat, and Mathew put his hand up.

"That won't be necessary," he said.

He looked at Len, who studied the girl with contempt.

"Go someplace else," he said. "I'll meet up with you when we get to Omaha."

Len looked at Mathew and started to say something.

"Go on," Mathew said, his voice calm and kind, as if he spoke not to an erratic giant, but a hot-tempered child.

Len looked at the girl, and something in his eyes made her palms leak sweat.

"Fine," he said through clenched teeth.

He stood up and walked out of the compartment, his boots bludgeoning the floor as he went.

Mathew waited for a moment, while the girl tried to make sense of the before and the now.

"Sorry about that," said Mathew. "He can be somewhat difficult at times."

The girl shook her head and eyed the entryway with contempt.

"He's a bastard," she said.

Mathew pursed his lips and nodded.

"Just don't let him hear you say it."

The two travelled in silence for the next hour, the girl's attention fused to yet another magazine, Mathew's on whatever unknown scraps of information his newspaper still held. An hour outside of Omaha, he began to consider Len's lingering absence, and worry set in.

"Where are you going?" asked the girl, as he stood.

"Bathroom."

Concern advanced across her face.

"What if your friend comes back?"

The words rushed out of her mouth with a suddenty she hadn't intended, and she repostured herself into an easy-looking disposition.

"I mean, is he dangerous or anything?"

Mathew thought for longer than she liked.

"Well?" asked the girl. "Is he?"

"I wouldn't worry about it," Mathew said. "He wouldn't do anything with all these people around."

With that, he left the girl alone in the compartment, her face taking on a sickly white color, as she contemplated his words.

Outside in the hallway, Mathew looked and listened. Everything seemed calm and quiet for the most part, and this brought him welcome relief. Then, he heard someone crying a few compartments away.

He tracked the little noises until he arrived at an open compartment. Inside, a middle-aged woman cradled a man's head in her lap like a new baby, reddened twists of tissue screwed up into his great swelling nostrils.

"Is everything alright?" Mathew asked.

The woman looked up with an expression of bewilderment.

"Yes," she said softly. "Yes, we're ok."

Mathew leaned out of the entryway and looked down both sides of the hallway.

"What happened?" he asked.

The man groaned through his injury, a symphony of snorts and gags filling the compartment.

"He hit me," said the man. "The son of a bitch broke my nose."

Mathew looked down and shook his head.

"Someone hit you?"

The woman shushed the man considerately.

"Yes," she said. "We were leaving the dining car, and some giant man came storming along, insisting that we give him a cigarette. Marvin told him he didn't have any, and the man called him a liar. Then, he reached back and hit Marvin without a second thought."

Marvin leaned over the nice lady's lap and spat blood on the floor.

"Son of a bitch broke my nose."

Mathew rubbed his forehead, as if he were pained by exhaustion.

"Do you know where the man went?

213

"The train's security person took him away," said the woman. "He had to get the cook and two porters to help him."

The man coughed and spat something objectionable into a handkerchief.

"They had to Tase the sumbitch over and over," he said. "He just wouldn't stop coming."

Mathew nodded.

"I'm very sorry for your troubles."

The woman gave a polite smile, and Mathew left them to their alliance against Len and the rest of the world's injustices.

Several cars down, he found the train's security man talking on the telephone.

"Yessir, that's correct," he said to someone on the other end of the line. "Yessir, just jumped on one of my passengers unprovoked."

He was a thinly built man with a push broom mustache, and when he noticed Mathew, he pulled the phone from his ear.

"It's gonna be a minute."

Mathew nodded and leaned against the wall of the car, while the security man returned to his call.

"Yessir, he's a large fella. Oh, I'd have to say about six-foot-four, gotta be 260 pounds at least. Yessir, took four of us to get him to the ground. Had to shock him three times to keep him there."

A member of the train's dining crew approached holding a bag of crushed ice. He handed it to the security man, who nodded his appreciation before placing the ice against the back of his neck.

"Yessir, I got him handcuffed. He ain't going nowhere. You can collect him when we get to the station."

At last, the conversation ended, and the man hung up the phone.

"What can I do for you?" he asked Mathew.

Mathew put his hands in his pockets.

"Well, I'm afraid I'm here to see the man you were just speaking about."

The security man pulled the bag of ice from his neck and set it aside.

"You know the fella?"

Mathew nodded.

"He's my traveling companion, unfortunately."

The security man scratched his head.

"Well, what's his problem? He on medication or something?"

Mathew shook his head.

"No, just a bit of a hothead."

214

"Well, I'm sorry, but he's got himself into some real trouble here. Assaulted one of my passengers. Knocked a tooth out of one of the porters trying to restrain him. I've got the police waiting for him in Omaha."

Mathew nodded.

"Can I see him?"

The man scratched his head again.

"Well, I suppose that'd be alright. Just try not to get him riled up again. He starts screaming, I'm gonna have to gag him. Can't have him causing a panic with the other passengers."

Mathew nodded, and the security man led him through the dining car and into a compartment. Inside the little room, Len lay on his stomach, his great wrists and ankles hogtied together with numerous nylon cable ties. Mathew looked him over and shook his head.

"I'm sorry for the restraints," the security man said. "We just can't have him loose on this train again."

Mathew nodded.

"I understand."

Len looked up.

"Well," he said. "How much longer you gonna let me stay like this."

Mathew rubbed his chin, while the security man shook his head.

"I told you," the man said. "You ain't getting loose until we get to Omaha. Then, you can reckon with the police."

Len flashed the man a chilling look.

"I wasn't asking you."

He looked at Mathew.

"Well?"

Mathew looked at the security man.

"How long until we reach the station?"

The man checked his watch.

"About 15 or 20 minutes."

Mathew nodded and looked down at Len.

"You know you're more trouble than you're worth."

Len's teeth flashed.

"Quit fucking around," he said, the words leaking out from between his teeth like vapor from an overheating engine.

An uneasiness began to crawl through the security man's chest, and he appraised Mathew anew. He was only average height and looked like he refused more meals than he accepted. But, something about his eyes made the security man take a step back.

"Listen," said the man. "I don't know what you fellas are getting on about, but don't do something stupid."

Mathew ignored his words and shook his head once more at Len. "I ought to leave you."

Len began writhing around in his restraints, his immense chest thumping audibly against the floor.

"God dammit, Matt, I can barely feel my fucking arms. Enough with this shit. I get it."

The security man's hand now hovered over the Taser holstered in his belt.

"Alright," he said. "That's enough. You're getting him riled up." He looked at Len. "I told you I was gonna put a gag in your mouth if you started making noise."

Again, Mathew ignored the man, his face relaxed and calm, as if he were sorting out trivialities on the most ordinary of days.

"Alright," Mathew said. "I guess I'll give you one more chance."

Now, the security man was out of patience.

"That's it," he said. "I'm gonna have to ask—"

He stopped talking, as if interrupted by a startling thought, his flesh turning stiff and still, brain growing foggy and disconnected from his body.

"Hurry up," Len said.

"Don't rush me," said Mathew, as his mind probed deeper into the man's brain. "We still have some time to kill before we reach Omaha."

Mathew approached the security man and looked him over. His body stood rigid, and his eyes had taken on a cloudy look, as if his mind had vanished within a fog of otherworld thinking. Mathew shoved a hand into the man's front pocket and searched around until he found a wallet. He removed it and thumbed it open. There were five crisp twenty-dollar bills inside. He withdrew all the cash and dropped the wallet on the floor.

"Get that box cutter over there," said Len.

Mathew looked over to see the item on a counter. He collected it and sliced away each of Len's restraints.

Once freed, Len stood up and stretched, his broad back cracking along the spine. He approached the security man.

"Keep him still," Len said to Mathew, as he swelled before the man.

Mathew watched as Len spat in the security man's face, the saliva dangling from his nose, like a sturdy thread of drying glue. But of this and anything else, the dormant man seemed unaware, his mind floating free somewhere, untethered to the happenings below.

A voice boomed from the train's intercom system, announcing their arrival at the Omaha station.

"Time to go," said Mathew, as the train began to slow.

216

They gathered up the security man and laid him on his stomach. One by one, they pulled his arms and legs behind his back and hogtied him, just as he had hogtied Len. When they had finished, Mathew stepped back and admired their work. Then, he ran his hand through his hair and relaxed.

As if jabbed with something sharp, the security man convulsed in a full-body flinch. He coughed and twitched about on the floor, as if he'd been set atop a hot skillet.

"Help!" he screamed, his eyes now alive with panic and fear. But before the words could travel, Len put him to sleep with his boot.

Mathew rubbed his temples like he had a headache.

"I was going to tape his mouth."

Len shrugged.

"Didn't see no tape."

The two men waited for the train to come to a stop, and then they left the compartment and lined up with the other travelers. Outside, six police officers waited for the passengers to exit, so they could enter and collect the security man's prisoner.

As the train doors opened, a sea of passengers flowed around them, each one hurrying ahead to his or her next thing. When the train had given up its contents, the officers entered one by one to find no prisoner, but a rambling lunatic with tales both large and tall.

CHAPTER 4

They pressed deeper into a pastoral landscape, the refined edges of the city drifting away into the horizon, like a great apparition vanishing into the fog. Outside, cattle grazed the land, their dull eyes gazing out with indifference at the world and all its happenings.

From her window, Mila watched a lonely hawk circling among the clouds, its sharp eyes searching the verdant ocean below.

"Will we drive all night?" she asked.

Claire flinched a little, as if a mute had spoken.

"No," she said. "We will stop for the night to eat and rest."

Mila looked outside at all the natural nothingness.

"Where?"

They breached a hill, revealing what seemed like endless miles of rural landscape.

"We'll camp outdoors, most likely," said Claire.

"Oh, God," said Mila.

Claire raised her eyebrows.

"You've never camped?"

Mila shook her head.

"It sounds awful."

"It's actually quite peaceful," said Claire," if you do it right."

Mila glanced into the backseat, which held only a backpack and a small bag of food.

"Will we be doing it right?"

Claire frowned.

"This is how you have to travel if you want to stay out of sight." She looked at the girl and gave a reassuring smile. "We'll get through it and find something better tomorrow."

An hour later, a tree line blossomed up on the horizon, its width snaking out for miles on either side of the road.

"There," said Claire.

As they grew closer, they could see a bridge and a small river, which wormed like a great nourishing artery amid the trees. Claire slowed the car and pulled off the road, driver and passenger jostling as the tires rolled over the dirt and grass. At last, she stopped several feet off the road, the car sitting neatly beneath the shade of some low pines.

"If it rains, we'll get stuck," said Mila.

Claire put the car in park.

"I can push it out."

They got out, and Mila stretched her legs, while Claire scanned the landscape around them. Beneath the golden light of late afternoon, the hills bowed up like the backs of giant beasts, their skins wrapped in blankets of lush green wool. She tilted her head upward and scanned the sky, a commercial jet soaring in the high away, some birds and nothing else. When she was satisfied they were truly alone, she turned toward the trees.

"Stand on the other side of the car."

Mila looked around.

"Why?"

Claire flashed her a look.

"If you're going to ask questions about everything, we'll never get anywhere."

Mila shook her head a little and walked behind the car.

"How's this?"

"You may want to crouch."

The girl looked puzzled.

"Alright."

She bent down slightly and waited.

"What now? Should I roll over?"

Claire turned and took hold of a gigantic tree branch, tearing it free with a swift and effortless motion. Mila shrieked, as a loud crack cut through the peace. She flinched, as wood fragments battered the car like a hail of little darts.

"What the hell was that?" the girl yelled.

Above their heads, birds fled the trees, their forms blending blackly, like a curious little storm in a clean summer sky.

Claire turned suddenly, the branch at her feet.

"You're a little young for all that, don't you think?"

The girl walked from behind the car with her hands to her sides.

"Really? That's what you're focused on?" She gestured to the tree branch. "You just ripped off a ginormous piece of tree like it was nothing. What is that? How did you do that?"

Claire bent over and started tearing smaller branches away.

"Just help me gather these up. We need to conceal the car."

Mila looked around.

"Conceal the car? From what? There's nobody out here."

Claire looked up.

"Just help, ok?"

The girl shook her head and started gathering limbs.

"Will you tell me how you did that, at least?"

"Maybe," said Claire. "If you listen and do what I tell you."

"Will you teach me to do it?"

219

Claire smiled a little.
"Just help me pick up these limbs."
The girl picked up limbs.

CHAPTER 5

The dark sky hung over the city like a lid, streetlights popping on one by one, painting the streets with sight.

Len looked up and shook his head.

"It's fixing to come down like gangbusters."

Lightning flashed, and big purple clouds glowed through the night sky for the briefest of moments, before vanishing within a gathering curtain of black.

"Yep," said Mathew without looking up.

Thunder roared in the heavens, and Len gave a little flinch.

"God damn it. Let's get off the street."

They called a taxi from a payphone outside a gas station, the first of the rain thrumming cars in the parking lot.

"Motherfucker'd better hurry," said Len.

Mathew looked around, but there was nothing much to see.

"This town is perfect," he said. "Let's go inside."

They entered the gas station and stood by the door, while the rain varnished the streets in a translucent enamel.

The old man at the register eyed them both with a scrunched-up face. After about ten minutes, he'd had enough.

"You boys gonna buy somethin?"

"No," Mathew said without looking back.

The old man put both palms flat on the counter.

"This is a business," he said. "No loitering."

Len flipped his head around.

"How much money you pull into this place?"

The old man straightened.

"What?"

"You deaf?" Len asked, as he turned his body around.

The old man reached below the counter.

"I got a 12-gauge settin right here," he said. "In case you got any other questions."

Len gave the man a toothy grin.

"Let's see it."

The old man pinched his face tight.

"You boys get out. That's the one and only time I'm gonna tell you."

Len took a step forward.

"Alright," Mathew said. "I'll buy this magazine if you let us wait here for our taxi."

The old man shook his head.

"Nope. Get out. Right now."

He withdrew the unseen shotgun and placed it flat across the countertop.

Len smiled.

"Maybe I'll just take that gun for myself," he said. "Sell it for a few dollars."

The old man stood with a stoic posture, a serious look on his weathered face.

"That's it. I'm calling the police."

Len started to say something else, but Mathew gave him an elbow. "Cab's here."

Len looked at the old man and grinned.

"We'll be seeing you again." he said, backing away. "We'll be seeing you real soon."

The old man watched the two walk out, his face holding its stern expression. But inside, his heart thumped wildly, as if it sought to escape at last and go it alone after all these years. And after the cab had gone, he raised a trembling hand to his chest, his age and vulnerabilities seeping out, despite his defiance against the world and all its modern failings. And, after a few minutes, he closed the gas station early and drove home to his wife.

CHAPTER 6

"Ouch!" cried Mila. "You're tearing my scalp out."

"Just be still," said Claire, as she worked the comb against the tangles in the girl's dark brown hair.

"Ouch!"

Claire withdrew the comb and set it aside.

"This is pointless. We're going to have to cut it."

She removed a small bone-handled pocketknife from her pocket.

"What?" said Mila, as she scuttled toward the river's edge. "No way."

Claire stood up.

"It's better anyway, just in case someone recognizes you."

Mila put her hands up.

"No one's going to recognize me, alright? And, you're not cutting my hair."

Claire stood up.

"You do understand that there are dangerous people hunting you right now, don't you?" She softened her expression and flattened the pitch of her voice. "Look, I understand how you feel. I was young once too. But you look ridiculous right now, and there's no way I can comb those tangles without taking hunks of your scalp with them."

The girl shook her head.

"I don't care. You're not cutting my hair."

Minutes later, Claire slipped the knife back into her pocket, while the girl sat sobbing at her reflection in the water.

"I'll give you a minute," said Claire, as she walked away.

She made her way through the trees and popped out into the grasses on the other side. She looked at the road, stretching out for miles into the seeable landscape. There were no cars coming and no helicopters in the sky. She took a breath and allowed herself to relax. Then, she reentered the tree line and walked back to the river, where Mila sat as before, holding strands of loosed hair, like the innocent casualties of a great injustice.

"Are you finished mourning your loss?" asked Claire. "Because if a car passes that bridge and sees you sitting out in the open, they are likely to stop and cause trouble for us."

Mila remained crouched down along the sandy banks, her eyes staring deep into the flowing water, like someone meditating on the true nature of the world.

Claire sighed and looked around. To the west, the sky flared gently, as the reddening sun plunged beneath the land. Within the trees, cicadas began chirping, and Claire could see that bats had begun to fall from their roosting spots beneath the bridge.

"You know, when it gets dark, the bugs start to come out."

Mila stood up and dusted her legs in a panic. Then, she calmed herself and folded her arms.

"I'm not scared of bugs."

Claire nodded.

"Alright," she said, as she approached Mila. "Do you see those birds right there?"

Mila looked up.

"Yes."

"Those aren't birds. They're bats. They live under the bridge." With that she turned and walked back into the trees.

Minutes later, the two sat together on a blanket next to the car, the sunlight nearly consumed by the gathering dark.

"Why can't we start a fire?" asked the girl.

Claire shook her head.

"Someone may see it."

Mila bent her knees up and curled her arms around them.

"I'm cold."

Claire handed her a blanket.

"Here."

The girl took it and wrinkled her nose.

"It stinks."

Claire shrugged, as she reached into her backpack.

"It's all we have."

The girl spread it over her legs.

"I'm hungry."

Claire nodded.

"I'm working on it."

She withdrew two cans of beans and cut the tops away with a can opener.

"Cold beans?" asked Mila. "This just keeps getting better."

Claire set the can opener aside.

"You know, you don't act like someone who's been surviving on the road."

The girl shoved a spoon in the can and shrugged.

"Well, maybe you're just not doing it right." She scooped up a spoonful of beans and looked it over. "I never had to eat cold beans before, at least."

Claire stood.

"Well, don't worry. I'm sure it will be four-course meals at Bloc 9."

A somber expression seized the girl's face. She dropped her spoon into the can and set it down.

"I'm sorry," said Claire. "I didn't mean it."

Mila stood up and walked way. Claire waited a moment and then followed her into the darkness.

"I'm sorry," she said, as she approached Mila from behind.

She placed a hand over Mila's shoulder, and the girl ripped herself away.

"Why are you even doing this?" She spun around, mouth spitting out flecks of saliva like bits of clear venom. "Is it to help me or to hurt them? Do you even know? Do you even care about what happens to me?"

Claire took a deep breath.

"Of course, I care. I'm sorry." She rubbed the back of her neck and tilted her head up. "Look, the truth is, I'm not used to being around children. I don't have any experience with this sort of thing. There's a lot of stuff I have to think of. A lot of planning and a lot of worry. This thing we're trying to do will not be easy. There are a lot of variables and a lot of risks. But I shouldn't have said that. I know this is not easy for you, and I'm sorry. Okay?"

Mila turned away and kicked the ground.

"I just want a normal life," she whispered.

Claire approached her slowly and touched her arm.

"I know," she said.

The girl turned, tears streaming from her eyes.

"What's going to happen to me at Bloc 9?" she asked. "I don't know anyone there. What if they hurt me?"

Claire put her hands over the girl's shoulders.

"They won't hurt you," she said. "They will help you."

The girl's chin trembled.

"How do you know?"

Claire knelt down and looked into the girl's eyes.

"I'll make sure of it."

Mila threw her arms around Claire and burst into tears.

"I'm scared," she said.

Claire hugged back.

"It's alright. Now, let's go eat those disgusting beans."

The girl smiled a little.

"You're terrible at camping," she said.

Claire stood up and smiled.

"Well, maybe we can figure it out together."

The girl wiped her face, and the two walked back to the car, where they ate their beans in silence.

CHAPTER 7

Out on the road, the cab driver looked casual and calm, despite his screaming intuitions.

"Where you fellas from?" he asked against his better judgment.

"Someplace else," said the big one.

They rode in silence for a while, and then the big man leaned forward.

"Where's a good place to get a drink?"

The cab driver flinched at the smell of Len's breath.

"What kind of place you into?" he asked, as he cracked his window against the stink.

Len scratched the black whiskers on his chin.

"Someplace with girls."

The driver shrugged.

"This ain't that kind of town, really. There's laws against strippin and such. There's the Firehouse, though. Lots of women there. They do free drinks for ladies on Thursdays. You should do pretty well there, if you have some money to spend."

Len leaned back in his seat.

"Well?" he asked Mathew.

"Whatever, as long as there's booze."

Len looked at the driver.

"Well, go there then."

About ten minutes later, The Firehouse appeared on the horizon, its shabby wooden exterior illuminated by what looked like twinkling white Christmas lights.

"That's it," said the driver.

Len leaned between the two front seats and squinted.

"Looks like a dump."

The driver swallowed.

"It's better on the inside."

They pulled into the parking lot and Mathew stepped out.

"Here," Len said, as he passed over the fare.

"You fellas have a good one," said the driver.

Len stepped out into the night without answering, the car rocking violently over the loss of his formidable weight.

"I don't know about this," Len said, as the cab sped away.

"As long as there's booze," said Mathew.

The two approached the entrance, as a pair of giggling college girls stepped outside, their skin soft and fair, eyes large and blue.

"Hello, ladies," Len said, his face contorted by an alarming grin.

The girls stiffened and rushed past, their eyes cast down to the ground.

"Fuckin little bitches," Len said, as he and Mathew entered the bar.

The cab driver had been right. It was better inside, though neither men could relate to what he saw. In one far corner, a young man in a cowboy hat clung to a frenzied mechanical bull. In another, couples danced to country music, their boots stirring sawdust from atop a wooden floor.

Len shook his head.

"Fuckin hillbillies."

They sat down at a corner booth, where the dim light softened their defects and scars.

A waitress approached.

"Hi there. What'll you have?"

Len grinned, and the waitress appeared to shutter.

"Hey there, pretty thing. How you doing this beautiful evening?"

The waitress gave a polite smile.

"Just fine, thanks. What can I get you?"

Len leaned back and threw his arms over the back of the booth.

"I'll have a beer and a shot of tequila, undressed."

"What kind of beer?" the waitress asked.

Len's smile widened.

"Why don't you just pick one for me?"

She turned to Mathew.

"And you?"

"Whiskey, neat."

She nodded and walked away, while Len eyeballed Mathew from the side.

"Quit staring at me," Mathew said, as he surveyed the room.

"Just take it slow," said Len. "I don't want no problems. This town's got potential. I don't want to blow everything in one night."

Mathew didn't answer.

"God damn, that waitress, though," Len continued. He bent over to get a better look, as she put their order in at the bar. "That ass and that hair." He hissed inward. "And that nose. I like it when their nose is kind of big."

Mathew gave her quick look.

"Yeah, she's got a look, I guess."

"A look?" Len said. "Shit, that bitch is packing a serious body under those clothes. Trust me."

She turned toward them, and Len sat up in a panic.

"Quiet. Here she comes."

The waitress carried over their drinks and set them on the table. Len picked up the beer and looked it over.

"This looks alright," he said. "You picked this out?"

The waitress offered no expression.

"Our bartender did."

Len frowned a little. He bent to the side and the bartender gave him a nod.

"Well, fuck," he said. "I guess beer's beer."

The waitress turned to Mathew.

"You all set?"

Mathew nodded, and she walked away.

"She acts like she ain't interested," Len said, "But I can tell there's something there. I got an instinct for this kind of thing."

Mathew lifted the glass of whiskey and poured it down his throat.

"God damn it, Matt," said Len. "Are you fucking kidding me? How many times have we been over this?"

Mathew set the glass down.

"Just worry about yourself, ok?"

Len lifted his shot of tequila and sucked it empty.

"I'll be at the bar."

He collected his beer and walked away, while Mathew motioned the waitress over again.

Two hours later, Mathew sat in the same booth, his face looking tired, eyes studying a wet circle on the table. Across the room, two men played billiards with a pair of perky-looking girls with big bashful eyes. Even amid all the clatter and noise, these two men stood out, their voices booming with arrogance and expletives. Mathew lifted his head and watched them. Both men were decorated with ridiculous tattoos, and both looked to have spent a considerable amount of time at the gym.

Mathew glanced over to the bar, but Len wasn't there anymore. He lifted his glass and sucked down the last sip of whiskey. Then he stood up and approached the billiard tables.

"I got next," he said, as he placed a twenty-dollar bill on the table.

The two men turned.

"Nah, we're playing with these two fine ladies," the taller one said. "There's another table over there. This one's ours for the night."

Mathew threw down another twenty.

"It's alright if you're scared," he said. "Or, maybe you just don't have the money."

The other man turned and pointed his finger at Mathew's face.

"Listen, fucker—."

"It's alright," said the taller man. "I don't mind taking this guy's money."

Mathew walked between the two men and collected a pool cue, while the tall man pulled the money from his wallet.

"Just give me a minute to dispose of this idiot," he told the girls, who seemed quite stimulated by the altercation.

The two girls walked over to a high-top table and sipped their drinks, while giggling to one another.

"What's the game?" asked the tall man, as he chalked his stick.

"Standard eight-ball," said Mathew.

"I'll hold the money," said the shorter man.

Mathew shrugged.

"Fine with me."

Within minutes, everyone could see that Mathew had made a tremendous mistake, as the tall man systematically cleared his balls from the table. Throughout the ordeal, his friend needled Mathew with boastful taunts, while the girls ooed and awed at the tall man's heroics. In no time at all, the man had lined up the eight ball for a simple shot that would close out the game.

"Get my money ready," he said, as he bent down over the table.

Everyone waited, while he studied the angle for what seemed an excessive amount of time.

"Come on, hurry up." said the shorter man.

The tall man persisted in his stance, his face locked in unwavering concentration.

"What's he doing?" whispered one of the girls.

The short man stood up and approached.

"You alright, man?" he asked.

At last, the tall man stood up, his face looking terrified, lungs sucking air. He turned to his friend.

"What's wrong? You alright?"

The tall man walked over to the high-top table and downed his drink, while Mathew watched with great amusement.

"What are you laughing at, fucker?" said the shorter man. "You are this close to getting your ass kicked."

He walked over to his friend.

"You alright?"

"Yeah," said the tall man, unconvincingly.

The girls watched the two men with great interest, one slipping a whisper into the other's ear that coaxed forth a little smile.

"Well, finish this fucker then, ok?"

The tall man placed both hands flat on the table, as if he were steadying himself on a bobbing ship.

"Yeah," he whispered. "Yeah, ok."

They turned to see that Mathew had collected the man's stick.

"Here you go," he said with a smile.

The shorter man walked over and snatched it away. He turned to his friend and offered it over.

"Here," he said, but the tall man only stared at the stick, his face locked in some sort of mute horror.

"I don't think he wants to play anymore," Mathew said.

The shorter man lowered the stick and approached his friend.

"What's wrong?" he asked, his voice low and discreet. "You need a doctor or something?"

The tall man stood silently staring at the place where his friend was before.

"I'll go ahead and take this," Mathew said, slipping the money from the shorter man's back pocket.

The short man spun around, his face aflame with anger and hate.

"Motherfucker, you ain't taking that money."

"Jackson!" yelled one of the girls. "There's something wrong with him. Forget that guy. We need to get him to a hospital or something."

Jackson turned to see his friend drooling all over his shirt. He approached him and slapped his cheek.

"Come on, man. Snap out of it. You're alright."

As Mathew returned to his booth, the tall man finally relaxed, his face regaining its color as his features perked up.

"See," said Jackson. "He don't need a doctor. He just needs another drink."

While Jackson and the girls tended to their friend, Mathew slipped back into his seat and flagged down the waitress. He ordered another whiskey and drank it down. Then he followed up with another, which he sipped a bit more considerately, at least for a while.

Now, the lights were bleary star bursts, and the sounds, a meaningless fusion of laughter, footsteps and dish clatter. He swung his head back and stared at the ceiling. He cried.

"You alright, mister?" asked the waitress, who seemed to appear as if from nowhere at the edge of his table.

Mathew whipped his head up to look at her.

"Yeah," he said. "I'm fine."

He reached into his pocket and pulled out a handful of crumpled twenty-dollar bills.

"Here," he said, slapping the entire wad on the table. "I gotta go."

He slid out of the booth and stumbled onto the floor, while the waitress made a false attempt to catch him.

"You alright?" she asked. "You need me to call a cab?"

"Nope," he said, as he climbed to his feet. "I'll be fine."

He walked away with his arms flared out to his sides, as if he balanced upon a shifting funhouse landscape with very real hazards on either side.

"Wait," said the waitress, her eyes big and bright. "This is way too much."

"Keep it," said Mathew, as he staggered away. "Buy something you don't need."

She watched him walk through the crowd of people, many assuming odd, wooden stances to let him pass. She waited until he pushed his way through the doors and into the outside world. Then, she gathered up the money, a broad smile forcing its way across her tired-looking face.

Outside, the storm had left big puddles in the street, and the air smelled of wet soil. He stood there for a while waiting for his senses to catch up with his body. But they never did, so he took a shaky step forward and collapsed onto the ground.

"Awe, look at this," said God, or a passing witness, or a voice within his mind. "Ain't this a sad sight?"

It was Jackson and his tall friend. They approached Mathew and stood above him.

"He don't look so cocky anymore, does he?" one said to the other.

Jackson drove a boot into Mathew's side and tossed him over onto his back.

"You fucked with the wrong people, you stupid piece of shit," he said.

The two girls stood watching from behind, their faces painted with genuine concern.

"You two are gonna get arrested," one said. "Just leave him be."

Jackson turned and held out his keys.

"You two go on to my house," he said. "Just take my car. We'll catch up with you after we finish with this motherfucker."

The girl put her hands on her slender hips.

"This is stupid, Jackson. You're gonna get thrown in jail."

Jackson stepped forward and yanked her arm from her hip.

"You go on now," he said, as he forced the keys into her hand. "Don't worry about us. We got it under control."

The girl took the keys and shook her head.

"Come on, Kailey," she said, and the two walked away.

Jackson turned and joined his friend.

232

"Time to pay, you stupid piece of shit."

Mathew gazed upward at the heavens, where starlight twinkled between a tapestry of drifting purple thunderclouds.

"Get him up," Jackson said.

The two men raised Mathew to his feet and forced him to the side of the building. His head lolled as they carried him down a dark alley, where the smell of sour dumpster content mingled with the scent of fresh rain.

"Hold him up," Jackson told the tall man, who yanked Mathew straight to expose his soft underneath.

Jackson glanced down both ends of the alley to make sure they were alone. Then, he took a hard step forward and jabbed his fist into Mathew, who coughed and wheezed, as the breath fled his body.

"Alright," said Jackson. "You're up."

The two men switched positions, while Mathew snorted and sucked at the air.

"Hold him higher," said the tall man, as he squared to deliver a blow.

Jackson hoisted Mathew as high as he could, while his friend swung his leg forward and sunk a boot into Mathew's genitals. A low moan seeped from between Mathew's lips, as the pain blossomed within his body. The tall man reached out and gathered a handful of Mathew's hair.

"You like that, fucker?" he said, as he yanked his head up.

He started to say more, but before he could, Mathew soaked his shirt with a foul stream of vomit.

"God damn it!" the tall man yelled.

Jackson released Mathew, who collapsed against concrete like a bag of bowling pins.

"Fuck!" yelled the tall man.

He wrestled his soiled shirt over his head, as little strings of vomit clung to his hair. He tossed the shirt aside and spat.

"You piece of shit," Jackson said.

He raised his boot and stomped on the buttons of Mathew's spine.

"Wait," said the tall man. "Leave some for me."

Jackson stepped back and folded his arms, while the tall man clutched his knees and heaved dryly. After a few moments, he gathered his composure and approached.

"I'm gonna fucking kill you," he said. "You hear me, motherfucker? You die right now."

He brought his leg back and drove it deep into Mathew, who cringed and coughed, his reddened eyes rolling about in their sockets, as if loosed from the wires in his head.

Suddenly, Jackson vanished backward into the darkness, his body plucked upward in a swift and soundless motion, as if God Himself had finally lost his taste for the violence of men. The tall man stopped kicking Mathew and spun around.

"Jackson?" he called out.

The darkness answered with muffled whimpers.

"Jackson, you alright?"

The darkness answered again, this time with a great clomp. And then it answered no more.

"Jackson?" the tall man muttered as he crept forward.

"He's not really in a talking mood right now," said Len, as he stepped from the shadows.

The tall man took a step backward, as Len's immense form transcended into the visible light.

"Who are—," the tall man began. But before he could finish, Len had him by the throat.

Now, he was rising off the ground, his hands clutching Len's thick wrists, legs bicycling in the air.

"You've made a big mistake," Len said, as he brought the man's face close to his. "See, that's my best friend right there."

He unclasped his right hand and held the man high with his left. He brought his arm back and plunged a fist into tall man's face, which tore apart from his lips to his nose. Garbled noises spilled out from his mutilated mouth, followed by blood and teeth and periodontal gore. Len held the man even higher and inspected his work with a false look of concern.

"My goodness. You ain't pretty no more."

He released the man's neck, and his body thumped the ground.

"Please," the man whistled through a torn and bloody mouth.

Len gestured toward Mathew.

"Did my friend say please when you was beatin him?"

As the tall man tried to speak, Len put a finger to his lips.

"Shhh."

He offered a friendly looking smile and then jabbed the man's head with his boot.

"It's sleepy time."

Len smiled to himself, as Mathew turned over and sat up. Len eyed him with contempt.

"Jesus Christ, Matt, what the hell is it with you? If you want to die so much, why don't you just do it yourself?"

Mathew sat in a puddle, his head bowed, legs splayed out. He spat blood in the water and watched it dilute to a soft pink.

"I don't know," he said. "Maybe I should."

Len shook his head.

"Christ," he said. "Come here."

He bent over and hauled Mathew up onto his feet.

"You got to get yourself together," said Len. "This shit's getting old."

He dusted away the street filth from his coat, while Mathew tottered about like a newborn deer. He placed his hand on Mathew's shoulder and squeezed.

"I hate seeing you like this. It's beneath someone like you."

Mathew ripped away from Len's grip and staggered away down the alley.

"Oh, is that how it is?" asked Len.

Behind him in the blackness, a horrible, desperate groan leaked out into the uncaring world.

"God damn it," Len said.

He approached the tall man and stood over him.

"Did I say you could wake up?"

He lodged his boot in the man's ribcage and turned him over onto his back.

"Go back to sleep motherfucker."

He raised his boot and stomped on center of the man's face, a sharp crack stabbing into the air, as the nose gave way. The man coughed out a little fountain of blood that bloomed up like oil from a fruitful well. Then, his eyes went cloudy and his chest fell still.

Len looked over at Jackson, still limp and unconscious on the wet pavement. He approached and straddled Jackson's torso.

"Nighty night to you, too," he said, as he gathered Jackson's head between his massive hands.

He gave the neck a sharp twist, and then stood up. Jackson lay dead on the ground. Len spat and looked ahead, where Mathew had collapsed onto his back.

"You gonna sleep here tonight?"

Mathew didn't answer.

"Shit," Len said, as he approached. "Come here, God damn it."

He bent down to collect his friend.

"Let's go, buddy. We gotta stick together."

Mathew shook his head.

"I'm not like you."

Len lifted him up and tossed him over his shoulder.

"Nah, you're worse."

CHAPTER 8

Mila looked out the window, where great pastures stretched into an indefinite horizon. As the cool wind tickled the grasses, young cows skipped about beneath the indifferent gazes of their elders, which stood like living statues, save for the workings of their jaws.

"I want a hamburger," said Mila.

Claire shook her head.

"We need to stay out of sight."

Mila slouched in her seat and released an impressive sigh.

"I can't eat any more beans," she said. "I won't eat them."

Claire shrugged.

"You will if you get hungry enough."

They rode in silence for a while, something wrong taking root between them.

"I can't wait for this to be over," said Mila.

"You and me both," said Claire.

Static seized the radio as they exceeded the station's broadcast limits. Claire flipped the dial in search of something stable.

"Can I at least listen to my music?" asked Mila.

Claire pulled her hand back.

"Knock yourself out."

Mila took the knob and spun it through a cacophony of foreign music and gospel radio.

"God," she said. "How could anyone live around here?"

At last, she settled on something modern and chaotic, the lyrics sexual, the singer inflecting wildly.

"No," said Claire. "Find something else."

Mila looked at her as if she'd just grown a second head.

"You don't like this?"

She turned the radio up.

"This is my song," she said. "I'm not even kidding. This song is about me."

Claire glanced at the radio, as the singer crooned about having sex with multiple men. She looked at Mila.

"Really?"

Mila folded her arms.

"Maybe," she said. "Does that surprise you?"

Claire turned toward the coming road.

"Yes," she said, her voice dry as stale bread.

Mila looked out the window and released another impressive sigh.

"There," she said. "Can we please stop there."

Up ahead, a little billboard stuck up from the earth. In ten miles, it promised, home-style cooking had a home at a place called Maxine's.

Mila perked up in her seat.

"We should avoid public places," said Claire, as she glanced at the sign.

As they raced past the sign, Mila flipped around in her seat and stared longingly at the bare wood backing.

"Please," she said. "I just want to eat some real food."

Claire looked over and frowned.

"Maybe," she said. "I'll decide when I see it."

Mila sat back in her seat and placed a hand over her stomach.

"Don't get your hopes up," said Claire. "If I don't like the way it looks, we're driving past."

Mila 's face turned dark.

"Oh God, please let this happen."

Several minutes later, they saw the restaurant sitting on the side of the road in the middle of the open landscape next to a small gas station with two working pumps. Mila looked at Claire with a sorrowful longing, her eyes wide and pleading and a little wet.

"Please?"

Claire scanned the surrounding landscape.

"Fine," she said. "But we need to be in and out as fast as possible. Okay?"

Mila nodded furiously.

"Thank you. Thank you. Thank you."

Claire slowed the car and exited the road. They pulled into the gravel parking lot, the wind whipping fine dirt fragments through their open windows and into their mouths.

"This is not something I would normally do," said Claire, as she filed the car into an open parking space. "You do as I say in here. Do you understand?"

Mila nodded.

"Open the glove box," said Claire.

Mila opened the glove box and a mass of hair flopped out.

"Hand it to me."

The girl lifted the wad of hair by the tips of her fingers, a wrinkled sneer spreading out from her lips.

"Gross," she said, as she tossed it into Claire's lap.

"It's just a wig," said Claire, as she tilted the rearview mirror her way.

Mila watched as Claire worked the wig over her head.

237

"Well?" Claire asked.

Mila started to say something and then considered the gnawing within her stomach.

"It's good," she said.

Claire took another look in the mirror.

"Maybe we should just go."

Mila put her hand on Claire's arm.

"It'll be fine," she said. "You look great. Like, I don't even feel I know you right now."

Claire looked at Mila and then back to the mirror. She took the wig with both hands and leveled it atop her head.

"Okay," she said, as she slid a pair of sunglasses over her nose. "Just don't say anything to anyone."

Mila nodded.

"No problem."

They left the car and crossed the lot, the sun sitting small and high in the sky, the heat like a weight on their shoulders. As the two approached the front door, a middle-aged couple stepped out, their faces indifferent to the strangers before them. The man stopped and held the door open for the woman and child. He wore a big black cowboy hat and a tiny smile that seemed more polite than sincere.

"Thank you," said Claire. Her eyes studied the ground, like a child caught doing something wrong.

"You're welcome" the man replied, but his face pinched inward with thought, as if he were crossing paths with a mental illness of some kind.

Claire and Mila moved swiftly through the open door, the man giving plenty of room, like someone concerned about a contagion in the air.

Mila took Claire's arm as they entered the restaurant.

"You need to relax."

"I can't," Claire whispered back.

Claire lowered her sunglasses and studied the interior, where a noisy collection of men, women and children had gathered amid a rustic setting with faux wood panels. In the center of the room, a little fireplace hissed and crackled. Above their heads, great taxidermized beasts laughed down, their bloodless face flesh gaunt and dry.

The two stepped forward, and a young woman swooped in to greet them.

"Hi there. Just the two of you?" she said in a thick southern accent.

Claire assessed the room once more.

"Yes," she said.

The young woman collected two large laminated menus that looked more like roadside placards for a car wash.

"Right this way."

They followed her through a maze of tables, where people socialized over huge plates of hamburgers, fried chicken, corn, mashed potatoes and cherry pie. As she moved past them, Claire watched closely in their faces signs of recognition, but most seemed to notice the two of them not at all, and this brought her considerable relief.

The hostess sat them at a table by the window and handed over their menus.

"Your waitress will be by in a minute."

She smiled and returned to her spot in front of the door.

Claire and Mila looked over the menu.

"Do they have breakfast?" asked the girl.

"It's afternoon," said Claire.

Mila shrugged.

"Some places serve it all day."

The waitress appeared with two glasses of water, her demeanor that of someone under great stress.

"Sorry," she said, as she plunked the glasses beneath their noses. "I'm in the weeds."

Claire leaned over to Mila.

"That means she's very busy."

Mila withdrew from Claire's whispering lips.

"I know what it means," she said loudly.

The waitress straightened her posture.

"I'll give you a couple minutes."

Claire waited until the woman had crossed the room and then leaned over the table.

"If you raise your voice again, you'll be eating nothing but cold beans for the rest of your short life." She raised a finger and stared deeply into Mila's eyes. "Do you understand?"

Mila nodded.

"Ok, look at the menu and figure out what you want. The sooner we leave here the better off we'll be."

They scanned the menus, as if there were little hour glasses upon the table, every falling grain of sand leading them closer to discovery.

"This is so dumb," Mila whispered finally. "No one here knows who we are. Can't we just relax for a little while?"

The waitress returned before Claire could reply.

"Ok, sorry about that." She took out her server pad. "Today's special is beef brisket with green beans and baked mac and cheese."

Claire glanced over the menu.

"What is your soup of the day?"

The woman looked puzzled.

"We got chili."

Claire nodded.

"Ok then, I'll just have the chicken sandwich."

She jotted it down.

"And your daughter?"

Mila opened her mouth to correct the waitress and then thought better of it.

"Do you have pancakes?"

The waitress pointed them out on the menu.

"Ok, I'll have the pancakes and bacon."

"How do you want your eggs?"

"No eggs," said the girl

The waitress looked at Claire.

"It comes with eggs."

"Scrambled is fine."

The waitress nodded and walked away.

"I don't want eggs," said Mila. "I hate eggs."

"I'll eat them if you don't," said Claire.

They sat together in silence amid the restaurant clatter. People muttering, some laughter, metal utensils clacking against glass plates.

"I hope they hurry," said Mila. "I'm starving."

"Me too," said Claire.

Across the room, a man stood up from his table and began walking toward them. He wore a camouflage hunting jacket, and his big belly hung heavily over a large metallic belt buckle. Claire watched him approach, her eyes assessing every detail of his appearance and behavior. Mila watched her watch him.

"He's just going to the bathroom," she whispered.

Sure enough, the man turned before reaching their table, but not before taking a quick glance over his shoulder as he opened the bathroom door.

"He noticed us," said Claire.

Mila shrugged.

"He just thinks you're pretty."

Minutes later the man exited the bathroom and returned to his table without looking back.

"See," said Mila. "It's nothing."

They sat in silence until the waitress brought their food.

"Alrighty," said the woman, as she slid the plates onto their table. "Everything look ok?"

Claire nodded.

"Yes, thank you."

The waitress nodded and walked away.

"Oh my God, this is so great," said Mila, as she slathered her pancakes with syrup.

Claire watched as the girl cut off a great hunk with her fork and jammed the entire thing in her mouth.

"Slow down," she said with a smile.

The girl shook her head.

"So good," she muttered, her mouth crowded to its limit.

Claire took up her sandwich and took a bite. She swallowed and looked at the girl.

"I have to admit, this definitely beats cold beans."

They both laughed, and the child shoved another forkful of pancakes into her mouth. Claire leaned back in her booth and smiled, an unfamiliar easiness tumbling over her body, despite every effort toward the otherwise. But then, in an instant, her smile dried up, like some green delicate thing in an unforgiving soil.

"I think I'm already full," said Mila, but Claire was studying something across the room. It was the fat man in the camouflage hunting jacket busy whispering in the bartender's ear.

"What is it?" Mila whispered, her cheeks pregnant with food.

"Shhh," Claire whispered. "Something's going on."

She watched the bartender's eyebrows furrow in response to whatever the fat man told him. All the while he had been polishing a glass mug with a soiled-looking towel, and he continued to do so, until the fat man gestured toward Claire and Mila. Then, the bartender's eyes trickled toward them, and his entire body froze.

Claire stared at the man without blinking, and his eyes darted down to his shoes. Then, she flicked her focus to the fat man, who was now hurrying toward the door.

"What do we do?" asked Mila.

"Wait a second," said Claire.

Now the bartender had adopted a look of exaggerated composure. He set the mug on the bar and approached a waitress. He gestured toward some dirty tables, and she quickly set off to clean them. He threw his soiled towel over his shoulder and exchanged some friendly words with a pair of men, who were both drinking whiskey and watching the television.

An old, rugged-looking farmer asked him for another beer. The bartender hurried over and poured his glass full, took his money and placed

241

it in the register. Then, with a most casual air, the bartender approached the telephone and started dialing.

"Let's go," said Claire.

She placed two twenty-dollar bills on table and they stood.

The bartender finished delivering his words and hung up the phone. Then, he nodded to the fat man, who was now standing in front of the door with his arms folded.

Claire and Mila crossed the restaurant without hurrying, the girl's hand tucked firmly within that of her caretaker. When they approached the door, the fat man put his hand up.

"I'm afraid you're gonna have to wait here."

Claire looked at his hand and then at his red, swollen face.

"Move."

The fat man put a finger to the bill of his camouflage baseball cap and tipped it up a bit.

"Listen, we know you're that woman from the news. The police are on their way. Don't make this hard on yourself. Not in front of the child."

The girl shrunk behind Claire, her eyes looking small and rodent-like.

Claire took a step forward.

"Move."

The sound of a pump-action shotgun filled the space behind them, as the bartender forced a shell into the firing chamber.

"You heard the man," he said. "Sit down on the floor right there and put your hands behind your back."

Within the restaurant, curious customers viewed the scene with mute terror, their chewing mouths stilled by disbelief.

Claire turned to face the bartender, who raised the shotgun to her face.

"Don't try to run, or I'll have to shoot."

Before the bartender could blink, Claire plucked the weapon from his grip and held it in her fingers like a child's toy.

The fat man gasped and took a step back, as the bartender studied his empty hands, the fingers still molded around an invisible gun. With a sudden motion, Claire jabbed the bartender in the forehead with the butt of the weapon, and he fell to the ground in an unconscious heap.

She looked at the seated customers, and they all turned toward their plates. She faced the fat man, who shied from the entryway and up against the wall. As Claire approached, he whimpered and turned away, his body impossibly still, as if he believed he might conceal his presence by will or by miracle or by the camouflaged clothing he wore.

Claire took Mila's hand and the two passed quickly through the entryway, leaving the restaurant guests to swallow, at last, the food within their mouths.

Outside, the two hurried across the parking lot, the sun-soaked gravel crunching beneath their shoes. They found their little car and slipped inside, the girl's face hiding poorly the worry on the other side.

"Just relax," said Claire.

She started the ignition, and they pulled out onto the street toward the lofty buildings on the horizon.

"We're going into the city?" asked Mila. "Why?"

"We have to."

Mila rubbed her forehead.

"But we'll be caught."

Claire checked the rearview mirror to make sure they were not being followed.

"If that man called the police, it will take less than 15 minutes for the others to find us," she said. "They'll start monitoring every road that leads from the city, hoping to catch us on the run. If they get us out in the open, they have more options. They can use helicopters and drones. They can hurt you, and they will use this as leverage to make us give up."

They approached a stop sign, marking a lonely four-way intersection in the barren open prairie. She brought the vehicle to a halt and let it idle, as the fragrant wind licked all around the open windows. She looked at Mila and gathered up her hand.

"If we go into the city, we can get lost in the crowd," she said. "That's our best play. We will blend in for a little while, and I will think of something."

The girl nodded, and Claire warmed her up with a bright, sunny smile.

"Don't worry."

She took the wheel and moved on, the girl watching the golden grasses through the open window and feeling much better with every passing mile. But, when she looked at Claire again, she noticed that her hands had bent the steering wheel, despite the easy expression on her face.

The story continues in the thrilling sequel:
THE GIRL OF FLESH AND BONE,
available NOW at AMAZON!

A Request from the Author:

Dear friend,

I rely on reviews to get the word out about my books. If you enjoyed this book, can I ask you to take a moment to leave a brief review on Amazon?

You can leave a quick customer review at the bottom of the page at https://www.amazon.com/dp/B094DY44FQ/

Also, to make sure you never miss a new release, please visit my website www.booksbyrjlaw.com to join my email list, so I can alert you when I publish my next book. I promise I only send messages when I have a new release. You can also follow on Amazon, at Bookbub and on Twitter at @RJLaw3,

Thank you so much for reading. I hope you enjoyed this book as much as I enjoyed writing it. Readers like you are what keeps me writing and I thank you for your support.

All the best to you and yours.

RJ LAW